T0329410

Knell.Ashes.Seppuku

Ashely Ropafadzo Tome

Langaa Research & Publishing CIG
Mankon, Bamenda

Publisher:
Langaa RPCIG
Langaa Research & Publishing Common Initiative Group
P.O. Box 902 Mankon
Bamenda
North West Region
Cameroon
Langaagrp@gmail.com
www.langaa-rpcig.net

Distributed in and outside N. America by African Books Collective
orders@africanbookscollective.com
www.africanbookscollective.com

ISBN-10: 9956-763-83-7

ISBN-13: 978-9956-763-83-2

© Ashely Ropafadzo Tome 2018

For My Mother, Father and Siblings
Alistar , Angelic and Adelis

1

Margaret was still awake, her eyes wide open. Her son Cephas had not come back home yet, it was now past three in the morning. She heaved a sigh as her eyes darted from corner to corner in her room. What was wrong with that boy? She had actually tried by all might to give him everything he wanted and had asked for albeit her relatives and friends complained about it, accusing her of spoiling the boy. They always said that he was a male child and as such had to learn how to live his life the hard way because one day he was going to be a father and a husband. Margaret turned and tossed in her bed, was she doing anything wrong in raising her children? Her first child Charity had six abortions and it all turned out to be a disaster when the doctor found out that her womb was rotten and responsible for her prolonged illness. The doctor said he had to remove the womb and burn it and that had been a sounding blow for Charity in that she was never going to be a mother for the rest of her life. Tears stung Margaret's eyes. She wanted to let them flow freely on her cheeks but suddenly she heard the gate open and knew that Cephas had come back home. She peeped through her window, she could not see properly since her bedroom light was switched on. She heard the sound of her car as her son drove in. Cephas had done it again, he went out to party with friends with Margaret's car without asking his mother for permission. He parked it just beside the fence surrounding the fishpond in the yard. Margaret was fuming with anger, she told herself to calm down and she took three deep breaths. The door creaked open as if some ghost had entered the house. Cephas gently shut the door and began to creep in the direction leading to his room. Margaret switched on the living room light, Cephas stopped and rolled his eyes as he turned his gaze away from his mother. There was a long moment of silence. Finally, Cephas decided to break the stony silence, "I thought you were sleeping already," he snapped. Margaret decided not to answer him though she kept staring in his direction. She was torn. Part of her wanted to walk towards her son and hug him because he had come back home unharmed while the other part of her wanted to punch him in the face. Cephas began to feel uneasy and enraged as his mother kept staring at him silently until eventually he decided to go to his room.

"Stop!" Margaret's voice boomed.

Cephas stopped with his back facing his mother.

"I want to ask you something Cephas."

"Go on mother," Cephas said throwing his hands in to the air in annoyance.

Margaret took a few steps towards him and held his elbow, turning him around so as to make him look at her in her face.

"What is it Cephas that I have done to …" she did not finish her sentence, she opened her eyes wide and realisation dawned on her.

"You are drunk? Cephas, you have been drinking again?"

"Mother please!"

"Oh, don't mother please me boy! You don't have any regard and respect for me as your mother so how dare you call me mother? How dare you? Answer me!" Margaret was now shaking violently with anger.

"Okay… Margaret, I'm tired right now and I'm feeling sleepy. I have to go to bed we will talk later okay? It's in the middle of the night for goodness sake!"

"I want to talk to you right now Cephas," Margaret demanded.

"You are freaking the neighbours!" Cephas said in a loud voice and staggering.

"What?" Margaret heaved a sigh, "Cephas you took my car with you, did I give you permission to drive it?"

"I don't have answers to your stupid questions Margaret."

"Stop calling me that or I will strangle you to death you wretched son!"

"You called me wretched?"

"Oh, so you are hurt? You are hurt Cephas? Huh?"

"I have no time for this," Cephas said as he walked away from Margaret.

"Of course you have," Margaret said as she ran her hand over his arm and then she pulled him by the elbow.

"Don't touch me you miserable witch!" Cephas shouted vehemently as he pushed his mother away from him.

Margaret lost her balance and fell on the couch.

"You pushed me?"

"What does it look like? Please I'm begging you to leave me alone, let me live my life the way I want and peacefully. I'll be grateful if you do that for me you hear?"

"Ceph…"

"Don't call my name! You are always bothering me Margaret. You make me think that I have to end your life so that I begin to live my life peacefully, " Cephas said with his eyes wide open and fiercely shining, "Don't push me mother, " he said waving his fore finger in Margaret's face and a dull cloud of wickedness filled his eyes. He had been holding both sides of the couch for he was leaning against it as he looked at his mother deep in her eyes.

Margaret felt an icy cold shiver flow along her spine. Cephas let go of the sides of the couch and straightened from his bent position. He kept staring at his awe-stricken mother and then he turned to go to his room. Margaret began to cry. She cried softly and quietly until she lost control and began to cry loudly. She did not sleep. She couldn't because of what Cephas had done and said to her. Her own son kill her? It was a taboo, this could not happen. It was never going to happen to her, Margaret kept telling herself that till she fell asleep right there on the couch.

2

I t was already nine in the morning when Margaret was woken up by her ringing phone - it was her daughter Charity calling her from the capital city, Harare.

"Charity how are you?" Margaret said as she answered her phone and yawned.

"Oh mother, you are still in bed?"

"Yes, my dear, I slept late last night."

"Cephas made you sleep late at night, right? Mother why can't you just get rid of that boy can't you see that he is messing up everything? I mean your happiness."

"How do you expect me to do that child? He is my biological son. I can't just dump him."

"Try finding some form of discipline mother rather than just watching him. He is growing up, he is already nineteen now mother."

"Charity I …"

"No mum. You're spoiling that boy. You're spoiling that boy and it's not good you know!"

"I know dear I'll try my best," Margaret just said the words even though they both knew that Cephas was no longer easy to deal with.

After a moment of silence Charity decided to continue with the conversation, "I was worried about you mum that's why I called you. I wanted to make sure that you were fine."

"You should not worry my child I'm fine. How is my son in-law doing?"

"He is doing great especially at work. Um, mother, my husband Nyasha said he doesn't want to adopt a child. He said he will wait for God's time. I'm so confused Ma," After a short silent internal debate, Charity finally blurted out, "You know I can't tell him what I did. He will kill me!" Charity said in a terrified voice.

"So, you haven't told him the truth?"

"Yes. He'll divorce me. You know how much I love this man mama. Not having kids is something that's beginning to destroy everything I have worked so hard to achieve, my marriage and business."

Margaret felt sorry for her daughter. She wanted to console her and scold her at the same time but she didn't feel like arguing and so she just said, "I'm sorry Charity, just keep on praying to God for mercy and grace."

"It's fine now. Anyway, I have called to inform you that your granddaughter Kuzivaishe has passed her grade seven. She had five units. Her father is so happy."

"Oh! Ululululu. Wow *makorokoto chokwadi!* She has made me proud!" Margaret said in a voice filled with happiness.

"I was overjoyed too when I got the news from her dad. She needs a place at a boarding school so I just thought that it would be great if you help us out mother. We want her to attend the best school in Gweru."

"Wow! Okay I will do that. She has made me proud Charity; what a beautiful girl, with a beautiful heart and is always determined to do good."

"Yes, ma I agree. Kuzi is a hard worker. Okay mother you know that I can always count on you."

"Okay my dear thanks for calling."

"You are my mother. So, it is my duty to call you and find out how you're doing."

There was a little moment of silence before they hung up.

Margaret decided to go to the kitchen and make herself a cup of coffee. Her legs were slightly swollen due to the discomfort she had had whilst sleeping on the couch, she walked uneasily. As she was making herself some coffee, Cephas walked in. He didn't even look at her. He just took the tea cake from the freezer and began to pour juice in a glass.

"Morning son," Margaret said quietly as she forced a smile on her face.

Cephas just looked at her and walked out of the kitchen. Margaret heaved a sigh and continued making herself a cup of coffee. She followed Cephas to the lounge and then she sat beside him.

"Son if you are upset because of what happened yesterday I'm sorry." Cephas neither responded nor raised his eyes which were keenly watching the crumbs of the tea cake fall from his hands and mouth to the table.

"All I want is for you to have a good life. You know what son? I love you so much and whenever I condemn you it's just me trying to show you the right path. I jus. . ."

"Hey!" Cephas stood up in a jerk, "What is your problem? Why can't you just let me have my breakfast in peace?! Can't you observe silence for just a second? You seem to have a problem with me living together with you under the same roof, I see, " Cephas said nodding his head, " Because every time you see me you just can't keep quiet!"

Margaret was not even surprised by Cephas' remark, "It's only the two of us in this house all your siblings have settled down and they now have their own homes. I don't understand it son why do you hate me so much?" Margaret asked with a voice filled with pain.

"You make my life a living hell because you can't just keep your mouth shut as if you have red hot blocks of coal in your mouth. You disgust me Margaret!" Cephas snapped and left.

Without warning Margaret's tears began to flow down her cheeks. She wiped them with the back of her hand. She sniffed loudly as she walked slowly towards her kitchen. But as she passed through her living room she stopped suddenly and turned her head to look at a huge portrait on the wall which had a golden rim. The image on the portrait was wearing a broad smile on its face. Margaret kept weeping as she went and stood before it as if it was an altar. She began to speak to the image.

"I know that I sinned against you my husband and I know that you're punishing me for that sin, please forgive me Lucas it wasn't my intention to hurt you, and I admit that the devil used me against you. I know very well that I made a huge mistake by turning the hearts of our children against you but a curse you laid on Cephas is making me suffer. I never meant to hurt you... Lucas I loved you so much. I know that I broke all our wedding vows by spending nights in another man's arms," Margaret was now in deep sorrow and so absorbed in her sobs that she didn't notice her third child Chipo who had just returned from Australia.

"Please Lucas my husband have mercy on me, " she shook violently with emotion and then she knelt down before the portrait, " Please Lucas do not punish me by turning this son away from me ...I know you died knowing that Cephas is not a real Khumalo. I'm sorry my husband for being unfaithful to you but with love you helped me raise the boy as if he were your own. Please don't let this child break my heart. Cephas is still our son regardless of him being an illegitimate child. Lucas please you used to call him your own so why are you turning in your grave? Why are y..." Margaret suddenly stopped. She felt that someone was watching her. She slowly turned her head and saw that it was her son Chipo, his cheeks were wet with

8

tears just like hers. Margaret quickly stood up and there was a little moment of silence...stony silence so Margaret decided to break it, "You're back?"

Chipo just looked at his mother as if she had said some magical words in a language he did not understand. Margaret then realised that Chipo must have heard her confession.

"I wasn't expecting you son, welcome!" Margaret ran towards Chipo to hug him but he stopped her.

"I'm not a fool mother."

"What do you mean son?" Chipo kept staring at his mother, "You don't want your mother to hug you? Wow!" Margaret bent down and picked up her coffee mug, " Okay then if you don't want me to hug you right now it's okay, call me by the time you are ready for your mother's hug, " Margaret turned to leave.

"You know exactly the reason why I didn't greet you mother. You said it with your own mouth. What is it that dad didn't do for you that made you crawl in another man's bed and let him rip off your pants!" This was more than a blow to Margaret.

She stopped walking and then turned back to look at her son. Margaret was silent for some time until she then walked towards her son with a narrowed expression on her face, "I can see that Australia has robbed you of your manners. Chipo you're my son and you talk to your mother like that!? No! That was wrong."

"Just answer the damn question mother!" Chipo was so enraged that he began to shake violently, "No wonder you keep spoiling the boy even though he humiliates you in public. You loved his father more than ours, right?"

Margaret turned her gaze away from her enraged son, "No son. I loved your father so much, he too knew that. I want to tell you everything but you need to promise me that no one is going to find out about this." Margaret turned to look back at her son.

Chipo wanted to refuse but he later agreed.

"I want you to find a place in your heart to forgive me," Chipo just looked at his mother but he didn't answer her.

"Twenty-six years ago, I got pregnant with you. I always had a feeling that you were a male child, even your father couldn't wait to hold you in his hands. Your father was a loving man son but he had one problem. He was a wife beater and cheater. His beatings were unbearable but I endured every pain he inflicted on me without question. I wanted to hate him but I couldn't - he was the man to whom I had given my all. I almost had a miscarriage when I was pregnant with you. I remember that day vividly. He had come back home again drunk and penniless. Until one day his closest friend Frederick Mangwende visited us. He knew that your father was a wicked man and he began to help with the groceries and everything till you, Charity and Christopher were able to go to school. You never heard me cry nor did you see my face with scars on it because he did it carefully so as to make sure that the neighbours, our friends and you my children didn't notice anything and I too was never sad," Margaret stopped as she waited for her son's reaction.

"You are lying to me mother. Father has always been a good man and if he ever did wrong why are you taking so long to tell me whatever that made you fall pregnant for another man and …"

"I'm human Chipo and I therefore am capable of making such mistakes. All I want is for you to listen to all that I have to say," Margaret sniffed loudly as her son rolled his eyes, "It was late at night when your father and I had had a fight. He

10

sent me packing and he threw me out of the house I had nowhere to go and so I went over to the streets. I was almost raped by a certain tramp but Fred saved me. He took me to his house and I confided in him. He seemed to be the only person who understood me. I don't know what happened but all I still remember is that one thing led to the other and I ended up in his bed with him. He took advantage of my pains and sorrows… it wasn't intentional and so this is how I got pregnant with your little brother, Cephas."

"So how did dad react when he found out?"

"He never did find out. He died under the impression that Cephas was his son."

"I knew it mother! I hope you still have an element of dignity in you. So shameless!" Chipo shouted in disgust.

"Actually I do that's why I have told you everything and that is the reason why I was confessing my sins to your father because I know that I did a shameful thing. I know that now you hate me so much Chipo but I'm still your mother so please forgive me, " Margaret began to cry. Chipo kept staring in her direction, "Everything you've said might be true but that which you said about dad abusing you I have a feeling that's telling me you're lying."

Margaret raised her face to look at her son, she stood up slowly from her crouching position, "Okay I'll show you, " Margaret slowly removed her gown over her shoulder until her entire back was uncovered and there was a huge black scar which ran across her back. Chipo wanted to cover his face with his hands, "No don't!" Margaret shouted and Chipo removed his hands from his face, "Your father pushed me in the well as we were fighting. I thank God that I didn't die. Do you believe me now that your father was a wicked man?" Chipo remained silent and then Margaret left. Chipo's tears gushed out as he fell down on the couch and cried.

3

That evening Chipo decided to leave, he told his mother that he wanted to go and see Charity his sister. Margaret bid him farewell and he went.

In Mambo Night Club Cephas was having a bottle of beer. This time he had decided not to bring his mother's car along. He sat on one of the clean glass tables and seemed to be in mild spirits. The bar was already full by half past seven in the evening. A certain woman walked in the bar, she seemed to be in her late forties. She came over and sat beside Cephas with a wide yellowish grin on her face, "I'm Brenda but many people call me Fassie!" she shouted because of the loud noise in the bar caused by the stereo.

"Oh," Cephas said showing the woman that he was impressed, "I'm Cephas!"

"Oooh you want to dance?" he asked pursing her large lips which had deep red lipstick put on them.

"Sure," Cephas said standing up and the two went on to the dance floor and began to dance. Cephas was already in ecstasy when he heard someone poking his back he turned around and saw Rusvingo his friend and the other boys from his neighbourhood and they were all roaring with laughter. Cephas then asked Fassie to be excuse him. They went outside and his friends could not help it.

"Hey what's funny?"

"Now that one is a stupid question," Rusvingo said, "That woman is almost your *gogo's* age man."

"Who cares man…I was having a great time man, what's up?"

"It's Bra S. He has more of that stuff so he said that I should tell you that we should meet at our usual spot and then share the goody goodies."

Cephas just nodded his head and then turned to leave, "Hey man you having a hard time at your *den*?" Rusvingo asked as soon as the other boys left.

"Yah my old lady's giving me a hard time."

"But I have always told you to ignore it. She cares for you...I myself wish to have a mother but..."

"It's getting out of hand she shouldn't force me to do the things I hate, she should stop pushing me around you know?"

There was a sudden tense atmosphere between the two boys, Rusvingo moved closer to Cephas and lowered his voice into a whisper, "You won't do it to your old lady will you?" Cephas was quiet for some time until he turned his gaze towards his friend and said "No." Rusvingo just shrugged and they both entered the bar.

Cephas sat with a plumb in his chair as Rusvingo ordered more beers for themselves and Fassie quickly left her other potential clients and ran over to Cephas to give him a shoulder massage and Rusvingo burst out laughing but before he had finished laughing another woman came over to him and he stood up and went away with her.

Cephas woke up the next morning in Fassie's bed but as he tried to go out she pulled him back in her bed, "You were so good. At this age I just can't believe that you're a Rambo in bed," she said grinning mischievously.

"I have to go now."

"How about this one la..."

"Get off me bitch! I have given you your coins and that's enough!" Cephas said pushing Fassie away and then he got dressed up.

14

"You are too aggressive for your age my dear."

"Now you listen to me," Cephas hissed, "You are nothing but a prostitute, a well into which every he-goat sinks his gourd to quench his thirst. So, mind your tongue."

Brenda was quiet for some time as she counted the money Cephas had given to her. He finished wearing his shoes and then he left.

Cephas entered Nowinnie's room without knocking, Rusvingo and Nowinnie were having an intimate moment.

"What is it now?" Rusvingo sneered as Nowinnie rolled her eyes.

"Time up man you said that we should go and meet Bra S today."

"Oh, yeah let's hurry," Rusvingo said and they both left.

Chipo had arrived late at night at his sister's home. He woke up with a slight headache his mind still reeling from what his mother had told him yesterday. He opened his bedroom window and then he then kept staring in the blank space.

"Watching the African sun?" Charity asked as she entered his room with two cups of coffee. Chipo then turned to look at his sister, "Yes…I miss it, "Chipo said as he forced a smile.

"Well you look sad to me, are you okay?"

"Yes, I'm good just that I have a slight headache."

"That reminds me, why didn't you spend the night at home?"

Chipo began to cough uncontrollably and then ran to the bathroom. He told Charity to leave and after she had left he heaved a sigh.

It was already eleven and Cephas had not come back home since the previous day. Margaret decided to do an investigation in Cephas' room because she suspected that he was doing drugs. Margaret tried to open his door but it was locked and so she searched for the spare keys. It's been ages since Margaret entered her son's bedroom. It had pictures of completely naked women stuck on the walls. The silver ash tray on the floor was filled with used-up cigarettes and small twisted papers of weed. His room was stinky and dusty. Margaret choked and then coughed violently, she then went over and lifted her son's mattress from its base and then she saw that it had been cut and sewn with twine. She tore it open and then saw that there were hundreds of little plastic papers filled with cocaine. She let out a loud cry as she fell down on her bottom in disbelief. She almost fainted. She then took a look in his drawers and then she saw different types of used condoms. Margaret became so pale. She then tidied up his room to avoid him from noticing that someone had invaded his space. Margaret was satisfied now, she had given birth to a monster, beast and devil!

Margaret decided to go and inform her best friend Danai who lived next door. Danai had always been like a sister to Margaret.

"Today I managed to get into Cephas' room and I have deduced something from this. My baby boy is now a grown-up he uses condoms on different women, his bedroom walls have pictures of naked women on them...as if that isn't enough...Cephas is now a criminal, he has stocks of cocaine in his mattress and he smokes weed...my son drinks alcohol and he sleeps outside like a stray dog."

Danai listened with her mouth agape. Fresh tears gushed out of Margaret's eyes as she finished narrating her story to Danai.

"What has gotten into your boy? Ei maybe he is cursed but if that's so who cursed him and why?"

Danai asked in a voice full of sympathy.

"That boy has killed me, Cephas has sounded a death knell for me. I am gone my friend!" Margaret wailed. Her tears had stopped flowing down her cheeks now.

After some time Danai told her friend that she had a plan.

"I think I have come up with an idea my sister that's going to stop Cephas from misbehaving."

Danai said this as she knelt beside Margaret who had been sitting on the floor with her legs out stretched.

"What's the idea Danai?" Margaret said in a low tone. Her voice was a little rough because she had cried too much.

"You should get Cephas arrested. That will teach him a lesson. The boy has caused you great pain Margaret."

Margaret was perplexed by the suggestion, "What? Are you insane Danai? Have you lost it?"

Danai fell silent. She looked at her friend and before she could say anything Margaret spoke out, "Think of something. I don't want my son to hate me or mistake me for some wicked mother."

"But that boy doesn't even treat you like a mother at all. Maggie you're spoiling that boy, if Cephas goes to jail he will learn his lessons and those lessons will help him change for the better. The lessons will force him to give up on the bad habits that he has gotten himself entangled with. He'll understand that you have done it out of love. Discipline from a parent is love but spoiling him is a different story."

"Cephas is just a kid. I can't send him to prison because he is still young. He is my son, my baby boy and my world. I know that the devil has turned my son away from me but I'm not going to let him succeed!" Margaret said vehemently.

"It's alright sister I understand," Danai said after remaining silent for a very long time, "Do you want some more coffee?

17

"Danai asked as she watched Margaret drink the dregs from her mug.

"Yes, and please make it stronger," Margaret said as she handed Danai her empty mug.

It had been a very busy day for Cephas, he sighed as he entered the living room. He noticed that his mother wasn't around and then he sighed again but this time it was a sigh of relief. Cephas realised that he hadn't eaten anything for the whole day and so he went to the kitchen and got himself a bottle of Redds which was his mother's favourite beer and then proceeded to heap slices of brown bread with cheese onto a plate. He then came to the living room and sat on the couch with a plump and began to attack his meal. There was suddenly a knock on the door. He scowled before opening it and then wore a smile when he saw that it was Rusvingo.

4

Rusvingo stayed with his uncle who was a drunkard and was accustomed to a habit of beating up his wife and children whenever he came home drunk and especially just after payday. Rusvingo would either run away and spend the night in the street or at Cephas' home. His uncle appeared to be a respectable man every time he visited them at the country side during Christmas. So, when Rusvingo lost his parents, his grandparents did not hesitate to send him to the city to go and stay with his uncle for in their eyes he was always the responsible son.

He too was hungry and so was glad that he had arrived on time when he saw Cephas' full plate on the table together with a bottle of beer. Back there at his uncle's house only his uncle could have a breakfast with more than two slices and a beer at his elbow. They both sat down and ate together. They discussed what they were going to do at night until they came to a conclusion. They were going to Mambo Night Club and not only were they going to drink there but they were also going to rob the bar!

After the tiresome night, Cephas decided to go and spend the night at Kindra's home. Kindra was coloured and had just turned twenty-one. She lived with her father Elvis James and brother Max. Max did not like Cephas because Cephas was in a rival gang. He had been sent to different rehabs by his father so that he would quit drugs and alcohol but to no avail. No one was around that night and so Kindra and Cephas had a peaceful night together and so Cephas woke up a little later and began to dress himself up.

"Cephas where were you coming from last night?" Kindra asked as she woke up and began to dress up too.

"Party. Bra S had arranged a late-night party for everyone so on my way back home we met the Samurais and so when they attacked us we escaped."

The Samurais were the rival gang in which Max had joined.

Kindra narrowed her gaze and then she walked towards Cephas, "Why is it that I don't believe you?"

Cephas turned his gaze away from her, "That is not my problem babe. I have told you all that you want to know."

"Okay," Kindra said in a firm but angry voice, "Get out damn it! You think I'm a fool? You think I don't know what you did last night? You think I don't know that you stole from that ba…"

Cephas rushed towards her and covered her mouth with his hand, "Damn it Kindra, do you want the police to come and get me?"

Kindra just looked at him and removed his hand from her mouth and then pursed her lips in annoyance, "How the hell did you get to know about this?"

"I listen to the news on radio my boy, you are WANTED!" Kindra said and then burst out laughing. Suddenly the gate was opened and the person was coming towards the kitchen door. Kindra quickly hid Cephas and then a loud knock was heard on the door. Kindra rushed to see who it was.

"Max is not around Fatso," Kindra said as soon as she opened the door.

Fatso was Max's friend, age mate and fellow gang member of the Samurais. He was around his late twenties and he had dreadlocks which were dyed blue at the tips.

"I'm not here for Max but for you my pretty chick," Fatso said as he tried to kiss Kindra on her cheek but she pushed him away.

"Get off me you lunatic! I have my boyfriend already I don't need you okay? Now leave!"

"Not so fast mabhebheeeza. How about I tell Max and your old man that I saw you change backs last night with your little puppy ...eh what is his name again? Yes Cephas."

Kindra was tongue tied she remembered that she had seen someone's shadow in her room from the window but had quickly dismissed the thought because she was having a good time with Cephas. She remained silent and then Fatso began to walk slowly towards the gate when Kindra followed him and asked what he wanted from her so that he would not tell Max and her father.

"Now you're talking," Fatso said widening his yellowish grin, "How about a jiggy night with me your Papa at the Mambo Night Club?"

Kindra just stood dumbfounded as if something had hit her in the face. She swallowed hard and when Fatso attempted to leave she pulled him by the arm and nodded her head.

"What?"

"We'll go together at the club and spend the night" Kindra said in a low voice.

"Good. I'll be expecting you my lovey!" Fatso said and left. Kindra almost bit her tongue, she just could not believe what she had said to Fatso.

When she returned, Cephas asked her who it was and what the person wanted, she lied and told him that it was Martha Max's girlfriend who had come looking for her boyfriend. Cephas quickly wore his shoes and left without saying another word to Kindra. He met Rusvingo just outside Kindra's gate and as soon as they finished greeting each other the police caught them and so they were taken to the police station.

Margaret arrived a little late with her nephew Tinashe whom she had gone to pick up at the Gweru bus terminus. He had come from Harare to stay with her and would be attending school in Gweru at the Midlands State University for he had done very well in his A 'level examinations. Margaret parked her car in the garage after she had dropped her nephew. Tinashe went over to his aunt and helped close the garage.

"You're welcome my son, this is your home," Margaret said after they had got in the house.

"Thank you aunt. Wow you have got a beautiful home," Tinashe said as he sat down.

"Thank you my child. It's been a tough time for your uncle and I for we thought that we were never going to finish building the house because of some financial problems that we had that time but we finished the whole task together," Margaret said as she shut her glass sliding door and then she turned to look at Tinashe who was sitting on the couch with a suitcase on his laps watching Margaret. "*Yohwe nhai mwana waMisheck* give me that suitcase," Margaret said as she took away the suitcase Tinashe was holding. She told him to follow her and then she showed him his room which had once belonged to Chipo.

"Wow the room is nice it's also bigger than the one we have in Harare, father said he wanted to extend the house but he hasn't found enough money just yet," Tinashe said and then smiled at his aunt. Margaret smiled back at him, "Your father must be very proud of you son," there was a moment of silence until Margaret broke it and said, "I'll make us some coffee."

"Oh no!" Tinashe ran and stood before his aunt, "You're tired aunt I'll do it."

He left everything that he was doing and made coffee for himself and his aunt. Misheck was Margaret's elder brother and her closest sibling. Tinashe was his third child and the first to do well at school in the family.

Margaret was sitting down in her living room with Tinashe having their coffee when her cell phone rang she quickly answered it and panicked as soon as she heard the message. She stood up in a jerk and ran for the door Tinashe held her and asked what the problem was and she told him that Cephas had been arrested. Tinashe decided to drive his aunt as she directed him to the station.

Nyasha was sitting in his study when Charity walked in holding a tray with two cups of coffee in her hands, "Oh, my darling aren't you going to rest? You have been busy since yesterday."

Nyasha looked up and smiled at his wife, "Charity how many times do you want me to tell you that I'm not doing this for myself but for my kids," Charity's smile disappeared and then she slowly put the tray on the table, "Honey? Did I say something wrong?"

"No it's just that I- I I'm not feeling well today. I have a headache," Charity said as she sat down.

"Oh sorry about that. So tell me, what do you think our kids would be like?" Nyasha asked as he went and sat beside Charity.

"Nyasha it's been ten years since we got married, we are never going to have children all our lives. Baby please I beg you let's adopt a baby, there are kids out there in need of a family you and I can ad..." Nyasha quickly changed the expression on his face and let go off Charity's lap he was holding.

"I want my own kids Charity not some other man's creations!" Tell me why you can't give me children. For ten years I have been married to you but your womb has never delivered even a cripple for me Charity!" Nyasha bellowed, "Is it trying to tell me that I Nyasha am not a man at all?"

Charity remained silent as tears flowed down her cheeks, she just stood up and left Nyasha panting like a tired athlete for he was so angry and devastated.

Margaret came back from the police station with Tinashe she had not expected it at all, all this proved to her that her son would never change for the better. When they had got inside the house Cephas decided to go to his room but Margaret stopped him, "Young man you know that I need an explanation. You can't avoid me like this you should at least say something."

"There is nothing to explain mother," Cephas answered and then left.

Margaret sat on the couch and sighed, "I just can't believe I have a dog for a son. "

Tinashe went over and sat beside his aunt, "Aunt is Cephas always this mean?"

Margaret looked at his awestricken face and smiled, "You shouldn't worry about him I will handle him."

Kindra was preparing supper and her father was reading a newspaper with a large brown cigarette lodged in his mouth. Max hadn't come back from the 'match'. Elvis stood up and took a glance from a clock hung over the wall, "Girly when did your brother say he was coming back from the match?"

This is how Kindra's father addressed her, "Um... dunno dad maybe he is having some problems with his car. It's an old car that you gave to him so he is bound to have problems with it on the road." Kindra winced as she said this to her father

24

who mumbled something as he flipped some pages and continued to read his paper.

The next day at noon Margaret and Tinashe were seated outside having some lunch as two lads and a young girl walked in through her gate. She curiously looked at them and when they had reached where she and her nephew were seated they exchanged greetings.

"How can I help you?" Margaret asked.

"Well *mama* we are looking for a house to rent. We are students at MSU. We heard that you needed tenants."

"No I don't need tenants. The people who have told you that have lied to you," Margaret said and the three looked at each other and as they were about to leave Margaret stopped them and then they turned to look at her, "I can be of help if you need it. I have a three-room cottage you can use that one but pay me $80 per month."

The girl screamed happily, "Of course *mama*. Thank you so much."

They then discussed on how they were going to live and behave and all agreed on it and then they left after paying and later on returned with a lorry filled with their property.

Later that evening Kindra received a call from Fatso. He asked her to meet him at the bar and do what they had agreed on. Kindra went to her room, took a jacket and peeped in her father's room and saw that he was fast asleep and was already snoring. She crept out of the house and went to the bar.

As she reached the bar her phone rang again but she couldn't hear what whoever had called was saying because of the noise from the bar. She got inside and saw Fatso sitting on one of the chairs close to the counter and as soon as he saw Kindra he winked, smiled, stood up and walked towards her.

"You are so hot mabhebheza eish I just can't believe that you have dressed up for me. You look hot! Eish ma…"

"Let's just get over with it Fatso. You're beginning to get on my nerves."

"Oh she's beginning to lose her temper, okay" Fatso turned around and then called out loud, "Fassie! Fassie!"

Fassie came running towards them, "What is it now Fatso?"

"We want a room."

Fassie looked astonished for some time and then said "Look, we don't have rooms for men to sleep with other bitches. If you want a room hire one of us we are not for display *shamwari.*"

Fatso looked at Fassie and gave her a five dollar note, "Now."

Fassie smiled, "Follow me."

Late that night Cephas came back home looking frustrated and barged into his room without even greeting his mother and cousin who were in the lounge. Later on Margaret decided to go to bed and left Tinashe watching a late night movie playing on a DVD player. He then stood up after the movie had finished playing and went to bed. But on his way to his bedroom, he saw Cephas cursing, sighing and sniffing. He then peeped through the slight opening of his bedroom door. He was amazed by what he saw, Cephas was a drug addict. Tinashe just saw it, ignored it and went to bed.

The next day Tinashe went to school and when he came back his aunt asked him how it had been and he said that he had a great time. Cephas walked into the kitchen took his slices of bread and some juice and left. Margaret just ignored him. She then called Tinashe and told him that she was going out to see Danai her friend and she left. Tinashe went over to the garden where Cephas was having his lunch.

"Cephas do you have a minute?"

There was a moment of silence, "What do you want Tinashe?"

"I want to talk to you. It's important."

Cephas stuffed more bread in his mouth and took a large gulp of juice and then turned to look at Tinashe who was still standing beside him.

"Speak."

"Why do you hate me? I mean since I came you never said hi to me. Is there something I should know?"

Cephas burst out laughing and then suddenly stopped, "Oh so you noticed that. Good, that's good. At least they don't call you Mr Bright for nothing man."

"Are you going to tell me or not?"

"Hey man stop getting on my nerves *wazvinzwa*. To tell you what, *hanty* you are very bright can't you at least tell me what's going on? You have come to take my mother away from me so that she keeps calling me a bad son. If you want me to love you go back to Harare *kuMbare kwenyu uko.*"

Tinashe smiled, "Cephas my bro grow up man. I never knew that my coming here posed a threat to you but allow me my man to tell you that what you have said is not correct. That's not my intention. Aunt told me that I'll be here to study and be your friend she actually mentioned something about loneliness but I know that a guy like you is probably the father of the hood," Tinashe said chuckling.

"All I can say for now is if you need anything come and tell me," Tinashe winked and left Cephas fuming in anger.

That afternoon Max went over to Mambo Night Club with some friends and there he met Nowinnie and Brenda. He was eavesdropping on their conversation because they were talking about him.

"*Makaradhi haana hunhu chokwadi.* His sister came with Fatso yesterday and when I passed through their room he was in ecstasy, groaning with pleasure."

"Fassie I hope you are not lying my dear, look the brother is a drunkard the sister a prostitute," the women said and burst out laughing.

Max felt that their conversation was getting out of hand and so he stood up and walked towards them, "Your boss said that he doesn't want trouble but you seem to enjoy discussing my family affairs in public. I am not going to do my job here but I will look for a suitable place and time. Remember I am a Samurai...*mathreats angu* are just not empty threats! That's a promise!" Max waved his finger towards them, beckoned to his friends and then he left together with them.

Kindra was lying on the couch having some ice cream when Max walked in shouting her name, "KiNDRA! KINDRA!"

Kindra rushed off to the kitchen to meet her brother, "What? Why are you shouting? Do you want to bring down the roof?"

"Will you shut up! Shut up! I thought you were different from those other girls in the hood but today you have proven me wrong."

Kindra remained silent as she stood looking at Max with her arms folded.

"Kinnie I am your brother please just tell me the truth."

"What truth?" Kindra said turning her gaze from Max and then rolled her eyes.

Max then jumped towards Kindra, "Did you have sex with Fatso?"

Kindra's heart began to beat fast, faster and ... She looked at her brother in horror as he took hold of her arm and firmly held it.

"Get off me Max! Leave my hand!" Kindra was now screaming.

Her father walked into the kitchen, "What's going on in here?"

No one answered Elvis, he was getting impatient, "Hey am I talking to myself? I said what's going on in here? Max tell me why are you holding her hand?"

Max just looked at his father, "Kindra I will be back for you and you know what, I want answers!" Max hissed in Kindra's ear, let go of her arm and left.

Kindra was left all alone with her father, "And that?"

Kindra shifted her weight from one leg to the other, "He didn't mention dad. Max just barged in and started accusing me of things I don't even know."

Her father was silent for some time and then he walked towards her, "I don't want trouble but why do I have a feeling that you are lying, girly?"

"Dad I'm still that princess you have always loved. I haven't changed," Kindra said forcing a smile.

"Mmmhh..." Elvis grumbled and left.

Max arrived at his gang's meeting place and saw Fatso talking with the other members he stood aside and kept watching him. Fatso saw Max and walked towards him, "Hey my bro *howzit?*"

Max pounced on Fatso and began punching him in the face. The other guys began howling like mad dogs as they cheered for Max and others encouraged Fatso to hit back but Fatso was already down. The gang's leader Lucifer then arrived the cheering stopped. Max was held by Lucifer's bodyguards.

"What is wrong guys? You are brothers so why the fighting?"

Fatso's face was covered with blood and he was finding it difficult to breathe, "This dog raped my sister," Max said panting at the same time.

Lucifer shut his eyes and burst out laughing. Everyone looked at each other and back at their boss and followed suit by roaring with laughter regardless of the fact that they did not know why their boss was laughing.

"The sister is now a woman, she is grown up. Kindra and I had an agreement my bro, I didn't r…"

"Will you sh…" Max fought the boys holding him but to no avail, he wanted to beat Fatso again and he was suddenly silenced by Lucifer who raised his hand.

"This will take us nowhere. This is our group's meeting place not a ring for skinny wrestlers like you. Brothers I want you to respect this holy ground. Do not misbehave *vapfanha*. If you repeat this again you will find yourselves in my dungeon or burning to ashes in my hell. Samurais are civilised soldiers…so I demand that you behave as such."

This statement sent a cold shiver along everyone present's spine. A chair was given to Lucifer to sit on.

"Now let's do today's business!" Lucifer demanded and everyone stood a little closer to his chair and listened attentively to what their leader was saying.

That night when almost everyone was fast asleep Margaret heard a fire crackling outside her house. She woke up and saw a bright light in her room shining outside. She then wore her slippers. At first she had thought that she was having a nightmare but she later on heard someone cursing and decided to go out and see. It was Cephas her son burning all his blankets. She asked him what was the problem but Cephas ran towards her with a burning stick he had used to turn his blankets to make sure they burn completely. He threatened to cut off his mother's legs, Margaret was so afraid that she let out a loud scream that woke up Tinashe and some of her neighbours. Her neighbours knew that her son was troublesome and so they didn't come to her rescue. Tinashe went over and saw what was happening, he rushed towards Cephas held him and then tied him up. He thought that Cephas had gone crazy. Cephas kept begging Tinashe to untie him but Tinashe refused. Margaret could not bear it and so she ordered Tinashe to untie him. Cephas was panting, "The fleas were biting me mother, I couldn't bear it."

"What fleas Cephas? I washed these blankets last month. Almost every month I wash them up."

"My room was last cleaned up a long time ago mum."

Everyone kept staring at Cephas, "You should have told us son you really scared us look Tinashe is new here and you scared him, he was thinking that you have lost it."

They all burst out laughing except for Cephas who returned to his room, "Those blankets were expensive but in spite of that I smiled. Yet, he is still mad at me. Tinashe my son do you think that Cephas is still himself?"

Tinashe sighed, "I don't know aunt but I hope so."

There was a long moment of silence and then Tinashe patted his aunt and told her to forget about everything and rather go to bed. Margaret was so scared. She didn't sleep the whole night, she could not figure out Cephas' real problem.

5

Early the next morning Danai came over to Margaret's house to find out what had happened last night.

"Burned his blankets? Ah *ukati mwana wako haana ngozi?* Margaret my sister do something. We should take him to a pastor or a witchdoctor. *Maprophets akazara muno wani* the boy is probably in dire need of divine intervention."

Margaret just cried and kept shaking her head, "That boy has killed me Danai. He lacks a conscience; he doesn't even know the difference between right and wrong. He tried to apologise this morning but later on rebuked me saying that I don't deserve his apology because I'm a wicked woman."

Danai was silent for some time until she said, "And you let him go? You should have slapped him in the face to wake his slumbering brains! How dare he insult the woman who carried him in her womb for nine solid months!" Danai said vehemently as she raised up nine fingers and waved them to Margaret.

"Margaret you are spoiling this boy. I just wish Lucas was alive so that maybe he'd help you tame that animal, Cephas!"

"Danai you a…"

"No Margaret your son is now an animal. A beast! How can a normal child behave in the way Cephas is doing? The boy is not himself anymore. He is possessed. He has to be cleansed my sister."

"No Danai I committed a sin in the past and I guess I'm being punished for that sin. Maybe God or even the ancestors are using Cephas for th…"

"There is nothing like that. I disagree with you. Sinners repent and are forgiven. That son of yours has an evil spirit inside him. I feel for you my sister. We should pray to God and consult our ancestors so that this ends."

"Danai," Margaret said in a low voice but it was scary.

"Yes my dear?"

"I don't know but I have a feeling that Cephas is going to kill me."

"What? No *shamwari* I don't think it has gone that far. Okay then but we can only avoid the tragic event by clean…"

"I have had enough Danai! There is no cleansing that's going to take place in my house! I don't believe in those things and I feel I need time to figure out why my son is behaving that way. Just give me time my sister. You are supposed to understand the love I have for Cephas is no ordinary love but a mother's love," Margaret was almost crying.

"I understand my sister," Danai patted Margaret's back, "I'll find us something to drink. What should I bring you?"

"A cold beer."

"Okay *sisi* relax *hanty?*" Margaret nodded and Danai went over to the kitchen and brought two brown bottles of beer and two glasses.

Chipo was sitting alone on one of the couch's in Charity's lounge when Charity approached him with two glasses filled with wine. Chipo did not see his sister until she made a sound by clearing up her throat, Chipo then turned his head and their gazes met. Chipo was a little bit startled but a weak smile formed across his lips as Charity put down the glasses on the table.

"Chipo are you okay? Since you came here you haven't been yourself is there any pr…?"

Charity asked in a low and gentle voice.

"I am fine sis it's just that I woke up wi…"

"With a headache," Charity completed the sentence for him as she put the two glasses on the table before them, "Chipo for how long are you going to carry on like this? Something is wrong somewhere and you don't want me to know about it. It's wrong you know. Did some girl dump you?" Charity said trying to create a humorous atmosphere.

Chipo just smiled, "No."

Charity stood up, "I'm sick and tired of your attitude! I am calling mum right now and you're going back home!"

"No sis. I want to tell you but mum asked me not to say it to anyone."

Charity turned to look at her brother, "But it's wrong because it's eating you up. We have always been there for each other Chipo. Besides if it's involving mother then it's a family affair so you can as well feel free to tell me."

Chipo sat down and then heaved a sigh, "It's Cephas."

"Cephas? I knew it! But I have sent her money this morning about a hundred dollars so that he stops causing mum trouble."

"It's not that sis," Chipo swallowed hard, "Cephas is- he-is not …No I can't believe I'm saying this. Even when mum said it I thought it was a joke."

Charity kept staring at Chipo with her eyes wide open, "You are not making any sense."

"Cephas is …" Chipo took a deep breath, "Not dad's real son. He is not our biological brother and …" Chipo did not finish his statement.

"What? "Charity was shocked, she couldn't believe her ears.

"Yes. I too could not believe it but …" Chipo shrugged.

"So whose son is he?"

"He is Mangwende's, dad's old friend who stays *kuMambo.*"

34

"But how did it all happen? I'm finding it hard to believe what you have just said, mum would never do that. I…I…I mean she would never be unfaithful to dad. It's so unlike her." Charity sat back in her chair looking confused.

"So are you saying I made up this whole thing?"

"No. There is only one solution to this whole problem. I am going to ask mum about this now. Right now."

Chipo pulled Charity by the arm as she reached for her cell phone, "Mum said I shouldn't tell a soul about it. Don't make any hasty decisions. It's a secret so let's keep it that way."

Charity and Chipo slowly sat down and there was a long moment of silence until Charity picked up one glass of wine and handed it to Chipo and then took one for herself, "I think we both need this," She said before taking a sip from it.

Max got home early that afternoon and saw Kindra having her lunch, "You had sex with Fatso right?"

Kindra was startled, she hadn't expected Max to come early because it was so unlike him.

"Max please stop troubling me. It's my life and only I have the right to choose which guy to go out with and have se…"

"Hey! You should stop messing around with me. I'm your brother this whole lot of mess is affecting everyone. Kindra people aren't just talking about you and Fatso, they are also pointing fingers at me. There is one thing I promise you, make sure you don't fall pregnant for Fatso and that monkey of a boyfriend Cephas."

"You must be crazy Max you're not my boyfriend and you should stop ordering me around. I am not Martha!"

"Okay girly," Max sneered as he said the word girly trying to imitate his father," Only time will tell who is the boss, between you and I. I am watching you," Max said pointing two of his fingers to Kindra and then went to his room.

"I hate you Max! I am not afraid of you. You don't scare me!" Kindra said after Max.

Tinashe had by this time become real friends with their tenants Abigale Musoncha, Lawrence Zambuko and Takunda Choto. Abigale was doing her bachelors degree in medicine, Takunda and Lawrence were both studying law, just like Tinashe.

They had gone out for lunch together on one Saturday noon, "*Nhai* Tinashe what's wrong with your cousin? He's always moody, cold and scary," Abigale asked as she stuffed a piece of the samosa into her mouth. Everyone then turned their attention to Tinashe who just shrugged and then took a sip from his juice.

"He doesn't have a problem, he's fine."

"Huh? *Haana* problem? No *sha* you can't say that. There is something wrong with his behaviour *kana kuti* he just doesn't like us."

"*Iii* maybe because he thinks *kuti takasara,*" Takunda said and they all burst out laughing.

"*Haaa* no guys. I also don't understand him maybe that's who he is, 'a guy with a cold personality'. All I can say is we just have to be tolerant because he sometimes gets on my nerves you know maybe because I'm staying at his home."

"I agree dear. But you have forgotten to explain to us something. He burned up his blankets that night – what was the reason for that?" Abigale asked as she took a gulp from her glass.

"Eish I don't know guys but all he told us was fleas and maybe lice had bit him because he last got his room cleaned up a long time ago, "Tinashe said and shrugged his shoulders.

"Umm and you believed that? *Kachatiitira zvechivanhu.* You never know, maybe he is being used by his ancestors," Lawrence said and again they all burst out laughing.

Christopher arrived at Charity's home as soon as Charity called her. When he entered they both sat down and then Charity called Chipo from his room and they then began their discussion. Christopher wasn't amazed at all when Charity told him that Cephas was their half- brother. He told them that he knew about it all this while. Charity and Chipo looked at each other and back at Christopher who stood up from his seat and began pacing across the room with one hand lodged in his pocket.

Christopher was Margaret's second child, he was a married and a successful businessman. He had two beautiful daughters Kuzivaishe and Kudzai who were aged thirteen and five respectively. His wife was also pregnant with another child and Margaret kept hoping that it was a son.

"I think we should confront mother now that we all know the truth," he suggested at last.

"Yes I agree the boy is causing her a lot of pain and almost every week we send her money to give to him so that he stops being a pain in the butt!" Charity said in agreement with what Christopher had suggested.

Chipo was silent,

"*Hezvo Chipo* are you part of this discussion or not?" asked Christopher, jerking Chipo from his thoughts

"I'm still thinking bro. Maybe we should wait until he does a mistake then it will be easier to throw him out of the house."

There was a moment of silence until Charity broke it, "I don't think that that is going to work because mum loves him so much she will prefer to go and stay with him in the bush rather than live without him."

They all nodded their heads and then Christopher said, "We should give each other time to think about this you know."

They all agreed and then Charity stood up, "I will make us something to eat."

6

Cephas woke up and got all dressed up as if he was going for a party. Margaret was sitting in her living room reading the daily paper with a cup of coffee beside her. She looked at him and smiled, "Anything special today?"

"What?"

"You're looking good my boy."

"I know. Mother I need money."

"More money Cephas? What happened to the two hundred I gave you last week? I don't have money right now… I'm not a bank remember?"

Cephas just glared at his mother as she flipped her newspaper pages and hummed an unknown hymn. He got out of the house and left. Margaret mumbled a few words and cursed.

Later that evening Cephas decided to visit one of his girlfriends, Lindiwe, a girl aged sixteen. She lived with her brother Mandla who worked in Silobela as a miner. He only turned up during the weekends and so usually Lindiwe would be alone. She lived in one of the high density suburbs in Gweru, Mkoba 9.

Cephas gently knocked on her door, Cephas was very angry and he needed someone to help him unburden his stress of not having money. He had wanted to visit Kindra but he had heard the rumour that her brother Max now watched her like a hawk had every information about her whereabouts.

When Lindiwe opened the door she was actually baffled to see Cephas in a drunken state, "Ceph-Cephas what are you doing here so late at night?"

"Oh shut up! Come on let me come inside," Cephas said as he pushed Lindiwe away for she was blocking the door's entrance.

"Cephas you can't just barge in. What if my brother was around? Mandla will go wild if he gets to find out about this," Lindiwe said after shutting the door.

"I love you and I'm here to spend the night with you," Cephas said sitting on the bed. Lindiwe lived in a two-roomed house and her brother slept on the bed whenever he was around and Lindiwe slept in the kitchen on the floor but whenever he was absent she'd always sleep on the bed.

"No Cephas this is wrong. When you told me that you loved me we never talked about you barging into my house any time at night. Please if you love me you should always show some respect for me."

There was a moment of silence until Lindiwe said, "I'm disappointed in you." She then walked towards the door and opened it up, "Please leave."

Cephas turned his red shot gaze towards her, "What? You are asking Cephas to leave? No I am not some herd boy you play around with Lindiwe, I am my own man and whatever I say goes."

"No. Not this time," Lindiwe swallowed hard, she sensed that something had gone wrong.

Cephas stood up from the bed and walked slowly towards Lindiwe and put his hand about her neck, Lindiwe began to shiver and then Cephas began to whisper something into her ear and began to kiss her everywhere. Lindiwe tried to push him away but she couldn't. When she tried to fight him he quickly slapped her across her face and then shut the door and then locked it up. Lindiwe tried to scream but he covered her mouth. Lindiwe gagged and in no time Cephas was undressing her but when he took off her underwear he jumped and cursed.

"Oh hell! Why didn't you tell me?" Cephas bellowed, "Disgusting!"

Lindiwe pulled her underwear up. She was shaking, "I tried to tell you bu…"

Cephas then pounced on the helpless young girl and began to beat her up. He mercilessly laid fists, kicks and ripping slaps on her body. Lindiwe screamed and cried out for help. Cephas spat on Lindiwe, "You have betrayed me you dirty, cheap and disgusting bitch, how dare you!" Cephas cursed and left. Lindiwe cried as blood oozed from her nose and mouth. She was badly hurt. Her neighbours came and took her to the hospital. Her brother was called and he arrived the next day.

Cephas arrived home, he was so angry that he just got into his room and banged the door. Margaret who was used to his late night comings just looked at him and shook her head. She didn't dare ask him any questions.

Mandla came to the hospital to see his sister but was told by the doctor that she was only going to be released the day after tomorrow.

Christopher reached home, he was so tired but the fact that his siblings now knew about Cephas' illegitimacy relieved him of the burden.

"Hi honey," his wife said as soon as he entered the living room. She was already dressed in her night gown, "You look tired Kiri. You must have had a busy day," she said helping him take off his coat.

"Yes," Christopher said in a hoarse voice and then he went and sank in one of the cosy couches in the lounge.

"I'm sorry honey, just give me a minute. I'll get you supper," Susan said as she headed to the kitchen.

Susan was Christopher's wife but her in-laws didn't like her that much because she was illiterate and only gave birth to female children but Christopher loved her so much and was very proud of her.

Susan came back in almost a second with a tray full of china dishes filled with delicacies.

"*Theya* you go," Susan said putting the tray on the table, "Your favourite."

Christopher opened the first basin and grinned slightly and when he opened another one he widened his grin.

"I love this stew …wow you added some spinach. But where did you get it from? There is no spinach in your little garden"

"The market of course," Susan said with a smile on her face.

"You are the best wife Susie," Christopher said already stuffing lumps of sadza in his mouth.

After he had finished having his supper Susan cleared the table and washed the dishes whilst Christopher was still sitting on the sofa.

"Susan do you ever rest?" Christopher said toying with a toothpick in his mouth and with his tongue. Susan looked at her husband and smiled, "Why do you ask? Of course I do rest."

"No. You are always running up and down fixing things."

Susan laughed, "Kirisi *askana,* a home is a woman's sanctuary. Have you forgotten that saying that goes *musha mukadzi?*"

"But you are pregnant now you should be resting. I told you that I'm going to get you a house helper but you always refuse."

Susan pulled a face, "This is my house and I don't need anyone to look after it for me. You married me and so it's my duty as a mother and wife to take care of you and the girls."

Christopher's grin widened as he stood up and hugged her, "You are like no other."

There was a long moment of silence. Susan asked Christopher if the family meeting had gone well but his mind was so far away that he didn't hear her ask and so he did not answer his wife.

"*Baba vaKuziva*. Hey. *Baba vaKuziva imi!*" she said shaking Christopher by the shoulder.

"What were you saying *zviya nhai* darling?"

"What's wrong? You haven't been yourself since you came back home."

"It's nothing my love. I'm fine."

"No. I have a feeling th…"

"Susan please, I have nothing on my mind. Why are you troubling me? I said I'm fine!" Christopher said exasperated.

"Oh and you want me to believe that? A marriage should have no secrets between a *hazibhande* and a *woifi*. You should *teringi* me what is bugging you. Come on *teri* me," Susan demanded.

Christopher looked at his wife with a scornful eye and did not respond her.

"I'm sick and tired of being treated like an invalid. So I have decided I am leaving you!" Susan said as she went to their bedroom. She opened the wardrobe and began to throw her clothes on the bed. She roughly removed her clothes from the hangers.

Christopher followed her to their bedroom, "Susan please calm down. Besides do you want to tear up those clothes?"

"Oh so you care a lot about my robes?"

"What are you saying Susan? Calm down please," Christopher holding her shoulders.

"*Kaumu dhauni?* Don't even touch me! I can't stay with a man who underestimates me only because I am illiterate. You don't even love me. You do not even trust me, you never tell me anything about your family, you don't tell me about your work, how you do it and what you do. You think that when problems arise in your family I won't be able to help you solve them. Well then Kirisi you are very wrong because it's not my fault that my parents could not afford sending me to school. I didn't even force you to love me nor did I force you to marry me. Kuziva our daughter is so intelligent but didn't she come from my womb?" Susan said shaking with rage.

"So what's your point?" Christopher snapped as he folded his arms in scorn.

"My point is that I have had enough and so I'm leaving you because I can't bear to stay with a man who doesn't appreciate me and also takes me for *girandidhi*," Susan said removing the wedding ring from her finger, "You know what Christopher? I am done," she said throwing the ring in her husband's face.

Christopher realised that the situation was now beyond his control, "Has it come to this Susan?"

"Hey Kirisi what does it look like? Besides you are an educated man you should read the situation" Susan said zipping off her suitcase and then carrying it on her head.

"Eish Susan you are stressing the baby. Remember what the doctor said about carrying heavy loads in that condition" Christopher pointed out in a calmer voice.

"*Ehe* professor. But what should I do now? It's been fifteen years and you treat me like some piece of garbage! Kiristofa I'm tired! I'm done okay? Enough is enough!" Susan said vehemently and got out of the bedroom.

She slept in the guestroom for the whole night and left very early the next day. Christopher was hurt and he felt guilty because of what he had done.

Nyasha and Charity were in their bedroom and Nyasha was getting ready for the golf match with his other workmates. They were talking about Margaret and Cephas.

"I'm trying but it's hard for me Nyasha. The boy is a lot of trouble. Mother has to go on with it. She should just send him awa…"

"No that's not right Charity. If mother in-law gets to know that all of you now know the truth she will be hurt. Remember Cee is also her son. Right now you are all angry and so I don't think it's wise to confront her about Cephas."

Suddenly the phone rang. She was shocked at first but later on she scowled her face in annoyance. She cursed under her breath when she hung up.

"Who was that and why do you look exasperated?"

"It's mother she is saying that your 'Cee' was arrested yesterday."

"For what?" Nyasha looked puzzle.

Charity cleared her throat, "He hit a girl. He tried to have sex with her but after finding out that she was having her monthly period he battered the girl and left her for dead. Mother says that she is badly hurt. The girl is all bruised up and messy."

"What?" Nyasha was perplexed.

"You see now the reason why I want that goon kicked out?" Charity said as she handed him his cap "Enjoy the match lovey," she said and got out of the room.

Mandla arrived at the hospital just in time for the doctor hadn't left. Lindiwe was discharged and so Mandla took her home.

"Lindiwe you haven't said anything to me yet. What were you doing with a boy in this house in my absence?!"

"He just came at night brother. He barged in after I had opened the door for him when he knocked. I thought that he was in trouble."

"Then?" Mandla asked impatiently.

"I found out that he was drunk. I asked him to leave but he refused. He then demanded that I sleep with him but I refused and so…and so…" Lindiwe broke down and began to cry.

Mandla hesitated but he went closer and hugged his sister. He forced himself on me. He wanted to rape me brother. He saw that I…I… I…"

"It's okay Lindi. Please stop crying. I will see what I can do to make sure that you are safe, okay?"

Lindiwe looked up at her brother with her eyes full of fear, "Just don't leave. You should promise me that you will never leave me again."

Mandla kept looking down at her and swallowed hard, "I promise you my princess we will stick together okay? Now you should stop crying" Mandla said, wiping off the tears from her face.

Margaret brought Cephas some food at the police station and then asked one of the policemen if it were possible to speak to her son to which he agreed. Cephas was called and when he came he sat on a chair opposite Margaret. Margaret did not know what to say to her son, she just kept staring him.

"*Hezvo asi* you've come here to just stare me?"

"No son, I'm just wondering why God made you my child." Margaret heaved a sigh as she picked her bag she had put on the floor and then she put it on the table, "I have brought you something to eat."

"I'm not hungry" Cephas said turning his gaze from his mother.

"Come on. Don't be stubborn just eat, you know you need energy be…"

"All I want is to get out of this place!"

"And I'm still trying to figure out how I can do that. I'm still…"

"No mother stop thinking and take action. Remember it's because of you that I got arrested. If you had given me some mon…"

"Will you shut up! You never think of anything besides money. Aren't you ashamed of yourself Cephas? You hit a girl and now you are blaming me for a crime that you have committed!" Margaret shook her head, "Shame on you!" Margaret stood up and left.

Cephas cursed as he heaved a sigh and pushed away the bag his mother had brought for him.

"What do you mean she just left?" Charity asked her brother as she put the tray she was holding on the coffee table in her lounge.

"She said that I don't respect her for the person she is."

"But why would she say that? I'm sure you said or did something that offended her. She is a village goat anyway she will never understand simple situations."

Christopher heaved a sigh, "I refused to tell her about Cephas' illegitimacy."

"What but how could you? I mean she is your wife, my husband already knows about it. Chris, you and Susie are one you should have told her you know."

"I regret it Charity."

"Just go over to her house and apologise. You should always remember that she's pregnant maybe that's why …"

"Oh!" Christopher said brightening up "I had forgotten. The doctor mentioned it the last time we went for the scan and the check-ups."

Charity smiled and Christopher stood up, "I will have to go now. I don't want to be late for work."

"Okay have a nice day."

"You too *sisi.*"

Nyasha walked in as soon as Christopher had left, "Oh honey I didn't know tha…"

"Hold it. People come into my house they talk about pregnancy and no feeling of guilt has ever crossed you. Chris and Susan are going to have a third child and us nothing, not even a blind baby. You are unpredictable! You might call Susan a village goat but she is a real woman. You are more of a man than a woman!" Nyasha said and left.

Margaret reluctantly opened her door, she asked herself what exactly she had done to be given a son like Cephas. She began to condemn her womb. She dropped her handbag on the floor and fell on the couch. She realised that she had left her windows wide open. She cursed from under her breath and then she went over to her kitchen to make herself something to eat. She decided to make herself a cup of tea because it was chilly outside. The kettle was switched on, she put some cooking oil in the frying pan and then switched on her gas stove as she broke two eggs and mixed them up with some garlic. "The oil needs some heating," she told herself out loud and then eased herself on a chair in her kitchen with both her eyes shut. She didn't hear the whistle of her kettle as hot steam came from its spout. The oil in the pan was burned up and the smell of burned oil engulfed the fragrance in her kitchen and then Danai who had visited her rushed inside.

"Margaret! *Mai* Cephas! *Yohwe!*" Danai called out as she switched off the stove and removed the pan "Are you okay my sister? Do you want to burn yourself?"

"No …I'm sorry I…"Margaret stammered.

"Sorry for yourself! Are you okay? You look stressed to me," Danai held both her friend's arms, "Come you need to sit down and rest."

"What is it *shamwari?*" Danai said later after they had sat down.

"It's Cephas… he got arrested yesterday."

"*Chii?* For what?"

"I'm even ashamed to mention it to you my friend. But what can I do? He hit a girl after she had refused to sleep with him. It's said that he hit her after finding out that she was having her menstrual period."

"Ah! *Iwe* is that boy still a human being? No your son is now an animal Margaret. Was that girl badly hurt?"

"I was actually going to ask you to accompany me there."

"*Kupi?*"At their home?"

"Yes. We have to go and make peace with her family."

"How old is the girl?"

"*Hanzi* she is sixteen."

"*Hezvo!* She is so young… I…I thought that she was also nineteen like Cephas. *Zvino hatidzinganiswe here nematemo?* Her parents will skin us alive the very moment they see us."

There was a moment of silence

"But my sister can you not see that you are spoiling this boy. Cephas has gone too far now."

Margaret remained silent and then turned her gaze away from Danai who just shook her head and cursed under her breath.

A few days later Margaret decided to visit one of her friends who stayed in the same neighbourhood as her. Rudo had three children and all had completed their studies and settled down with their new families. Kurai her first son got married to a Shona girl and this had made Solomon her husband very proud of his son. Sarudzai her second child was married to a Ndebele man who besides being a fireman had inherited a mining station from his father and so was very rich. Her last born child Zororai had married a white girl and this had actually cost Rudo and her husband their reputation. Solomon was so enraged that he attempted to disown his son.

"Zoro you have failed me! The Mbirimis are well known for their decency, pride and honour for their culture. Couldn't you find yourself a beautiful Shona girl son? A Shona girl who is capable of giving me grandchildren carrying Mbirimi blood in their veins. With this Lolita you will be cuckolded in broad daylight!" Solomon had shouted vehemently on that day when Zororai had brought Layla Arden to his parents' house.

"Eh, father take it easy on her please. Layla is also a woman and I don..."Zororai protested but Solomon kept shaking his head in disagreement.

"Are you really going to argue with me about this boy? Take that white Lolita back where you found her. I refuse to give you my blessing for this marriage. How are the people going to react if they ever find out that my son brought me *kamurungu zvako?* People are going to laugh at me, at us, at your mother!" Solomon said pointing at Rudo who had not uttered a word since Layla had entered her house.

"But father I love Layla with all my heart, she loves me too. Besides, you told me that I should find a girl of my own choice. You promised me father that …"

"Hey Zororai! I asked you to bring an indigenous girl, one with black skin like yours and mine not some hot white American wanton *mhani!*" Solomon bellowed as he threw his hand in Zororai's face.

Layla's tears began to sting her eyes because she could feel the tense atmosphere around her. Rudo also disapproved of their marriage because they did not know anything about her family's whereabouts for she said that she had left them in the USA.

"Okay father I have heard you but the culture and doctrine of our tribe will not stop me from marrying Layla," Zororai replied as a fiery spark shone in his eyes.

"Well go ahead son. But I swear on my great grandfather Nyaudzaivamwe Mbirimi that I won't consider you as my son ever again from the day you decide to marry this white cockroach. I'll disown you Zororai. So choose between your family and that little mermaid," Solomon said using his walking stick to point at Layla. Zororai winced in pain, "I am done!" he said as he was leaving and then shut the door behind him with a loud bang.

After about two days, Rudo began to notice a sudden change in her son's behaviour. Zororai stopped having his meals at home and he even started to drink alcohol, this was so unlike him for he was a cultured boy with good manners and was also reserved. Rudo became very worried until she forced herself to accept the white girl Layla as her daughter in-law. Solomon was very disappointed especially when he discovered that Rudo had supported Zororai's white wedding with Layla. No lobola was paid since Layla's parents were in the States. Solomon threatened to divorce Rudo and send her back to her parents.

"Go ahead Solomon! You can send me back but I myself and God know that I have done a good thing as a mother. Didn't his breakdown mean anything to you? The tears and his ego too? I had to do something to assure him that he still has a mother in this world a…"

"Will you shut up Rudo! I regret the day I met you and paid lobola to your people. I am your husband, you should have supported me first before supporting that brat! You promised to stand with me through thick and thin. What happened to the vow?"

There was a little moment of silence before Rudo answered, "Solomon I know that I vowed but to supress my son's interests in maintaining vows is something I can't do. *Vana vangu* are my life. Remember you have other children with that your chocolate. What's her name by the way? *Hooo ehe* Christabel," Rudo said after remembering the name, "You're secure but I am not. I only have Kura, Saru and Zoro. You've nine of them but I only have three, that is you have three with me, three with Christa, two with Chenesai and one with Mary."

Solomon's face was awestricken. He hadn't expected it at all. So Rudo knew about all his filthy games. Eish, women could be so heartless sometimes he thought to himself as he scratched his chin. Solomon was quiet for some time until Rudo broke the silence herself.

"Oh so you thought I didn't know? I know my husband. Now tell me between you and I who has violated the vows the most?" Solomon remained silent as he felt his hair rise with shame.

"Well then," Rudo said removing the suitcase from the top of their old wardrobe, "Since you said that I should go back to my people I will, but I can't go without the bus fare."

"Eh no *amai* Kura. We can talk about this please. We can settle this. I said all that in anger, at least you should have told me that Zoro and that Luhila wanted to get married. Please don't leave."

Rudo burst out laughing and Solomon looked at her confused, "What? Did I say something wrong?"

"*Anonzi* Layla. The girl's name."

"Oh sorry, but I do accept what you have said and done," Solomon said with difficulty and left.

Rudo had told Margaret all this and Margaret burst out laughing, "*Haaa ende wakamugona.* Men are a problem, that was great my friend," Margaret said pouring herself some drinking water in a glass.

"Thanks my dear for the compliment," Rudo said, also pouring some water in her glass.

Margaret cleared her throat before telling Rudo that she had come to collect her money since it was now her turn to receive the joint amount of cash. Rudo gave it to her and then Margaret decided to leave but Rudo stopped her.

"*Nhai amai Cephas* is everything okay at home? I have heard that Cephas is a lot of trouble."

Margaret sighed and sat back down on one of the sofas in Rudo's living room, "Cephas has always been a lot of trouble for me but I really don't want to talk about it right now," Margaret said standing up from where she was sitting, "I better be on my way *sisi* thanks very much for your concern."

Rudo just shook her head as Margaret left.

Margaret arrived home and as she was going to her bedroom she noticed that Cephas' bedroom door was wide open and Cephas was sleeping on his bed. She tiptoed and dropped her handbag on the bed and then locked her bedroom door. She came to the kitchen and poured herself some cold beer in a glass and then sank in one of the couches in her lounge.

Tinashe then entered with his satchel slung over his shoulder, "Ah aunty you're back already?"

"Yes and you, you're so late. I hope everything is fine?"

"Yes all is well. Um is Cephas…"Tinashe said pointing in the direction of Cephas' room.

"Yes but he is asleep right now, "Margaret said sipping the cold drink from her glass.

"Um okay aunt. I'll go and change my clothes and then prepare supper."

"No. I'm not hungry. Here," Margaret said giving Tinashe a ten dollar note, "Go buy yourself something to eat. I don't think Cephas is hungry either."

"Thank you aunty," Tinashe said clapping his hands before taking the money from Margaret.

"You're welcome son," Margaret said with a smile on her face and Tinashe left.

That night when everyone was asleep a loud shrill voice was heard from Margaret's home. Cephas had entered her room holding a knife with a sharp blade shining in the dark for her lamp was switched off. Cephas lowered the knife towards his mother's throat and partly sunk the blade in her flesh. Tinashe rushed off to his aunt's bedroom and he quickly switched on her lamp. Cephas scared him off with the knife, "Don't even think about it buster, or I will sink this in your ribs."

"Just drop the knife Cephas please," Tinashe said in a gentle voice.

"Don't tell me what to do Tinashe, you're just a relative. You don't know what's going on in here so just zip it!"

"Okay Cephas what do you want? I'm your mother and you want to stab me with a knife even God is not so pleased by this action son. What is it that I have done to you that you want me dead!"

"Why did you give birth to me mother? Why? You give money to some relative's son and not me? I asked you for money but you didn't give it to me why?"

Margaret was quiet for some time, "Tinashe is not just a relative's son he is more of a son to me than a nephew. Is it because I gave Tinashe some money that you want to kill me? Huh?" Cephas kept quiet, "*Taurazve nhai* Cephas. Speak why are you quiet now?"

Cephas looked at his mother with a dark expression on his face, Margaret felt that something was wrong. She started shaking with fear, "Tinashe…Tina please get me my handbag."

Tinashe hesitated, "But where is your handbag aunty?"

"Cephas if it's the money that you want just tell me son I'll give it to you all of it but please my son do not kill me."

"$500," Cephas demanded as he continued to deepen the knife into her flesh. His mother trembled frantically with fear.

"Behind the door in that drawer Tinashe hurry up *kani!*" Margaret shouted impatiently.

Tinashe then found the handbag and as he was walking towards Margaret with the bag Cephas scared him off with the knife, Tinashe then threw Margaret the handbag. Margaret began searching quickly for the money in her handbag, she quickly counted the notes and handed them to Cephas. Cephas snatched the notes from her shaky grip and left. Margaret heaved a sigh and began to cry. There was a long moment of silence before Tinashe broke it, "I know exactly what to do aunt I am going to call the police."

Margaret quickly stopped him. "No don't call the police please."

Tinashe was dumbfounded, he seemed to have lost his speech for some time, "But why aunt?"

"He didn't mean any harm, I know."

"What? Aunt what guarantee do you have that Cephas won't try to kill you again?"

Margaret raised up her gaze to Tinashe's face, "Cephas is my biological son. Blood is thicker than water. Besides I have never heard of sons or daughters who kill their parents."

"But aun… Cephas can be the first one to do it. He's your son but yo…" Tinashe was cut in the middle of his statement by Margaret who raised her hand in protest. "Okay," Tinashe said, "You are afraid you'll lose Cephas forever right aunt?"

Margaret's tears began to flow, "Yes my dear. He is so young. I love him so much but he doesn't understand. I was shocked today by his actions. Cephas wanted to kill me?! Cephas wanted to stab me! Tinashe I am a cursed woman. I am a cursed mother!" Margaret began to cry violently whilst in Tinashe's arms as he tried to console her.

As he got back to his room Tinashe sat down with a plump on his bed. He heaved a sigh and then pulled his suitcase from under his bed, he took a photo album and began to look at his childhood photos. He then noticed a photo in which he had his childhood friend Tashinga Makombe and her doll Bobby. Bobby was like her soul mate, she never wanted to part from her. He had last seen her eight years ago when she was eleven and him twelve. She had lost her mother and so her step-father had decided to stay in Gweru. Tashinga was not very happy because she had lost everything – her mother, her home, her friends and her sweet memories. Tinashe heaved another sigh as he removed the photo from the photo album and put it in the bible he kept under his pillow and went to sleep

7

The next morning Cephas came back sober and saw Tinashe sitting in the lounge having a cup of coffee. Their eyes met and stares locked and it was Cephas who dropped his gaze first. Tinashe then stood up to leave but Cephas stopped him. There was a moment of silence for Cephas was looking for the best words to convince Tinashe that it wasn't his intention to kill his mother.

"I know you are angry with me because of what I did last night."

"Oh no," Tinashe said quickly, "Who am I to be angry with you? It's just that I have realised that I am so late for the lectures today," Tinashe said putting his half empty mug on the table.

"What I did last night was a mistake…it was wrong, I don't know what had got inside me," Tinashe narrowed his gaze, "Cousie to tell the truth mother is so special to me and I can't live my life without her," Tinashe took a glance from his watch and looked away, "I know you are avoiding me but I mean every word," Cephas decided to kneel down.

"Please forgive me my cousin. I can't live my life without my mother. Don't turn a deaf ear to my apology please forgive me and I promise you that it will never happen again."

"What guarantee do I have Cephas that you won't try to kill anyone again?"

Cephas was silent for some time. He was crying uncontrollably, Tinashe then softened his gaze. He decided to help Cephas stand up on his feet, "Okay I forgive you, but on one condition."

Cephas raised his gaze to look at Tinashe for he was also taller than him.

"Go to aunt and apologise and promise her that you won't attempt to murder her or anyone else again."

Cephas nodded his head, "Thanks so much Tinashe," Cephas said trying to kneel down again.

"No that's not necessary," Tinashe held him by the shoulders, forced a smile and then left without saying another word to Cephas. He met Alice and her colleagues just outside the gate, they greeted each other and left. Cephas then went over to his mother's room and saw her praying. She was holding her bible and her entire room was filled up with lit up candles.

"Oh my God, *Nkosi yama nkosi*. Please my God protect me together with my family. Protect me my Father. That son you gave me tried to kill me and maybe he's still trying to kill me, *Mwari Baba* help me, please me Jehovah. I trust in you only my God. I no longer trust him I no longer trust that son but all I can say is prote…" Margaret heard Cephas clear his throat. She turned to look at her son but her eyes were full of fright.

"Get out! Get out you wicked son. Go away *nemadhimoni ako!*"

"No mother hear me out!" Cephas said kneeling down a little distance away from his fretting mother.

Margaret stood up with the bible in her hands, "Hear you out? You tried to kill me last night! And now you must have come back to finish your job. You know what Cephas? If God had shown me in a dream or vision the kind of a son you were going to be I would have aborted you rather than keep you. Look at the shame and stress you have let me go through," Margaret stopped for some time and took a deep breath, "I am so unlucky to have you as a son Cephas. I feel so ashamed to call you my son," Margaret then sat down on her bed as her shaky palms covered her completely shut eyes. Hot tears began to spill down from her eyes. Tears began to sting Cephas' eyes.

"I am sorry mother I don't know what came over me. I am still your son mama so please do not abandon me for this silly mistake that I have done. I did it without thinking and I promise you mother that it's never going to happen again."

"I know that you weren't yourself son. Drugs have actually turned you into a beast!" Margaret said turning her gaze to look at Cephas who had a surprised look on his face, "Yes son I know…I know all the things that you do… you use cocaine, cannabis and some stuff I don't know. You are a drug addict Cephas. What is it that I have failed to give to you Cephas?"

Cephas then stood up in a jerk, "You are becoming too emotional mama…I… I don't know what you are talking about." Cephas stammered as he turned his gaze away from Margaret whose eyes seemed to cut through her son in search of the truth.

"I am not a fool Cephas of course you know what I am talking about."

Cephas winced as if in pain as she rubbed his head, "No *mhani!* This is a moment I hate. You keep pushing me. You like fighting with me…you like figh…" Cephas was waving a finger in warning to Margaret.

"Just accept the truth damn it… you use drugs!"

"Tinashe told you that right?"

"Keep him out of this discussion. I found out about it before he came here to stay with us."

"You got in my room?"

"The door was open… besides, this is my house I have got every right to …"

"Mother! Mother please just stop it! You don't have to get inside my room it's not right. This is our house, not your house. We live here together remember? I am going to inherit this house soon because since you're old, you are likely to fall down and die," Margaret was frightened by this statement.

"You are not even a repentant soul Cephas, just now you were apologising kneeling down and begging me and now what has happened?"

"Tinashe told me to do it, he said it was the right thing to do. Now I am beginning to realise how wrong I was to have accepted his advice. This apologising thing is a nuisance," Margaret was tongue tied. Tears began to flow down her cheeks and then Cephas cursed under his breath and left. Margaret began to chant her prayers once again asking God to protect her from her wicked son.

The next day early in the morning Tinashe was having his coffee in the garden when Abigale approached him still wearing her morning gown.

"Hi Tinashe how are you this morning?" She said extending her hand to him.

"Hi Abigale, I am good and you?"

"I'm fine, " There was a little moment of silence before Abigale spoke again, "I'm sorry to disturb you but I think I heard some screaming and shouting from your house the night before yesterday, " Tinashe remained silent, "Well I actually didn't ask you yesterday because I thought that it'd maybe offend you since we were with Law and Taku."

Tinashe raised his eyebrows and took another sip from his mug, "What's your story Aby?"

"What happened in your house that night Tinashe?"

"Oh, it's nothing serious Aby."

"What do you mean 'nothing serious Aby'? You are hiding something from me. I also live here remember?"

"I know but the thing is um… an um… a scorpion crept in my aunt's bed and so she screamed out loud because she was frightened."

"But I think I heard someone mention the word 'kill'," Abigale said with a quizzical expression on her face.

"Well that must have been Cephas, um oh yes he must have been commanding me to kill the scorpion. You know Cephas, he's afraid of reptiles," Tinashe said grinning sheepishly.

"Oh so is your aunt okay? I hear scorpions are very poisonous."

"Yes of course Aby she's fine maybe because we killed it before it had sunk it's forked weapons in her skin."

"Wow that's great Tina well I'll see you later boy. Do you have any plans this evening?"

"Nope."

"Well the boys and I will be going out today so I just thought *kuti* it'd be fun to have you come along together with your cousy Cephas."

"I'll have to ask him first but I'm on it."

"Great," Abigale said with a smile, "So you should be ready by six."

"Ok Aby I will."

"Um… great, so I'll see you later."

"Ok," Tinashe said and heaved a sigh as soon as Abigale left him. Cephas suddenly emerged from behind some hedges applauding.

"That was good I never knew you were so good man"

"It's not funny Cephas. You wouldn't want people to know right?"

64

"Of course, well thanks my bro you saved my ass," Cephas said and burst out laughing.

"Like I said it's not funny, that woman really loves you. Aunt is so proud of you to an extent that …"

"Hey I know, just stop preaching. Well since you have done me a favour I have decided to do something great for you in return."

Tinashe looked at him suspiciously, "And that is?"

"Take you out."

"Oh Aby has already…"

"I know…I heard you talk about it but can you please cancel that one with them and come along with me?"

"I don't know about that…"

"Please Tinashe you know I need this one."

"Okay but I will have to tell her first," Tinashe said looking in the direction of the cottage where Abigale stayed.

"That's great I'll go and change now," Cephas said leaving.

"Ok I'll join you soon."

Tinashe and Cephas arrived at the bar, it had an expensive food outlet nearby, "Oh no Cephas… before I forget is it aunt's money that you want to spend with me here?"

"No. I borrowed it from my friend, Rusvingo you know him right?"

"No I do not believe you."

"My mother's money is safe with me at home. I haven't returned it just yet because I feel so ashamed because of what I did that night."

Tinashe looked at Cephas and then away, "The bill is on me, I'm paying."

Cephas wanted to protest but Tinashe insisted that he was the one who was going to pay the bill. Delicious food was served which they both enjoyed until Cephas requested that they go and have some drinks in the bar and so they went.

Cephas began to dance with some girls who were dressed in miniskirts and high heeled shoes who seemed to be having a good time until he came to chat with Tinashe who was sitting alone.

"You should stop being a nerd my bro, come on."

"No. I don't feel like dancing."

"Ok so maybe I should just sit down with you," Cephas said sitting on a chair opposite Tinashe.

Suddenly there was some screaming and cheering in the bar as the strippers came on stage to dance and show case their booties. Cephas could not resist this kind of temptation and so he quickly stood up and went over to where the crowd was cheering. Tinashe shook his head and he continued drinking from his glass. Cephas was now drinking and dancing with about four ladies, the crowd had dispersed. Then another stripper walked in, she had a green wig and an orange bikini. She looked younger than the other strippers and seemed naïve. She began to dance around a pole with a bottle of beer in her hand. The audience booed for she appeared to have forgotten the steps. Tinashe first ignored her until he noticed something familiar about her. Men ran over to her threw some money at her, some grabbed her arms and legs and kissed them she then dropped the beer bottle on the floor and it smashed into a thousand pieces. She screamed out loud for help until a security agent came and pulled her from the crowd for they had crowded over her to the extent that she was finding it very difficult to breathe. Tinashe then realised that he knew the lady, it was Tashinga. His childhood friend a stripper? What happened to her? How did she end up like this…? Tashi, a girl who did very well in school now a stripper? Her stepdad had loved her, well did he really? Tinashe stood up quickly and decided to follow her and the security guard who was dragging her out of the bar.

Tashinga and the guard went over to a nearby cottage. It wasn't so bad. The guard opened a room and helped her to get in, "Your keys," He said throwing her a bunch of keys.

"Thanks," she said in a hoarse voice.

"Aren't you going to lock it now? You know that madam does not want trouble."

"No I'm fine no one will find me here, I will lock it now."

"Ok, so when are you going to sort me? I saved your ass tonight," the guard said in a lowered voice.

"Not now Tutsi, I'm tired we'll talk about this tomorrow."

"Ok but be sure to pay me back," the guard said but Tashinga remained quiet and so the guard left.

Tinashe then emerged from behind a wall where he had been hiding he then ran into Tashinga's room as soon as she was about to lock her door. She tried to scream but Tinashe covered her mouth and switched on the lamp which was beside her bed.

"It's me. Tinashe," Tinashe whispered.

Tashinga's eyes ran over his face and they showed a sign of relief as she recognised him. Tinashe then slowly removed his hand from her mouth. Tashinga sat up straight, "Tinashe? Oh my God I can't believe it's you. Where have you been all along? Tinashe oh my God I'm so happy to see you."

"Me too," there was a moment of silence until Tinashe spoke again, "And so what are you doing here Tashi? I mean what happened to you, your dad and Bobby?"

"They all died. They were involved in a tragic accident."

Tinashe sighed and Tashinga's tears began to flow, "Everything became a nightmare for me Tinashe. I lost everything my family, my happiness, my identity and… just everything you know," Tashinga then turned to look at Tinashe, "You are so lucky you know you've got a home, you are probably going to school right now, you have a family, warm blankets, peace of mind… you are just so perfect Tinashe."

Tinashe found it even hard to swallow because he realised that Tashinga had been suffering all this while, "No I am not perfect Tashinga. You're not telling me the exact thing that happened to you."

There was a moment of silence until Tashinga cleared her throat and looked away from Tinashe whose eyes were looking deeper into hers.

Tashinga sniffed and began to cry again, "I was raped on that same day I came to stay in this city, Gweru."

Tinashe felt as if a loud blow had hit him, "What?"

"My dad had just gone out to buy us some food I was so hungry and so he left me with his friend James. His son raped me, he actually forced himself on me. He was fifteen by that time and I was only eleven."

"And where had this James guy gone to?"

"I told him I was cold and so he had gone to buy me some hot coffee at a nearby store. He took time there because there was a power problem. James was a mechanic and so he did not have the utensils you know. Until then Max walked in…and yes I can never forget his name it was Max. I huddled Bobby, but…but he snatched her away and then he…he…he ra..pped me. He started by to…" Tashinga could not finish statement until then Tinashe's tears began to flow down his cheeks.

"You're crying Tinashe? Come on, you should man up because I am moving on with my own life," Tashinga said amidst her sobs.

"And your dad?" Tinashe asked in a hoarse voice because he was also crying.

"It was raining heavily and so he could not see the road clearly, he swerved off the road and hit against a tree and died. I continued to stay with James and his son continued to torture me. I did not have any option I had to run away. His daughter was a little mean towards me I had to run away Tinashe and live my life alone."

"So you never got a chance to attend school?"

"School...damn you're askin' me bout school... that's why I said you are perfect."

"Don't tell me you left school...I mean dropped out a long time ago?"

Tashinga looked at him with the corner of her eye and clicked her tongue as if Tinashe had asked a stupid question, "*Shaa* going to school is a privilege...where do you think I'd get money for schooling whilst I'm struggling to buy myself something to eat...not to mention a roof over my head!"

There was a little moment of silence as Tinashe stared blankly at Tashinga who seemed to be so absorbed in her smoking that she appeared to have forgotten Tinashe's presence.

"And the madam?"

"What madam?" she was getting drowsy.

"I don't know I just heard that guard mention her."

"Oh... her name is Rudo she is a landlord not... a pimp. She does not want people to fight that's all."

"Ok," Tinashe sighed again, "So you want to go back to school?"

Tashinnga looked at him and burst out laughing, "You want to send me to school, no it's impossible. . . I'm past that age, besides I have moved on," she said reaching out for a box of cigarette which was on her bed. She took out another cigarette and lit it up. She extended it to Tinashe after smoking a little bit but he shook his head.

"We are just the same you can start by revising and writing exams please Tashi, you know that in this country you can never be a better person without school. I want to help you."

"I don't want to go back to school Tinashe, I'm coping," Tashinga said reluctantly.

"The kind of life you are living is dangerous."

"I have been through so much to consider my lifestyle dangerous," she snapped as she let smoke pour out of her mouth slowly.

"I'm sorry but…" Tinashe was choked by the smoke and then he heard Cephas' voice, "I better get going right now. Here is my phone number," Tinashe said as he entered his phone number in Tashinga's phone, "Call me when you need anything and don't hesitate," Tinashe said and left. Tashinga just nodded as she got inside her thin blanket and continued with her smoking. She was feeling drowsy already and she did not even notice him leave. Tinashe stopped and then walked back to where she was lying. He gently removed the burning cigarette from her lips, stepped on it and then he shut the door behind him.

As Tinashe got outside he met Cephas, "Where have you been cousy? I have been looking for you everywhere."

"I had come outside for some air, "Cephas' facial expression told Tinashe that he wasn't convinced by the statement, "Come on let's go and enjoy, we came here for fun didn't we?"

"Yes that's the spirit!" Cephas said in a loud voice full of excitement and they went back inside the bar but he turned his head to see where Tinashe was coming from and smiled.

The next morning Rudo decided to visit Danai at her house. They too were friends in many ways including the fact that they went to the same church. She knocked on the front door and Sekai who was Danai's second child opened it.

"Hello Sekai," Rudo said with a smile, "Is your mother inside?"

"No she's at Ceph..." Sekai stopped as soon as the gate opened. It was Danai, "Oh there she is."

"Oh," Rudo said as she turned to look at Danai, "Okay child I'll see her right now," Sekai then went back into their house.

"*Mai* Sekai where were you? I have been looking for you *askana.*"

"I am coming from Margaret's house my dear. Things are actually upside down there. Hey, may God have mercy upon her, that woman is suffering *veduwe.*"

"What do you mean Danai, what are you saying exactly?"

"We cannot talk outside come on in," Danai beckoned her friend to come inside and they both entered the house. They went and sat down in the lounge and Sekai brought them glasses filled with juice and some loose biscuits.

"Eh, Sekai why are you here?" Rudo said jokingly, "How is your husband?"

"He is fine mama, actually I am here bec..."

"Rudo when will you stop poking you nose in other people's businesses and affairs? Huh? Okay since you have asked my daughter I will answer those questions for her."

"I'm all ears," Rudo said as she chuckled.

"Sekai's pregnant with her first child as you can see and so she is here so that her husband can perform the rites... *kusungira.*"

"Oh I am so happy for you my sister you're going to be a *gogo* very soon," Rudo said as she playfully hit Danai on her shoulder, "Well done Sekai."

Rudo then stood up and began to dance ululating at the same time.

"Come on stop it!"

"Why? We're going to be grandparents soon," Sekai giggled shyly and then went back to her room.

"You can say that again," Danai said amidst her chewing.

Rudo sat back down, "Eh... you were about to tell me something about Margaret."

"Um yes... *zvakaoma askana.* We could have been at her funeral right now. Margaret almost got killed the day before yesterday."

"*Chii?* I don't understand."

"Cephas tried to stab his mother with a knife. If Tinashe had not been around Margaret would have been dead by now."

"What are you saying Danai, Cephas wanted to kill our sister Margaret? But for what in particular?"

"*Aikaka,* money my sister. *Hanzi* he got angry because Margaret gave money to her nephew and not him."

"Don't tell me," Rudo said holding her chest, "That child Cephas is so evil. He is a real incarnation of the devil."

"You can say that again my dear, how can a person attempt to kill his mother who carried him for nine solid months in her womb?"

"So did she call the police? She should let him stay in a cell for some time, maybe when he gets out he'll be able to realise his mistakes and might be able to obey his mother let alone respect his elders," Rudo snapped as she picked a biscuit from the plate on the table.

"What? You're dreaming my dear, I told her to do the same thing but she refused. She says she can't bear to see her son behind bars."

"You lie!"

"Yes I'm telling you the truth."

"Margaret is spoiling this boy, she is spoiling this boy. It's just too much for a mischievous and disrespectful son."

"I guess it's time I wash my hands," Danai gestured the washing of hands and then wrung them before Rudo, "I won't give her my advice anymore because she doesn't even listen and follow it at all."

"No my dear we have to go and talk to her together, she is our friend."

"No *hazviite* I give up I have tried my best even God knows how much I have tried to help her. Honestly Rudo I give up."

"Okay, if you insist," Rudo said easing herself on the couch and then took a sip from her glass of juice.

Margaret was cooking in her kitchen with her favourite glass filled with beer when her mobile phone began to ring. She reluctantly picked it up and answered it.

"Yes Charity."

"Hello mum I have called you because I wanted to find out if you're fine. I have heard about what Cephas did to you so I thought that it'd be great if I visited you."

"No my dear that's not necessary, Tinashe is here he has always made everything seem right."

"Oh I hear he is a good mannered someone," Charity pointed out.

"Yes it's true."

"Mother I think you should come and stay with us because home is no longer a safe place for you. Cephas is a maniac, he'll kill you. He's too violent an…"

"Charity I said I'm fine. He just wanted money."

"So are you telling me that if you don't have money he'll definitely kill you? Ma your son is beginning to scare us. Only robbers do that to strangers and not their parents."

Margaret seemed to be absent-minded, whilst on the phone she just mumbled as she walked around her kitchen with her hands holding cups, bowls, spoons and her glass of beer.

"Like I said I'm fine."

"Okay then. The other reason I called was to tell you that Susan and Chris are getting divorced."

Some dishes and plates fell from Margaret's hands and crashed on the floor, "What? But why?"

"You will have to come here mom and see for yourself."

"I just hope it's not your plan to make me visit you."

"No mom it's not."

"So who is with the kids?"

"A nanny. They are fine though."

"I warned Christopher before he married that wench! I told him to marry a beautiful and an educated young woman but what did he do? He simply turned a deaf ear to me. Now look at what is happening… his home is turning upside down!" Margaret said in a high-pitched voice.

"And Kuziva did you find a place for her?"

"I tried, the headmistress said she'll call me within forty-five minutes so I'm still waiting."

"Ok then mother so when are you coming? Chris needs you here."

"Maybe tomorrow or the day after tomorrow."

"Great we look forward to seeing you mama," she said and then they hung up. Margaret then heard her gate open up and she saw Rudo come inside. Margaret went outside to meet her, they greeted each other.

"Let's sit on the verandah," Margaret offered and they then sat on the luxurious chairs on the verandah.

"So how is everyone?" Rudo asked as soon as they had sat down.

"Everyone is fine I was just talking to Charity on the phone a minute ago. She's fine and she wants me to look for a place for Kuziva at one of the best schools in Gweru."

"Oh I heard that Kuziva did well in her exams, congratulations my friend."

"Thank you," Margaret said with a smile as she rubbed her hands on her laps.

There was another moment of silence but it was lengthy before Rudo spoke, "I heard about what Cephas did to you I'm so sorry my dear."

Margaret heaved a sigh, "Cephas is a lot of trouble my friend. *Hona* I look like a ninety-year old hag instead of sixty!"

"No Maggie *askana* the opportunity has come now. I Rudo am your friend and I have never betrayed you before. This is the right time to deal with Cephas. Help him correct his mistakes before they develop into the worst of crimes."

"But how? What do you mean Rudo?"

Rudo cleared her throat, "You can only do this by letting Cephas go to prison and stay there for some time. Do not bail him out, he won't be grateful to you at all and I think you know your son better than anyone else Margaret."

Margaret quickly looked at her friend, "You have been discussing this with Danai right?"

"Not in a bad way Margaret. We're your friends, your trouble is ours too. Take a look at all the bad things he has done too. He hasn't offended you only but the community at large. Your son fights in bars and he also steals from us, he…"

"Hey did you come here to tell me the types and the number of crimes that my son has committed so far?"

"No *sisi*. The thing is that I too am concerned about your joy and happiness. Cephas has ruined your joy. We as mothers, Danai and I want you to experience the joys of being a mom. Telling you to leave Cephas behind those bars is not that bad because it's for his own good. Your son is not fit for a job…*ndeupi* employer *angade kupinza zvakadaro basa?* He'll be sacked soon after the interview…or might stay behind bars forever because he'd have committed a very huge crime. A short period in prison can be of help to your son Maggie. *Mujeri* people are likely to realise their mistakes and then let go off them," Rudo said in a gentle voice.

Margaret was quiet but appeared to be in deep thought, Tinashe suddenly walked out and greeted Rudo. Rudo asked him how school was and requested that he bring her a glass of cold water.

"I'll have to think about this Rudo," Margaret said after some time.

"Yes please do my sister but be sure not to make any hasty decisions."

"Yes," Margaret said as she moved her legs so that Tinashe could pass through and hand over the glass of water to Rudo who thanked him with a smile on her face.

"Tinashe please make her something to eat," Margaret called out as Tinashe was getting inside.

"No," Rudo said quickly, "I had some juice and biscuits at Danai's."

"Oh so you only eat at Danai's house and not mine?"

"Margaret please come on," Rudo said laughing out loud.

"Tinashe bring us some snacks then," Margaret said to Tinashe and then turned to look at Rudo who squirmed playfully and they both laughed.

It was now lunch time and so Tinashe decided to go and meet Tashinga. They met at a nearby food outlet, they ate in silence as Tashinga could only concentrate on the food due to her hunger. After she had finished she called on for the waiter, "Hey I called you a thousand times can't you at least do your work properly?"

"I'm sorry. What can I offer you?"

"A glass of water and s…oh yes just a glass of water."

The waiter rushed to give her a glass of water, she gulped it down and then poured herself another one and after she had poured a third glass she asked the waiter to go by waving him away with her hand.

She took a deep breath and then she looked at Tinashe who was staring at her, "What?"

"You have changed."

"Really? Well thanks for the lunch. So have you hired the crib?"

"What crib?"

"No. You should stop behaving like a small kid. Every time a man does me some charity he asks for his reward so what makes you different?"

"Tashi you're my friend, you're my sister. I can never do that to you"

"Oh stop playing Christian with me. You're shy?" Tashinga grinned mischievously as she reached for his knee and squeezed it seductively.

"I said no!" Tinashe bellowed that everyone looked at him quizzically including Tashinga, "I'm sorry I did not mean to shout. Now let's talk business. About sending you back to school... I have found a good tutor who'll help you write exams for O and A level in two years. Then you will be ripe for a degree – that is if you work hard and pass."

"Where will you get the money?" Tashinga said as her tongue toyed with a chewing gum in her mouth.

"That's my business. All I want is for you to go to school. But I'd try looking for a job so that you'll be able to sustain yourself."

"I do not need a job Nashe... I am fine. I hate it when people, especially men tell me what to do with my life."

"I'm sorry if I'm being too forward but I want the best for you, really. All you got to do is trust me," Tinashe looked into her eyes for an answer but Tashinga just looked at him rolling her eyes in annoyance.

Tashinga sighed and Tinashe kept his eyes on her and then said in a gentle voice, "So we meet here again at exactly eight in the morning, don't be late."

Tashinga kept staring at him as he stood up and put the money on the table for the bill. She watched him leave and as she stood up she took the money, put it in her bra and left.

It was seven in the evening when Cephas and his gang attacked Rudo on her way to the bar, "Hi virgin Maria."

Rudo was startled. She tried to run but the boys grabbed and pushed her. She lost her balance and fell on the hard and dusty ground.

"Please don't kill me," she begged the young men who surrounded her as if she was their prey.

"You're afraid of death Maria? Look at you, you actually go to my mother and tell her to hang me? Sending someone to prison is murder! You want Cephas to die in prison… but listen to me Maria I will not go to prison without your blood on my hands!"

Rudo let out a cry of fear, "Gents pour the petrol!" Cephas ordered and Rusvingo whistled as one of the boys handed him a five litre bottle half filled with the 'petrol'. They poured it on her as she silently hugged herself and shivered. Cephas lit up the match stick but as soon as he dropped it on Rudo it went out. The boys then burst out laughing and began to run away as they heard some people approaching, Rudo realised that they had poured their urine on her, she frowned in disgust as she stood up and walked in clumsy steps in her bar's direction. She cursed under her breath and then began to drag her feet to the bar as she shook off the dust from her bottom.

That night Margaret received a call from the police that Cephas had been arrested for theft and fighting. Margaret told them that she was on her way but she didn't go there. Cephas waited and waited but no one visited him at the station that day. The next day Margaret woke up and went over to Harare to where Charity had called her. She arrived safely and everyone welcomed her. She together with her children went over to Susan's home in Domboshava where they were received with mild joy. They went along with their uncles and their oldest aunt. Susan's uncles arrived a little later and they began to discuss the issue. Susan stated her case and Christopher was told that he had wronged Susan. He listened to every detail with his head bowed down and he admitted that he never liked sharing his major problems with Susan because she was Illiterate and probably that was the reason why he underestimated her. People were told to go and have a break, Margaret then met Susan, on her way to the bathroom.

"Susan I wasn't expecting such bad behaviour from you. Your mother didn't teach you manners at all. She ac…"

"No do not drag my mother into this please *vamwene*. She taught me very *gudhu* manners and they are the reason why I managed to stay with Kirisi for years in that hell of a marriage in which he takes me for *girandidhi*. And talking about manners mama, does Cephas have any?" Susan said in a gentle and polite tone but with her eyebrows raised in scorn and this really embarrassed Margaret for their conversation had attracted most people's attention.

"Susan!" Christopher shouted, and when he was about to slap Susan his mother held his hand.

"No she is right my son. Cephas is a disgrace and he shows that I have failed in his upbringing," Margaret said and then she left. Christopher walked towards Susan, "That was bad."

"Are you saying this to me because she is your mother? I gave you back your *ringi*. And remember nothing's going on between us," Susan said in a firm voice. But as Christopher was about to say something when someone came and told her that she was wanted in the kitchen to serve the food to the visitors and so she left him.

Charity who was listening to their conversation approached her brother.

"Christopher, I cannot believe this. Susan insulted mother and you did and said nothing about it?" Charity asked with her arms folded but no one answered her and so she decided to continue, "*Heede* that woman has gone too far. You should do something about it and she said that she is going to divorce you. I think it's great news, you will have to let her go… I myself do not like her much because she is ill…"

"Charity!" Christopher shouted vehemently," Take that back! It's not my business that you hate Susan. I myself love

80

her because she is my wife and the mother of my children, I really wasn't expecting that from you," Christopher said disappointed and left.

Chipo was shaking his head when Charity looked at him for approval, "Chipo did I say anything wrong? I was just saying my mind."

"Well, that mind and those words are terrible. You should excuse me please," Chipo said as he followed his brother.

Charity was left alone. She folded her arms and rolled her eyes. Margret approached her, "Yes, why are you sulking like some grounded teenage girl?"

"I wonder what that village goat gave to my brothers. That *muti* must be very strong."

"I heard everything and all you've said. That was so mean."

Charity was surprised at her mother's statement, "I do not think so mama, she insulted you."

After a moment of silence Charity turned her gaze away from her mother and stood with her back facing her, "To tell you the truth mama, I hate Susan because she has the things I know that no matter how much I try I'm never going to get them."

Margaret patted Charity's shoulder and then she turned and looked at her mother, "I knew it but I have been silent all this while so that you could tell me yourself. All I can say child is move on."

"But how mama? Nyasha and I are not even getting along anymore because of a child. He wants an heir and heiress but *ini* I just cannot give him that. My past is now haunting me mama. I'm scared because if Nyasha gets to find out about this I'm finished," Charity said as tears spilled from her eyes messing some of the make-up she had applied.

Margaret moved closer with her arms outstretched and then she hugged her daughter and told her that everything was going to be fine.

Christopher decided to go and talk to his wife Susan who was serving dinner for her in-laws.

"Eh, Susan can I…I… I can I have a minute with you please?"

Susan just ignored him and continued with her serving until Christopher called her again.

"What? What Kirisi? What do you want? *Hanty* you showed me *kuti* I disgust you. Your mother dislikes me why then didn't you follow her advice… why didn't you just dump me? The wound have been healed by now?" Susan said as she dished out some relish in her niece's plate who had just come.

"Hi Gladys tell mum I'm coming to greet her ok?"

"Yes aunt em, aunty mama bought a car. A big one."

"Really?" Susan smiled, "Tell her I'm coming and as for the big car I can't wait to see it!"

Susan looked at the six year old as she ran towards her mother with a plate with some relish and sadza cooked with sorghum powder, "Susan please, "Christopher said as he walked towards her.

"I said I am sorry," Susan looked away from his direction, "It's never going to happen again," Christopher said in a gentle voice.

As she was about to answer Christopher Uncle Themba came by, "Aha! That's what I call a blissful marriage you two should always be like this and Susan you're a great child don't allow bad things to change that."

"Ehoyi baba," Susan said curtseying before the old man who grinned and then winked at Christopher who winked back.

"Our baby needs both parents Susan please I need you to come back home and I promise I'll make it up to you," Christopher said after the old man had left.

Susan just smiled, "I am not going to fall for that Kirisi, *ekisikuze mei* please," she said trying to avoid Christopher.

Susan was leaving but Christopher pulled her by her arm. Their gazes locked and for some time they were both silent until Christopher spoke.

"Susan I love you. I need you to forgive me. What I did was wrong and I promise you that it's never going to happen again."

Susan kept staring at his face. She liked it whenever they argued for she knew that Christopher would become so gentle, romantic and… She really did not want it to show that she was enjoying it until she looked down and smiled, "I wanted you to say that… now I'm satisfied Kirisi because I now know *kuti* you really *ravhu* me."

"So is my apology accepted?" Christopher said searching for her eyes.

Susan looked up at her husband's face shyly nodding her head, "*Ehe.*"

Christopher then bent his head and as he was about to kiss Susan, Margaret walked in.

"Oh sorry, but am I actually interrupting something?"

Susan looked away embarrassed, "Um… no mama em… we were just…just…just um…" Christopher stammered.

Margaret burst out laughing, "*Tibvire apa,* since when did you start stammering?"

Christopher and Susan both looked down and Margaret smiled, "That's what I want my children. Happiness. Chris, Susan is an incredible woman and you should respect her for the perfect woman she is. And Susan I'm proud and I thank my God every time for making you my daughter in-law."

Susan raised her gaze and then she looked at Margaret in disbelief, "I know you can't believe your ears Susan but I mean every word. We elders are not always correct…I shouldn't have insulted you earlier but…"

Susan's tears began to sting her eyes and Margaret walked towards her, "Isn't it just wonderful to have a daughter like you?"

Christopher looked up and saw Margaret and Susan's arms round each other. They stayed like that for a long time until Susan looked up at her mother in-law, "I did not mean those words mother… the one's about Cephas I was…was ang…"

"I know child," Margaret said wiping the tears off Susan's face and then they hugged each other again.

It was chilly cold in the cells, Cephas realised he missed home so much. Was it his fault that he ended up in cells every time he has wild fun? He felt anger rise from within him and then he punched his fist against the wall. He was grounded for real, the police had caught him this time. That week he had gone to his former high school, and took one of the teachers' car and went for a long ride. He had with him about four 'hot chicks 'Daisy, Chiedza, Oleny and Lorna who was coloured and Kindra's cousin. They were wearing nothing but bras and mini-skirts. They were having fun until a police car began following them but Cephas did not notice it. They arrived later whilst they were having some fun, and then took Cephas along with his hands in cuffs. When the police grabbed him Cephas found out the ladies had left him all alone. Unfortunately they had left all the meat on the braai stand and a lot of booze in a cooler box, he wished he hadn't bought so much and…

Cephas then realised how much he hated the police. Their navy blue uniforms were too much for him, they were so alarming, disgusting and as for their sirens they made an unbearable noise that made his eardrums itch!

Suddenly Cephas saw that he was surrounded by some men who had fiery tattoos on their necks, wrists, legs and arms and one of them had the one of a dragon emitting fire from its mouth... it looked like Cephas'. Most of them had spider tattoos drawn even on their faces. The faces were unfamiliar but Cephas had learned one of the thugs' name. His name was Zenze and he had a python's tattoo on his back. He was the leader of all these men who were surrounding Cephas like predators. One of the men was stepping on a little stool and was also leaning on his leg. The previous day Zenze and his men had hit Cephas to a pulp and so he was so frightened that he squealed as they got nearer him. The other men in the cell were so busy talking to each other that they did not notice what was happening to Cephas until Zenze spoke in a loud voice.

"Hey kid do you know who the fuck I am? Do you know who the fuck I am?" Zenze said vehemently as all the noise in the cell was dying down.

Cephas remained silent and the he turned his gaze away from Zenze who then grabbed him by the collar of his soiled golf t-shirt. Zenze held Cephas' collar in both his black and callused palms. Cephas noticed that Zenze had a set of golden teeth in his mouth and some of his teeth were yellow maybe due to heavy smoking. He also smelt of sweat and dirt. He had long dreadlocks on the centre of his shaven head and these were tied into a ponytail and tinted with the ginger tint.

"You don' turn away nor look away when da man is talkin' kid. Do you hear me kid?"

Cephas' tears began to sting his eyes. He just nodded his head.

"I saw you hit and bang de walls wis dis your fists. You wanna show me dat you de no lion bah you de tiger. Huh?"

This time Cephas did not respond. Anger began to well up inside Zenze.

"You gotta talk to de real tiger kid! Oh is it cuz you do not know dem rules? Ok lemme brief you bout dem... no buddie de shut up when Zenze asks dem to say somting. So now I demand dat you speak kid! Speak!" Zenze said fiercely as he shook Cephas.

Cephas then looked at him with tears streaming down his cheeks, "What... do you want?"

Zenze burst out laughing including his colleagues who roared with laughter together with him only because he himself had laughed. Cephas looked confused. He wasn't sure if what he had said was at all so funny. The men suddenly stopped and Zenze's facial expression darkened...it became so evil.

"Good question kiddo," Zenze mimicked the Jamaican tone, "Give me paradise. I want that dust of salvation," Zenze leaned towards Cephas' ear, "I want to sniff. I need cocaine."

Cephas looked up at him as he let out an evil laugh, "You de one dat asked me what I wanted... so give it," Zenze demanded as he stretched out his long arm in front of Cephas.

"But...bu... I mean... I do not have that stuff right now," Cephas said looking from side to side to look at the other men surrounding him.

Zenze quickly put his strong hand right round Cephas' neck as if to strangle him. Cephas was now gagging for air. Zenze was even trembling, "I said give it !"

"B…bo…boss um the kid doesn't have it right now… but I am sure he will arrange something for you so that you get it. Isn't it so kiddo?" One of Zenze's man injected.

"Yes…Ye… Yes I will do zat. ." Cephas said and then Zenze left him. Cephas fell down with his right and left hands holding his neck.

"Wizzy I feel that we mustn't leave him but should kill this son of a bi…" the police suddenly arrived at the door of the cell as one of Zenze's men was about to kick Cephas on the neck. Zenze was beaten to a pulp together with his men. One of the police officers picked up Cephas and then put him in another cell. Cephas lied on the floor groaning. The police officer crouched down to where Cephas was lying down, "You see what you get for doing silly things like committing crime. You stole a car, I don't blame your mother, she is probably fed up with you, pthu," the police officer said as he spat on Cephas and left after locking his cell.

8

It was already one in the morning when Margaret woke up screaming. She was calling Cephas' name. Tinashe rushed to her room only to find his aunt holding her blanket, sweating and calling her son's name with her eyes closed. Tinashe gently held her and calmed her down. She looked restless. Tinashe then stood up and brought her a glass of water.

"It was a bad dream," Tinashe said quietly after some time.

"Yes. They wanted to kill my son. *Mwana wangu.* He is not safe Tinashe, my son is not safe at all."

"No don't worry at all aunt. I think you had this nightmare because you are constantly thinking about Cephas. He's going to be fine."

"No my dreams can not lie to me. I know *kuti* people think I'm crazy but my baby is never safe in those places. I have to call my lawyer at eight. I'll see to it that he gets out."

Tinashe heaved a sigh. He waited until Margaret went back to sleep and then he went back to his room.

Kindra was having her breakfast when Max walked in. She quickly stood, picked up her satchel and headed for the door.

"Not so fast girly," Max said imitating his father. He turned to look at his sister who was rolling her eyes.

"What?"

"Where are you going?"

"How is that your business Max?"

"Just answer the damn question," Max said fiercely.

Kindra turned her gaze away from her brother, "To the police station."

"Why?"

"To see my boyfriend."

"How did you get to know he was there?"

Kindra looked at Max in annoyance, "Max are you insane? That's a whole lot of questions. What for anyway?"

"I just don't like it when you jump into bed with all men," Max snapped, "My reputation is on the line *saka* I'm just being careful," Max said and then went to his room as he left Kindra dumbfounded.

Rusvingo decided to go and see Cephas at the police station.

"I could not find the time to pay you a visit man. My uncle has been giving us hell for the past three days. So how are you?"

Cephas just looked at his friend and cursed.

"Come on Cipho, you know you can tell me. Are the cops giving you a hard time?" Rusvingo said pointing at the scars on Cephas' face.

"No. The jerks are."

"What and you let them beat you?"

"They were millions man, all around me. They outnumbered me."

"So they hit you for what?"

"Cocaine."

There was a little moment of silence before Rusvingo burst out laughing.

"What's funny?"

"*Iweweka* just look at you, for the past two weeks you were having fun and now you're all swells and sores and in a cell," Rusvingo said laughing again.

"So you find my suffering funny, right?"

"Eh no man. Of course not. It's just that I miss you and all the fun."

Cephas shook his head, "You're beginning to sound like them bitches," and they both roared with laughter, "So are you going to bring the dust?"

"Of course anything for you my soul brother."

Cephas smiled as he nodded his head and then leaned on the chair with his back, "Yeah, soul brother for real."

Kindra met Rusvingo at the police station's gate. They greeted each other and then they began to talk.

"Cocaine? So are you going to bring it over here for him?"

"Yes. But I thought you should bring it."

"Um… why? "

"Because I do not want the cops to suspect anything. I have just come out so if I go back they might get to think that I am up to something."

"Well I hope the stuff is nearby because I don't want to be late for the lectures."

"Yes it's nearby, I have just called Welly he is going to meet us at that corner," Rusvingo pointed in the corner's direction and they both went there.

Margaret then visited her son with the lawyer and they met Kindra walking in through the gate they were about to leave the station.

"Good day mama, hi Ceecee…"she said sweetly as soon as she saw Cephas.

Margaret looked at Kindra in annoyance and then she looked away. Kindra was staring at Cephas until he realised that she had brought him the cocaine.

"Um… mama this is Kindra she is my…she is my girlfriend. Kindra meet mama."

"Oh nice to meet you mum."

Margaret forced a smile and then left without saying anything. Her lawyer followed her outside the gate to where they had parked their cars. Cephas winked at Kindra who walked over to the officer at the reception counter.

"Afternoon officer, I am here to see Ezekiel Bhosvo."

"What do you want to give to him?" the police officer said as he looked at the lunch box.

"Food," Kindra said with a smile.

"Open it!" The police officer demanded ignoring Kindra's impish smile.

There was pasta with a large chicken drumstick lodged in the pasta and some uncooked vegetables (lettuce).

"Taste it!"

"Okay," Kindra said and then picked up a fork and tasted the food. The officer nodded in agreement and then called out to another police officer to call Zenze because he had a visitor. When Zenze was called Kindra sat together with him and then winked at each other so that they make up a conversation.

"The kids miss you honey."

"And you, don't you miss me?"

"No I am disappointed in you. Mama is the one who told me to come and see you otherwise I am done. I should get going now."

"Lizzy please don't leave me… I know I made a mistake but…"

"It's too late Ezekiel. It's over!" Kindra said as some crocodile tears rolled down her cheeks and then she stood up and left. Zenze buried his face in his hands and then stood up after some time as a police guard escorted him back to his cell but with the lunch box in his hands.

Margaret thanked her lawyer and then he got into her car together with Cephas who looked impatient.

"What was she doing at the station?" Margaret asked as they got home.

"She wanted to see her uncle," Cephas said dismissively and went to the kitchen.

"What did he do?"

"Shoplifting. His crime is meant for women not men."

"Oh so you call yourself a man because you stole your former teacher's car?"

"No. I didn't say that," Cephas' cell phone began to ring. He did not answer it but he merely looked at it and said, "Um... I better go and meet my friends ma. They are calling me." Cephas said ready to leave but Margaret stopped him.

"I don't want any more trouble beca..."

"You're never going to bail me out again," Cephas finished the sentence for her, "I'm not going anywhere far... and one more thing ma... I'm not a baby anymore," Cephas said and left.

Kindra went back home late that night. She was coming from the night club. All the lights in their house were switched off and so she crept inside and walked stealthily into the living room but before she had gone any far the lights were switched on. Kindra almost jumped in fear.

"Oh! Dad you scared me!"

"I scared you? Tell me now girly, where are you coming from at this hour?"

Kindra's eyes began to move about, "At a friend's home dad, she was um...having a party. It was so decent dad. It had about ten church girls. Three from *Johwani masowe*, six from ZAOGA and one was from your favourite, Roman Catholic."

Elvis looked at his daughter in disbelief, "You don't sound saintly to me, you sound drunk and stupid!" Elvis said in anger.

Kindra gasped, "Why poppa?"

"I have warned you a thousand times not to call me that!" Elvis said exasperated

"But why? Before mother died she had always told me to call you that. She was Italian dad, that makes me Italian too."

"You drank alcohol at that party right Kindra?"

"Yes, I had a few drinks but only because I miss mum."

"Don't bring your mother into this!"

Kindra began to cry, "I miss her so much dad. I can't bear to live this terrible life without her."

Elvis quickly ran to where Kindra was standing, he hugged his daughter, "I know you're hurt girly but drinking is not the right way to deal with your grief. You hear? And please stop calling your life terrible."

Kindra nodded as her father kissed her and went back to bed, she smiled at herself as she hissed a yes.

The next day Tinashe decided to visit his aunt at her work place, it had a placard on the gate written in bold letters, **MARGARET'S DELICACIES AND CATERING SERVICES FOR HIRE.** Margaret was very happy to see Tinashe. She welcomed him to her inn and they occupied an empty table.

"Now this is what I call excellent aunt, your inn is very beautiful," Tinashe said looking around.

Margaret smiled, "Well thanks dear for the compliment. After my retirement as a teacher at that primary school I couldn't bear staying at home so one of my friends Catherine Jones gave me this inn. She went to stay in Britain, she said she is never coming back to Zimbabwe."

"But why? Is it because our country is boring?"

Margaret laughed, "No. She has a terminal disease… she has breast cancer, and so she said she wanted to die in Britain so that she can be buried there. It's her home you know."

"I'm sorry aunt. She must be so depressed."

"Yes poor Cathy. She and her husband were just adorable."

There was a moment of silence until Margaret called one of her waitresses, "Anita please give my son something to eat."

"No aunt I had sadza back there at home. It's a Saturday and so I had all the time to cook myself something."

"Your wife will be the luckiest woman in this world," Margaret said waving Anita away.

"Um…aunty can you please do me a favour?"

"Yes? Anything for you my darling."

Tinashe blushed and then later on cleared his throat, "I have a friend and she is looking for a job, is there something she can do?"

"What kind of a friend is this Tinashe?"

"Former classmate. Um… it's urgent she is really desperate aunt, please."

"Like I said, anything for you. Just bring her tomorrow at our house."

"Okay thanks aunt, but…um…she um…"

"What?"

"She was working in a bar."

"What kind of job was she doing in that bar?"

"She was selling the beer," Tinashe said and then swallowed hard.

"Ah. That's great it also implies that she has some experience."

"Ok aunt I guess I should be on my way right now."

"Ok my dear thanks you came to see me *pabasa pangu.*" Margaret said as Tinashe left.

Late that evening when Fassie and Nowinnie were driving they saw something that looked like a roadblock and four men dressed like policemen stopped their car. The man signalled for them to come out of the car and as soon as they stepped on the ground the man grabbed them and took them inside the bush. The two women tried to scream but one of the men took out a knife and hushed them. This man had a mask on his face, he removed it and the two women saw that they knew the man. It was Max!

"Ma…Ma…Max? Um…what is going on he…he…here?" Fassie asked stammering as she pointed at the other men.

"Oh beautiful ladies you forget so soon. Don't tell me *kuti* you had forgotten my promise to you?" Max asked as he smiled callously.

The women's facial expressions showed signs of realisation, "Oh no Max we did not mean it at all I swear," Nowinnie said crossing her trembling fingers in front of Max.

"It meant something to me ladies. You know what *vakadzi vemuMambo* you talk too much *manje nhasi* I want to show you that no one messes around with Max James."

"No…no no no Max please do not hurt us. We said we're sorry."

Max looked at the four men who had carried Fassie and Nowinnie, "*Akomana* help yourselves."

The men grinned and laughed wildly as they pushed the two women and they fell down. They loosened the belts fastening their trousers and they even fought among themselves as they asked who was going to be first. Fassie and Nowinnie tried to scream but Max told them that no one was ever going to hear them. The four men raped Fassie and her friend continuously without stopping. Suddenly one of the men who was on top of Fassie stopped. He put his hand against her neck so as to check her pulse.

"Eish *varume* she is dead."

"What?" All the men asked with their voices filled with fear. Nowinnie's heart began to beat fast she too quickly shut her eyes and the man who had claimed that Fassie was dead shouted to his colleagues, "She is also dead."

Max looked confused, "Let's bury them."

"But where exactly boss?" one of the men asked.

"No let us just stab them so that they will not wake up. Boss if these ladies wake up we're in trouble," one of the men suggested.

Max sent a man to his car who brought him a hammer. Max grabbed it from the man but as he was about to hit Fassie with it they heard voices and so they all ran away. Nowinnie remained silent for some time until she woke up and began to shake Fassie. Nowinnie saw that Fassie's body remained stiff. Oh no it was true her friend was dead. The truth landed on her like a loud blow. Nowinnie wanted to scream out loud but she just stood up and ran away. She ran in the opposite direction of the voices.

9

As Charity opened her living room door she saw Nyasha sitting on the couch with a bottle of whisky in his hand. She sighed as she walked towards him.

"Hi honey? I missed you so much," Charity said as she sat down beside him and then extended her arms to him and began to rub his chest.

"I missed you too. I was so lonely here," Nyasha said after kissing her lightly on the forehead. "So how was th…"

There was a loud knock on their door, Charity sat up straight as she looked at Nyasha with a quizzical expression on her face.

"Are you expecting someone?"

"Umm…no," Nyasha said as the loud knock was heard again at the door, louder this time. Nyasha stood up and went to see who was at the door, and as he opened it, the owner of the knock barged inside. Charity stood up in a jerk as if to run away.

"Hey Charity *muroyi wekwaKhumalo*. I knew it! I knew that you were still here!" the woman quickly turned to look at Nyasha, "And you, what is this rug still doing here? She is useless my dear you should just throw her away. Nyasha it's been ten years, ten good years and still I haven't heard the sound of a baby crying."

"Mother please is this the way one should visit her son?"

"*Wena mfana* don't patronise me *wazvinzwa?* What do I look like, bush fowl *he-e?*"

"No. Who said that to you mum?"

"Anyway I did not come here to play *nhodo*, I am here to talk business," the woman then turned to look at Charity,

"What is wrong with you? Huh? What is wrong with your womb *mhani?*"

Charity looked at Nyasha with her sparkling eyes as tears began to sting her eyes. Nyasha walked over to his mother, "Mama ple…"

"Hey *iwe,*" the woman waved Nyasha away, "I am talking to our barren queen here Charity. I want answers Charity. Do you know that your bareness is an insult to my family? People are laughing at my family and I, they are saying that my son married a man. *Amadhodha!*"

Charity's tears began to flow down her cheeks, she looked away from her mother in-law, "Hey *iwe* look at me. Who do you think you are? Huh? Is this what your useless mother Margaret taught you *kuti,* you just look away when your elders are talking to you?"

Charity lost control she then burst into tears and began to cry loudly, "Mother please!" Nyasha shouted, he came over to where Charity was now crying sitting down on the floor. He helped her up and as he was about to escort her to their bedroom Nomagugu stopped them.

"I have good news for you my babies, I am here to stay because *wena* you are not working hard enough to make this your sweet burger pregnant so I'm here full time to supervise," Nomagugu said before sitting down laughing very hard. Nyasha just shook his head as he took his wife to their room.

Chipo's phone was ringing but no one was around to pick it up so his friend Muza picked it up.

"Hello?""

"Hey Chips. It's Florence, at Ruregerero Holdings."

"Um… Chipo is not in sorry…but um…you can leave a message," Muza said biting his nails.

"Um… ok just tell him that he has got the job."

"What? Are you serious, man he's going to be head over heels. Well thanks and bye," Muza screamed out loud, he was so happy. He could not wait to tell Chipo the great new.

Chipo then arrived, Muza stood up quickly but before he could say anything Chipo spoke first, "And that?"

"What?"

"My mobile is in your hands."

"Oh, yeah Florence just called."

Chipo rolled his eyes and pursed his lips, "Well, what did she want this time? She told me it's hard to get a j…"

"Well, you got the job!" Muza exclaimed as he hugged Chipo.

"Whoa stop it Muza. Who told you that? Is this a joke or something?"

"Do I look like a clown to you Chips?"

Chipo was silent for some time but as Muza turned his back on Chipo, Chipo hurried towards him and hugged him, "Of course I believe you queenie!"

They hugged and began to laugh out loud as Chipo's eyes showed a sign of relief in them.

Late that evening, Tinashe went over to where Tashinga was living. Her door was open so he just walked in. She was sitting on her bed smoking weed.

"Tashinga! What the hell are you doing?" Tinashe asked with his palm over his face covering his nose.

"Shh… It's prayer time buster! Do not make noise," Tashinga said almost in a whisper.

Tinashe ignored her and sat on the bed, "What you're doing right now is not right at all."

"There is no right and wrong in this world boy. Like I said shut up! I'm praying, I want to feel it as I breathe, you want to try?" Tashinga asked extending her hand to Tinashe. Tinashe grabbed the rolled paper with weed in it and stamped on it with his feet.

"Heeey?" Tashinga said a little surprised by his behaviour.

"You're coming with me. This has to stop it's so disgusting," Tinashe said as he pulled Tashinga with her hand and they went outside.

Tashinga pulled her hand out of Tinashe's, "Stop! You say you care about me but you really don't!"

Tinashe looked at her with a quizzical expression on his face, Tashinga began to cry and when Tinashe walked a little closer so that he could comfort her Tashinga told him to back off.

"Don't you dare! You betrayed me. Nashe you betrayed me. We were friends but you let him take me away from home. Where were you when he raped me? I was raped and everything was gone," Tashinga knelt down as if in prayer crying, "My dreams, hopes, *magoals angu?* Huh? Where were you?"

Tinashe stopped as he quietly looked at her crying, she looked helpless and pitiful.

Tinashe came closer and knelt down beside her, "You never told me your step-dad raped you Tashi. Why?"

"I…I did not think it right to tell you, I was scared. I'm scared right now."

"What? Tashi I'm your friend…I am not your enemy, you should trust me…and Max?"

Tashinga looked up at him, "Yes. He raped me too."

"Wha…I'm sorry…I know you're in great pain right now but I really want to help you out!"

101

Tashinga looked up at him with wet cheeks and bloodshot eyes which were filled with nothing but fright and hope. She was willing to trust him but something inside her was not sure about his intentions. Tinashe felt tears sting his eyes, he tried helping Tashinga to get up but she couldn't stand up on her feet and so Tinashe carried her in his arms and took her to her room. He put her on the bed and then in her blankets. He decided to leave when she stopped him and told him that she did not want to be left all alone for she was very scared that her step-dad and Max would come and get her. Tinashe walked towards her bed, he wanted to tell her something. He began to talk about the wild and great experiences they had when they were still small children. He said something funny and laughed out loud. He was in the middle of his story when he heard her snoring. He quickly turned to look at her and saw that she had fallen asleep already. He stood up from the bed and watched as she sighed peacefully as she turned to look at the other side.

Charity and Nyasha were asleep in their bedroom when they heard a knock on their door. They woke up as soon as their door was opened.

"Hey *wena mthakathi!* Charity! You're asleep, why aren't you doing what my son paid for. Nyasha paid lobola didn't he?"

Nyasha woke up groaning he switched on the lamp and looked at the clock at the head of their bed, "Eish mama, it's one in the morning for goodness sake."

"*Inyi hwani in ithi moningi for gudhunesi seki.* Oh come on save my breath, I didn't come here for nothing Nyasha. I want to have my own grandchildren because you haven't given me one just yet."

"Mother please, this is going too far, please. This needs to stop!"

"No. Nothing is going to stop until her womb stops withholding what is rightfully ours as the Machinguras," Nomagugu said firmly and then sat on the bed. Nyasha just looked at Charity and shrugged.

At dawn Nyasha woke up only to see Charity pulling fully packed bags along their corridor.

"Baby what is the meaning of this? What do you think you're doing?"

"I am leaving you with your mother. I can't stay here anymore Nyasha. Your mother is treating me like I am some piece of trash."

"No, honey please. You know I need you."

Charity looked at her husband as tears were flowing down her cheeks, "Not anymore Nyasha. Your mother is right, I am useless. I guess I should be leaving right now," Charity said picking up her bags. Nyasha took hold of her hands and told her that she was not going anywhere. Nomagugu came out of her room only to see Nyasha and Charity fighting over the bags.

She burst out laughing, "*Yohwe zvangu*. Why? Do you want me to die of laughter?"

Charity and Nyasha just looked at her and they both kept holding the bags in their hands.

"Now the witch is ready to leave. Hey Nyasha, *iwe* leave those bags. *Hanty* she said she wants to leave. *Kasiye kaende mhani!* You should let her go! She is useless."

"Mother please. . . Charity is my wife."

"Wife my foot. Come on, you are beginning to get on my nerves, go to your bedroom," Nomagugu said as Charity went over to the garage with her bags, started her car and left.

Chipo decided to call his siblings to tell them about his new job. Charity's mobile was unavailable and so he only managed to tell Christopher.

"Well congratulations my bro. Um… so do you have any plans for the day?"

"Yes we could visit Charity and Nyasha and celebrate there."

"Yes but I think it will be fine if we do it at my house."

"Wow ok, so I'll try calling sister or even Nyasha."

"Ok, bro. Bye," Christopher said and hung up.

Tashinga decided to visit Tinashe at his aunt's house. Cephas opened the door.

"Hi I'm Tashi can I please see Tinashe?"

"Oh, yes. Just give me a sec," Cephas said and then left.

Tinashe came in no time to meet her in the lounge, "Hi Tashi. Wow you did a great job, you came! Well, just wait here for about two minutes, I have to go and change."

"Ok," Tashinga said with a smile on her face and began to look around the room. Tinashe finished dressing up and then they went out. They went to a nearby food outlet and ordered some snacks and soft drinks.

"I have come to apologise to you about yesterday. I actually blamed you for m…"

Tinashe hushed her by putting a finger on her lips, "No, it's okay. We're not here to worry about the past. Let's let bygones be bygones. Anyways, I found a job for you."

Tashinga stopped drinking her juice and looked at Tinashe who could not stop grinning, "What kind of job is that?"

"Waitressing, in my aunt's inn."

Tashinga looked at him and then away.

"Now what is the problem?"

"I don't think I can do it."

"Oh come on Tashinga, you've always been a genius. I want the police off your hook. Remember all workers are getting arrested, I know you don't want to be the cops' victim."

"Just say it in full. Sex workers," Tashinga said as she took out a cigarette and put it in her mouth, "I think I heard a campaign is going on so that our profession is legalised."

Tinashe took hold of her hand, "You should give up the habit…It's not your profession. That's not your destiny Tashinga. You know that better than I do."

Tashinga nodded her head as she removed the cigarette from her mouth, "So when are we going there?"

"As soon as you are full."

Tashinga nodded and resumed eating as she toyed with the cigarette between her fingers.

Charity was already in her hotel room when she decided to go for shopping. She had come from the church where her mother had told her to go and seek God's grace. There at the store she bumped into a certain woman who seemed to be very ill. As she was passing her by, the woman fell down. Charity gasped and ran to her, "Hey, are you okay?" she asked, worried.

The woman just shook her head but did not say anything to Charity. Charity called out to some of the people in the store to come and help her carry the woman to her car. The woman was put into Charity's car and so Charity rushed her to the hospital. One of the nurses told Charity to sit down on some benches in the waiting room. Charity was trembling, she failed to understand the problem facing the woman until the doctor called her.

"Are you the one who brought Ms Dube here?"

"Um… I think so. I don't know her name. She just fainted and so I just picked her up and thought it wise to bring her here."

"Well, thank you. You did the right thing because she has cervical cancer and it is at an advanced stage. Are you the one who's going to pay her hospital bills?"

Charity was dumb-folded, "Em doctor, what do you mean it's now at an advanced stage? Does it mean that her life cannot be saved?"

"All I'm saying is it's too late to treat it now but if you're the one who is going to pay we can try our best."

Charity looked at the doctor with a terrified look on her face, "I will pay. Please doctor, save her life."

The doctor nodded his head, "We will try chemotherapy, it goes for $1600."

Charity gasped, "Now that's a whole lot of cash."

The doctor was silent and then Charity spoke up, "Get on with the treatment, I'm going to the bank to withdraw the cash. I'll be back soon," Charity said and left.

Nyasha was already at his workplace when his mobile phone started ringing. He took it out of his pocket and answered it.

"Hello?"

"Hello, we are calling from Parirenyatwa Hospital. Your wife has been admitted and so she told us to inform you."

"Charity? No. Wha…what happened to her? Is she okay?"

"We will inform you with the rest when you come here sir," the nurse said and hung up.

Nyasha felt numb, he prayed in his heart that Charity had not been involved in a car accident or attempted to commit suicide because of his mother. He shivered at the thought. He quickly took the car keys from his desk and drove to the hospital. He called the hospital again and asked the number of the ward. On his way to the ward he met the doctor.

"Mr Machingura?"

"Yes," Nyasha said as they greeted each other with a handshake.

"Your wife's condition is critical. Have you ever tried taking her for diagnosis recently?"

Nyasha was tongue tied, he stared at the doctor as he shook his head, "What diagnosis doctor?"

"Your wife has cervical cancer or didn't you know about it?"

Nyasha was perplexed, he looked for a place to sit and then wiped the sweat from his forehead with the back of his hand, "No. She never mentioned it to me."

"Oh," the doctor said as he raised his gaze and then he saw Charity, "Ah, pardon me. Your wife fainted and someone volunteered to pay her bill. Here she is sir."

Nyasha raised his face and then his and Charity's gazes locked.

"Baby?" they said together, "What are you doing here?"

There was a moment of silence as they digested the whole incident. Nyasha decided to speak first, "I thought you were the one in the ward. I was so worried," Nyasha turned to look at the doctor, "Doctor this is my wife."

Charity looked at Nyasha, "But how did you know I was here?"

"The hospital called me and told me that you were admitted here…and that your condition was critical."

"How come?" Charity turned to look at the doctor, "I didn't give you my name nor my details for there to be a cause of misinformation."

The doctor looked at the couple with a calm expression on his face, "The patient in that ward over there did."

Nyasha and Charity looked at each other and then walked to the ward. The doctor escorted them and as soon as they arrived the patient's bed she opened her eyes.

"Aaron. Aaron, I knew you would make it here," the woman said forcing a smile but with great joy present in her voice. Charity looked at Nyasha with surprise in her eyes as he smiled at the patient.

"Nomaqhawe? This can't be. How are you?"

The patient groaned in pain before answering Nyasha, "I am sick. The nurses were saying I am not going to make it. I am going to die," the patient said sounding helpless.

The patient suddenly broke into tears and Charity felt tears stinging her eyes and so she went out of the ward and waited for Nyasha. He got out after some time.

"Charity I …"

"Now tell me, what was the meaning of that? How did you get to know that woman?"

"That is what I want to explain to you," Nyasha said and then heaved a sigh, "She is an old friend of mine."

Charity laughed an evil laugh and then looked at her husband, "Nyasha that woman knows your second name, Aaron. I and your mother are the only women who call you by that name. How did this woman get to know your second name? Is there something you're not telling me Nyasha? Something that I should know?"

Nyasha looked away from his wife, "She is my ex-girlfriend. We had an affair when we were still high school students until we met again, five years ago. From there we started communicating. We met in Silobela, she was a cook at a nearby school which is actually closer to our mining station."

Charity was now shaking with anger, she turned to look at her husband, "Did you have sex with her?"

Nyasha quickly looked at Charity, "What?"

"You heard me! I said did you have sex with that woman?!" it was louder this time and the people in the waiting room and the reception area which was adjacent to the waiting room looked at them. Nyasha was about to say something when, a nurse approached them.

"This is a hospital, please lower your voices."

Charity looked at Nyasha and then the doctor approached them, he asked if anything was wrong but no one answered him. He then asked about the bill. Charity handed him the money and then left without saying a word.

Tashinga told Tinashe that she enjoyed working for his aunt. With the help from Margaret, Tashinga decided to quit drugs. Margaret gave her a small bible with the words **HOLY BIBLE** on it and the letters **NKJV**.

"I love reading it. It reminds me of brother Joze at our Sunday school," she told Tinashe smiling.

Tinashe nodded his head, "He was good at quoting scripture."

There was a moment of silence until Tashinga spoke, "About school, I really feel I should go back."

Tinashe looked up at her with disbelief, "Are you serious?"

"Yes… aunt made me realise how important education is in one's life."

"Wow, so I just couldn't convince you that much?"

"No. You have been a shoulder to lean on Tinashe, and remember *kuti* it's because of you that I met Aunty Maggie and the reason why I have a job."

Tinashe smiled, "You should also thank God Tashi," Tinashe took a glance at his watch, "Lunch time is over I should get going and as for you back to work."

"Ok. Bye," Tashinga said as they both stood up and Tinashe waved at her and left.

Margaret received a call from Charity who was telling her that she had arrived in Gweru.

"What…but how?"

"What do you mean but how ma? Nyasha doesn't love me anymore. He has another woman in his life."

"What? Nyasha did what? But he…"

"I'm on my way home ma. I'm coming and I am going to tell you everything when I get there," Charity said as she hung up.

Margaret sat down with a plump on her couch. Maybe her son in-law had found out the truth about her daughter's abortions. But who had told him? She later on decided to wait for her daughter to come and tell her herself.

Margaret waited for Charity to come home and as soon as she entered she stood up to help her with the bags.

"Eish so many bags. I didn't think it was that bad."

"No mama, Nyasha is not the reason behind the number of bags, it's his mother. She called me useless because I am barren."

"What? Nomagugu *anowonererwa fani*. Why does she keep getting on my nerves? *Hanty* you now see it Charity, your mother is now being insulted because of your silly and selfish actions."

"I wasn't ready to become a mother," Charity said as she put down the bags.

"So why did you rush to bed with, Oskido?"

Charity looked away from her mother, "Mama please, I actually came here because I needed some peace of mind."

"So what did I do?"

"You're adding to the stress!"

"Hey, this is my house, I didn't invite you here!" Margaret shouted after Charity as she carried her bags to her room.

Nyasha decided to visit Nomaqhawe at the hospital again. This time she asked a nurse to help her sit up straight. Nyasha had brought her some fruits, juice and a bouquet of flowers.

"Thanks," Nomaqhawe said smiling weakly.

"No, don't mention it," Nyasha said as he put these on the table, "So how old is he now?"

There was a moment of silence as Nomaqhawe gathered the strength to speak, "Oh, you mean Nkosilathi? He… is five years old now. He looks ju…st just like you. He used to ask me where his… father was, I told him far away in the city. He's… so excited." she forced a smile.

"You brought him here?"

"Yes, I knew my… days were… numbered. I am never going…to… to survive this. Cervical cancer is the wo…rst disease."

"Thank you Qhawe, you brought me my flesh and blood."

There was a moment of silence until Nomaqhawe broke it.

"I still remember when we… were still in fo…rm three, I almost fell in a…a…a mining shaft but you saved my life. I just… can't stop imagining myself dead already," Noma forced another smile, "I o…we you Aaron. We had always loved each other but, I'm failing to understand…to understand what happened to us. You were a genius but I…I would not even come to school for the whole month, my mother was… a widow. Aaron …do…do you still remember?"

Nyasha looked at her with gentleness and nodded as he patted her weak arm with his strong hand, "Yes, I remember everything."

"There is something I would like you to tell your wi…fe, that… I did not come here to create any forms of mis…misunderstandings between the two of you. You should also thank her for me for saving my life and…since…since you do not have a child I leave her my son, Nkosilathi. Nkosi is…a diamond… my diamond you should look after him for me Aaron," Noma said with some difficulty and began to cough. A nurse rushed inside as Noma and Nyasha clasped one another's hands so firmly. Tears began to sting Nyasha's eyes as the nurse parted their hands from each other. Nyasha went and stood outside as he broke down and cried, his sobs were very loud. A certain woman and a man came and helped him up. They helped him sit on one of the leather chairs in the waiting room and still he continued to cry.

It was already three in the afternoon when Kindra came running to Max with a newspaper. Her father rushed out of his room to see what was happening for she was making a lot of noise with her screams.

"Max! Max! Look," Kindra was panting now but her father grabbed the paper before Max took hold of it. It had on it a headline which made Max's heart skip a beat *RAPISTS LEAVE WOMAN'S BODY IN A BUSH.*"

Max had peeped and read the headline. Max pretended not to care and then went to sit down on a chair in their kitchen.

"Do you know the person's body that was found Max?" Kindra said walking towards him.

"No," Max shrugged and said too quickly, "I did not murder the person so how do you expect me to know."

Kindra sat in the chair opposite Max, "It's Fassie's."

"What?" Max pretended to be surprised.

"Yes, Max I never knew prostitutes can be made victims of rape. Those men are so wicked," Kindra's tears began to flow. Max stood up quickly took his coat from behind the door and left. Kindra looked at her brother, a little bit surprised by his actions.

Tinashe met Tashinga at her workplace. It was her half-day since it was on a Friday and so they decided to go out together. They had a great time, Tinashe had bought Tashinga a gift. She unwrapped it and as soon as she saw it tears began to stream down her cheeks. It was a doll which looked almost the same as Bobby.

"Thanks Nashe it really means a lot to me. I always thought that no one was ever going to be able to replace Bob," she said wiping the tears off her face with the back of her hand.

"All I want is for you to be happy, I hate it when people think negatively of themselves. You know I used to think that I was my father's burden until he made me realise how special I was to him and to the world too."

They looked at each other and smiled. Tashinga saw a vendor selling candy and told Tinashe that she wanted some. Tinashe indulged her. They went to the park and there Tashinga was chased around by Tinashe. When he caught her he would pick her up and turn her around like a small girl. They were having their blissful moments.

That night when Cephas went to the night club with Rusvingo they met Fatso and everyone there was talking about Fassie's mysterious death and Nowinnie's sudden disappearance. It was so strange for nothing like that had never happened in the little ghetto of Mambo before.

"Cephas, do you mind if I buy you one?" Fatso asked pointing at his bottle.

"No thanks I'm fine. I can afford that one," Cephas said turning away but Fatso held him by the shoulder.

"There is something that you do not know about our girlfriend Kindra."

Cephas then turned to look at him, "Sorry? Did I…"

"No, you heard well, I said it loud and clear. Oh, you think you're unique in this hood. You think you don't share your bitches with any one. *Haiwa mhani* you should stop lying to yourself. I am a Samurai Cephas, and Samurais are…" Fatso was slapped right across his face. He staggered and most of the people sniggered and laughed.

"How dare you open that stinky hole you call a mouth and vomit trash? Huh, Fatso?" Kindra said waving her forefinger in front of Fatso.

"*Hezvo, ko* Kindra how did you…"

"How did I what? *Pfutseki!* You should stay away from me and my man *mhani,*" Kindra said holding Cephas' hand in her own and they both left him.

Cephas and Kindra started dancing but Cephas stopped and walked away from the dance floor. Kindra followed him.

"What's the problem baby?" Kindra said touching Cephas' collar.

"Did you have sex with that dog?"

"What? What are you saying Cephas? What do you take me for, a whore?"

"No, all I want is the truth Kin."

Kindra looked away, "No, Cephas I didn't have sex with him," Kindra turned to look at him, "Are you satisfied now?"

Cephas was quiet for some time and then he smiled, nodded and they went back to the dance floor.

Charity was sitting on the couch hugging her late father's portrait in her hands. Margaret walked in wearing her night dress.

"And now? What's that?"

"Dad's portrait. I miss him so much."

"*Heede seka hako* Maggie. Are you trying to tell me that you now miss your father because you're in trouble?" Margaret said as she eased herself on the couch.

"Mama, I have always loved my dad regardless of the fact that we were always at loggerheads with each other."

"Charity, I warned you. *Chiona manje.* Look at yourself now, I always warned you against those abortions. Where are you now? Aren't you supposed to be at your matrimonial home with your husband?"

Charity's tears began to flow down her cheeks, "You should be giving me some advice mama instead of blaming me. I know what I did was wrong but it happened long ago."

Margaret looked away from her child, "I am sorry child but there is nothing I can do about it."

Charity looked at her mother, cursed under her breath and left the lounge.

The next morning Nyasha woke up early and went to see Nomaqhawe, he had another bouquet of flowers in his hands and more juice. He quietly walked into her ward and shut the door. But as he turned to look at her bed he saw that she was no longer there. He dropped the flowers on the floor and a nurse walked in.

115

"Em, *nhai* nurse where is the patient…the female patient suffering from cancer. When I came yesterday she was lying here."

The nurse heaved a sigh, "She is gone."

There was a little moment of silence. Nyasha walked towards the bed and began to pat it gently. He suddenly turned to look back at the nurse who stood aimlessly behind him "Gone? *Kupi?* I want to see the doctor, can you please show me his office."

Nyasha was now trembling, the nurse agreed and as she was taking him to the doctor's office he kept mumbling the same words to himself, "It can't be. I hope it's not what I am thinking…"

The nurse knocked on the doctor's door and then they both walked inside. The nurse and the doctor nodded at each other and as she was about to leave Nyasha held her back.

"Stop! I want you to repeat those same words you said earlier about Nomaqhawe."

The nurse looked frightened and then she raised her gaze to look at the doctor, "I only told him that his wi…the woman is gone sir."

The doctor nodded his head, "Yes, Mr Machingura your friend could not make it."

Nyasha kept staring at the doctor. The nurse left and Nyasha tried to stop his tears from flowing but he could not. His legs felt so weak that he held the doctor's table for support as he slowly sat down on a chair behind it. He cried quietly but he could not stop the shaking. When he had finished crying the doctor handed him a note which was roughly scribbled on and the writing was a little bit shabby. It read:

To you Aaron

I have always loved you but fate has always kept us away from each other. I was happy though when I learned that I was carrying your child in my womb. This time I told myself that fate had failed to keep the two of us away from each other. I could not make it...I mean death has won. But my love for you lives forever. I leave our son in your care. . . I believe that as his father you'll be able to show him the brighter side of this world because all he knows is poverty and suffering. . . He is staying in Mbare with my aunt, here is the address: 6A Seke Street Mbare Jouburg lines. His name is Nkosilathi Aaron Machingura, I named him just in the way I knew you would if we were together. I know you have a lot of experiences that you wanted to share with me, but because of a little time we have had together you could not say it all. I love you and maybe I'll miss you...

Love

Nomaqhawe (Qhawe)

Nyasha slowly crushed the piece of paper in his hand as small beads of tears rolled down his cheeks. He quickly stood up from where he was sitting, thanked the doctor and left.

Kindra woke up the next morning not feeling well. She was nauseous. She rushed off to her bathroom and vomited. She was feeling very weird even though she could not tell her real problem. She sat down slowly on the floor, opened a drawer which was below the sink beside her. Kindra took out a mirror to see her face. Her skin had changed, it was becoming so light and beautiful. She smiled to herself, but the smile suddenly disappeared when the thought of being pregnant crossed her mind. She had missed her period for about two months. She quickly stood up from where she was sitting and went back to her room. There she quickly changed in to neat clothes and headed for the nearby clinic. There was a short queue to the nurse's office. Her turn to consult the nurse came and she walked so slowly towards her office that the nurse had to shout the word 'next!' thrice.

"You're scared?" the nurse said and a gentle smile appeared on her face.

Kindra forced a smile, "No. It's just that, it's a little bit cold today," Kindra said sitting down.

"Ok, so what can I do for you?"

"I am not sure if I am pregnant, so I want to get tested."

"*Asi* you do not make use of *macontraceptives?*"

Kindra looked at the nurse who was smiling at her, "Of…of course I use contraceptives…it's just that…I feel I should…have the test, um I…" Kindra stammered.

"No. It's okay. I understand. We can do it right now…I hope you're fine with it?"

"Yes…it's okay," Kindra said feeling a little bit frightened.

The nurse looked at her and smiled, "Don't worry the pregnancy test won't take time. You will just have to come after two days and check on your results."

Kindra nodded as the nurse stood up and came closer to her, stretching the plastic gloves in her hand. She told her to lie on the bed and Kindra did as she was told.

Max was pacing about in his bedroom. He was questioning himself on how and why one body was found in that bush. Where had Nowinnie's body gone? Could she have fainted and then woken up and run away? His heart began to beat faster. He reached for the newspaper again and saw that it was only Fassie's picture which appeared. He scratched his chin, hit against the wall with his fist and then kicked his bed's base with his left leg. Max did not notice Martha when she walked in. She touched him on his shoulder and he quickly turned and almost choked her to death. He let go of her neck after he had recognised her. Martha stood up from the bed holding her neck.

"I am sorry Martha, I did not see you come inside."

Martha was still coughing, she just looked at him and said, "I think this isn't the right time to talk to you. You almost killed me Max."

Max looked at her and then away.

"Baby are you okay? Is something bothering you?"

"No. It's just that… you know what, I agree with you. This is not the right time, so can you please leave."

"What? Max, you want me to leave…just like that?"

"Leave now!" Max shouted fiercely.

"Ok ok, I get it. There is no need to be mad about it," Martha said as she picked up her purse from the floor which had fallen down when Max had pounced on her and left. Max heaved a sigh as he looked at his hands. His hands were shaking, he had almost killed Martha. He sat down on his bed as tears began to flow down his cheeks.

Tinashe was preparing breakfast when Charity walked in the kitchen.

"You're one in a million cousy. You cook, sweep and do all women's stuff. Do you know that mama has been praising you since I came here? I like that."

"Thanks," Tinashe said with a smile on his face, "So how is uncle?"

"He's good," there was a little moment of silence until Charity decided to continue, "I miss my home, my husband…I just miss everything you know."

Tinashe turned to look at his cousin, "Then I suggest you try and make things right."

"But how? *He-e.* I am barren, I can't give birth to a child. I am beginning to think that my mother in-law was right... *ndiri* useless," Charity said as tears flowed down her cheeks, "Please tell me *sekuru* Tinashe how to get my marriage, joy and normal life back."

Tinashe looked at her with a sad look on his face, "All I can say is pray to God. He is the only one who can help you with everything. He understands our mistakes, forgives all our sins and can transform our lives in a second. That is, if you truly believe in Him."

Charity looked up at Tinashe as she sniffed, "I am going to try my best *sekuru*, because my heart is aching for my man," she said getting off the table where she was sitting. Margaret suddenly walked into the kitchen with an angry expression on her face.

"What is it mama?"

"Cephas. He has taken my car again. He took it without even asking me. That son is a disgrace for sure. Can you imagine?! He doesn't even respect me at all."

"I do not blame him at all mama. It's you, you just keep spoiling him by forgiving him every time he commits even the worst sins."

"Will you shut up Charity, do not make me embarrass you in front of your cousin here," Margaret said pointing at Tinashe who shyly turned his attention back to the food he had been preparing for everyone to have as breakfast.

"I'll be in my room," Charity said and then left Margaret peeping through the window for any signs of Cephas arriving with her car but there was nothing.

Nyasha was still thinking about his son. He hadn't gone to meet him from the day he had received a note from Qhawe.

He heaved a sigh before taking another gulp of whisky from his glass. Nomagugu walked in her son's bedroom holding a tray with a teapot and two cups in it.

"Here is some tea for you Aaron," Nomagugu said as she put the tray on the bed.

Nyasha reluctantly looked at it and then away, "I don't want tea mother."

"*Hausikuda* tea? But why? Come on my son, you should eat something. Whisky is not good for you."

Nyasha remained quiet, Nomagugu decided to pour some for him. He ignored her when she put the cup near his mouth. Nomagugu put the cup back in the tray and then took out an envelope from the apron she was putting on.

"Son I have good news. Your brother's wedding is going to be held this month. Look he has sent us the wedding card," Noma said handing her son the wedding card which had pink ribbons tied around it.

Nyasha smiled, and then put the card on the table. Nomagugu tried to impress him but to no avail. She got fed up and then she walked out of his room. Nyasha looked at Charity's portrait on the wall and mumbled something before taking a gulp from his glass which was filled with whisky.

Two days later Kindra went back to the clinic to check up on her results. The nurse told her that she was two months pregnant and that she was also HIV positive. Kindra could not believe her ears. She stood up in a jerk but as she was about to get out of the nurse's office, the nurse stopped her. Kindra sat back down in her chair as the nurse told her that her baby could be delivered without getting affected by the virus. Kindra was advised to come back to the clinic for another test. She just nodded her head and then left. She quickly got home. She could not believe what the nurse had told her. There was no one at home and so she took the chance and screamed out loud. She had tried telling Fatso about her predicament…including her fears and all the other stuff but he had ignored her. Now she had to go and tell him but how was he going to listen to her? She had even tried to explain to him how the condom had broke in the middle of everything. She went over to the kitchen, opened one of the drawers and took a knife. What was this for? She had asked herself, just to scare him so that he accepts responsibility of everything, especially the pregnancy. She had told herself and so she went to his home to tell him the shocking news.

Fatso was putting his clothes on the washing line to dry up, when Kindra arrived.

"Hi mabhebheza," he said patting Kindra's shoulder with his wet palms.

Kindra quickly removed his hand and wiped the water he had splattered on her, "I'm not here to play games Fatso."

"Well, if it's about yesterday I am sorry but I hate Cephas."

"Why did you do it Fatso? Why didn't you tell me?"

"Tell you what?" Fatso said exasperated.

"That you're HIV positive… you never mentioned it before going to bed wi…"

"Hey! Are you stupid? *Hanty* if I had told you, you would have refused to go to bed with me. Besides we used a condom so what went wrong?"

"The condom broke. Have you forgotten? I thought you were fine that's why I just let us continue."

Fatso looked at Kindra, away and then back at her, "So is that the reason why you came all the way here to tell me?"

"I am coming from that clinic. I…I even found out *kuti* I am pregnant for you."

"*He-ee. Wati chii?* Ah I think you're mistaken, besides I am not the only guy with whom you have sex with."

"What? No, Fatso. It's only you and Cephas that I..." Kindra said illustrating her point with her fingers, "I did it many times with Cephas without using any contraceptives but I never got pregnant because Cephas is impotent."

Fatso burst out laughing. He even held the washing line for support. His landlord who had been watching them shouted out loud, "Hey Fatso leave that wire, *haisi* swing *kaiyi* you will loosen it!"

Fatso quickly let go of the wire and then the smile quickly disappeared from his lips, "Kindra stop playing games with me. This pregnancy of which you are blabbering about, I don't know anything about it. I am a Samurai, you should be careful when playing dirty tricks on me," Fatso waved a finger in her face.

Kindra held his arm, "I am not lying...I am also not going anywhere until you accept what you did. This pregnancy belongs to you Fatso."

Fatso slapped her across the face and so she fell down, he crouched beside her as she lay in the dirt and waved his finger. "You're very stupid. You have sex with all the men in the hood without a condom, you get pregnant and contract the disease and then you come here to accuse me of all that. Don't mess up with me little girl. You're a messy pig. Pthu!" Fatso spat on her and as he stood up to leave, Kindra took a knife from her purse, she ran after him and stabbed him in the back. Fatso lost his balance and fell and so she sat on top of him and then stabbed him several times on his chest. He let out a loud cry but when his landlord came out it was too late. He was still breathing though a lot of blood oozed from his body. Kindra escaped and she was running very fast with both the blood and knife in her hands. Her cheeks were already drenched with tears which kept streaming down her cheeks.

Nyasha decided to call Charity to find out how she was doing. She was not fine of course, especially without him. He even told her about Qhawe's death. Charity felt guilty but was both happy and scared that Nomaqhawe had left them a child. She feared that Nyasha would end up loving the boy more than her. Nyasha also mentioned to her that his younger brother was getting married the following week. She hung up, after Nyasha had told her that he was coming to fetch her from her home in Gweru after the wedding. She was very excited. She was however discouraged by the thought of how her mother in-law would react to seeing her back home.

10

When the postman had left, Margaret rushed to see what he had brought. It was a letter which had a wedding invitation in it. Margaret ululated as soon as she saw the names of the bride and the groom. The letter read:

Dear Aunty Maggie and Family

You're kindly invited to the wedding of Kundai Chigorimbo and Tanaka Machingura. It will be held on 16 January 2016 at exactly 9am at the Roman Catholic Chapel. The map is behind the wedding card.

See you there.

NB: NO KIDS ALLOWED

Love

Kundi & Tanaka

Margaret put the letter back in its envelope as she went into the house and showed it to Charity. Charity told her mother that she had talked to her husband about it on the phone, she even said that she was sad because she wasn't part of the preparations for the great day. Margaret's phone rang, it was the bride who was asking for her help with the catering services. Margaret asked why she had requested too late and the bride said she had discovered that Margaret's services were more reliable than the one she had hired before. Margaret agreed and then she hung up.

That afternoon Danai visited Margaret at her house. They greeted each other and then they sat on the chairs on the verandah.

"Hey, it's been long my sister. Well, what did I do wrong that you had to abandon me like this?" Margaret asked as soon as they sat down.

Danai sighed, "It's your son Cephas. He came to my house and warned me. He said I should never set foot here or else he will have his hands covered with my blood. I do not want to die just yet my friend."

Margaret looked at her friend with a quizzical expression on her face, "So why are you here?"

"I miss *youka*. I noticed that he has not been around for some time now."

"Yes, dear. He even took my car with him. Where? I do not even know my sister."

Danai shook her head, "My case is better than Rudo's. Cephas and his gang followed her to the bar and poured their urine on her."

Margaret just looked on with her mouth agape. She could not believe it.

Danai decided to continue, "I knew you did not know anything, I knew it," Danai said clicking her fingers confidently before Margaret.

Margaret heaved a sigh, "I do not even know where to start from. I do not even know what to say. I am sorry my sisters. Please forgive me."

Danai looked away and then back at Margaret, "It is not your fault my sister. It's not. He is even causing trouble for you."

Margaret nodded in agreement, and Charity then came out to greet Danai who assumed that she had merely visited her mother. After having a few drinks Danai decided to leave.

Charity was sitting in her room when Margaret walked in. She was smiling, but her thoughts seemed to be so far away.

Margaret patted her gently on her shoulder. Charity turned to look at her mother, as Margaret sat on the bed.

"Why are you smiling?"

Charity's smile widened, "I am thinking about my wedding day. We had it in that chapel, which has been abandoned for a long time. People were amazed when they saw Nyasha and I choose it as our venue. They thought we had gone crazy."

"Yes, why not? *Hanty* the place is said to be haunted by ghosts."

"But, not anymore. We just wanted to show people that ghosts do not exist."

Margaret looked at her daughter in disbelief, "You are crazy. I myself believe that ghosts exist. I was so scared, I thought your marriage wasn't going to last at all. I thought *kuti* those spirits were going to destroy it..." Margaret heaved a sigh, "The things you do some times Charity they are just so unpredictable," Margaret said standing up from the bed.

"I still remember when Nyasha and I met in the States, we told ourselves to stop believing in barbaric things. We had the same dreams, aspirations, interests and we were both adventurous..."

Margaret shook her head smiling, "Is that the reason why you chose the haunted chapel as your wedding venue?"

Charity nodded her head, "Yes, to prove you and them wrong."

Margaret and Charity looked at each other and smiled. Margaret bent a little and kissed her daughter on her cheek, "Sometimes I hate being a mother but you just make it easier for me to carry the burden of being one...thank you."

Charity looked at her mother, "I should be the one thanking you for everything...thanks mama."

Margaret smiled at her daughter and left. Charity kept on staring behind her mother until she had left the house. She suddenly felt engulfed by a strange feeling of loneliness. She bit her lower lip as she felt tears sting her eyes.

Fatso was rushed at the hospital. The doctor went inside the ward and then he returned after a few minutes.

"How is he doctor?" Fatso's landlord asked impatiently.

"We are trying our level best."

The landlord together with his neighbours who had helped him take Fatso to the hospital shook their heads as they cursed under their breaths.

The doctor looked at them with sympathy, "He has lost a lot of blood. But how did this happen?"

"A girl stabbed him. I saw *kuti* they were fighting over something. I did not think *kuti* it was that serious. I later heard him scream and *kamusikana kacho kangakatorova pasi kudhara.* She escaped doctor, but I think I know her."

"That's good because we need a police report, so can you go and get it please before we continue with the treatment."

The landlord and his friends nodded their heads and left.

Cephas was parking his mother's car at a nearby bottle store when Zenze approached him. He tried to escape but it was too late. One of Zenze's men held him by the neck and Zenze took a pen knife out from his pocket. He was pointing it at Cephas' throat as if to slice it in half.

"H...hey gents what's the problem? Why do you want to kill me? W...wha...what have I done?" Cephas stammered as Zenze continued to press the pen knife against his skin.

"Shut up *mukwenyani.* They do not call me Zenze for *nasing,*" Zenze said pointing his men one by one with the pen

129

knife, "I want some more of that stuff kid. You promised to give it remember?"

"But I did…I gave you the stuff," Cephas said in a bolder tone. Zenze let him go and began to laugh together with his men. Cephas swallowed hard as Zenze hugged him.

"You should be a man *mfana,* you're more of a woman than a man," Zenze said as he let go of Cephas, "You're our friend now, from that day in the cell. Actually in 'Soweto 'that's how we greet each other."

"In Soweto?" Cephas asked with a quizzical expression on his face.

"Oh, you do not know Soweto? Mbare Musika is our Soweto here in Zimbabwe boy," Zenze said making some moves he called *maclakcs.*

Cephas smiled, "Wow that's a great move."

Zenze widened his yellowish and golden grin, "Don't flatter me boy," and all the members of his gang who had been once surrounding Cephas dispersed, cheering him.

It has been two days and still Kindra hadn't come back home. Max felt something was wrong and then there was a knock on the door. Max went to look who was at the door. As he opened it his frightened locked gazes with one of the police officers standing on his door step. Max was silent until the police asked him if this was where Kindra James stayed.

"Ye…yes," Max stammered, "Is there any pro…problem?"

"Yes. Her body has been found in Gweru river… she drowned …"

"What? Kindra…sorry officer but are you really talking about my sister Kindra?"

The officers were quiet for some time until they asked Max to follow them at the mortuary so as to identify his sister's body.

They arrived at the mortuary which was in the nearest hospital in no time. The police officer who was driving drove as though possessed by some spirit. As they got off the car Max could not stop trembling, they walked to the reception and the nurse called the doctor who later went with them to the mortuary. Kindra's face was opened for Max to see, at first he could not recognise her and then he later saw that it was his sister. He let out a loud cry. The other policemen comforted him and after he had calmed down, Max was taken to the police station and there he was told what had happened to Kindra.

"She was pregnant? She never…um but for who?"

"One Mr Fatso. I hear he is your friend."

Max gritted his teeth though it was so hard to believe what he had heard. He used the back of his hand to wipe away the sweat from his forehead.

"Your sister was impregnated by that man Fatso and he also infected her with the virus. She was informed by the clinic staff when she had gone there for a pregnancy test. So she decided to go and inform Fatso who refused to accept the responsibility. This explains the reason why she stabbed him nine times on his chest and two times on his back, " the police officer paused his narration as he swallowed. Max could not believe his ears.

"Kindra stabbed Fatso? So how did she get drowned?"

"She was trying to wash her hands and the knife in the water. The river is flooded and so maybe she was trying to wash it whilst standing in the middle so that the fishermen who were present would not see what she was doing."

Max stood up and slapped the walls. He cursed under his breath, "Damn it Kindra!"

When the police had finished explaining everything to Max, he went back home. When he had reached home, Max went to his sister's room. He picked up his sister's photo which was in the photo frame. Their mother had bought them similar picture frames when Kindra was only eight. He looked at her smiling face in the photo, he put it back to its place upside down and began to cry. His sobs were so loud as he cried uncontrollably.

After some time Max called his aunt, Erica who was Elvis' sister. She rushed to their home and they agreed that Elvis wasn't supposed to know about Kindra's death for he would die of heart attack since he had heart problems.

"I doubt that we will be able to keep this news from dad for too long aunty."

Erica dropped her hand bag on the kitchen table and then walked over to stand by the sink which was opposite the table, "Do you still remember what happened on the day your father learned about Marilyn's death. He almost died, now do you want to get rid of him that much?"

Max turned his gaze away from his aunt, "No…but this is a ghetto. I mean …people talk, people read papers. Dad will find out about it one way or the other. You won't be able to silence everyone aunty."

Erica heaved a sigh, "Where is he right now?" she asked in a whisper.

"In his room."

"Make sure he doesn't read today's paper," Erica paused for some time and then continued, "I think I have got a plan, I will call Uncle Silas in Zambia. Elvis can go to Lusaka for a holiday," Erica said with a smile as Max clapped his hands which made a little noise.

"Hush buster, you might wake him up," Erica said as she sat down and poured herself some water which was in a bottle on the table.

That afternoon Nyasha went to Mbare Msika, to take his son Nkosilathi. He was a little scared and took three deep breaths before getting out of his car. He took a brown doll which he had put on the passenger seat and a box of chocolates. Nomaqhawe had mentioned that he was madly in love with chocolates. Nyasha cursed under his breath as one of the dogs began to bark wildly, it had startled him. Lucky enough it was next door, he thought. He opened the little gate made of tin and then walked inside the yard. It was a very small house which had about two rooms and then another single room which was built a little further away from the rest. As he was about to knock on the door of the main house the door of the separate one roomed house opened. A thin young woman came out of it, she looked shrivelled and a Madison cigarette was lodged at the corner of her mouth. Nyasha cleared his throat as he inhaled the smoke.

"Hello, can I please see Mrs Majuru?"

The woman smiled, "You mean *amai* Divah?"

Nyasha was about to speak when the woman walked towards the main house shouting, "*Amai* Divah! *Amai* Divah *kani!*" she removed the burning cigarette from her dry lips and then began to bang the door calling out at the same time.

The sound of shuffling feet was heard and then a lazy voice, "*Tirikuuya.*"

The woman widened her yellow grin as she extended her hand towards Nyasha, "*Bond coin, bhudhi.*"

Nyasha kept staring her hand for he had not understood what she wanted, *"Ndati givhu me ka25 senzi kana* fifty."

Nyasha then nodded in agreement as he took out a two dollar note from his pocket and gave it to her, the door of the main house suddenly opened and before Nyasha had completely handed the lady the money she grabbed it and ran away.

"Pfutseki!" the woman who had just come out of the house said running after the lady with shrivelled hair. She stood at her gate with her both hands on her hips, *"Imbwa yemunhu!* Shame on you, *haunyari.* Shameless whore!" Nyasha swallowed hard as the woman hurled more insults.

She then came back and stood before Nyasha with a widened smile on her face, "You must be Mr Machingura."

Nyasha was silent for some time until he said, "Um…yes…yes yes it's me," and then they greeted each other with a hand shake.

"Here for Nkosi?" the woman said as she rubbed her hands together.

"Ehe," Nyasha said as he looked around the yard.

"He has gone out but will be back soon. Come on in," she said as she moved her head in the direction of the house.

Nyasha was given a metal stool to sit on and the woman asked if he wanted anything to drink but Nyasha smiled and told her that he was fine. She then told Nyasha that he had to wait for a few minutes since Nkosilathi had gone to buy bread at the shops with her eldest son, Divine. They began to discuss how people are suffering these days. After a few minutes the children came back. Nkosilathi was introduced to his father and Divine his uncle. The woman then packed Nkosilathi's clothes in a plastic bag just beside their bed. Nkosilathi suddenly let out a wild noise full of excitement when he saw a rat jump on the bed and then went through a hole which was caused by the cracks in the walls. Everyone in the house laughed except Nyasha who forced a smile. Nyasha then left Nomaqhawe's sister some money to thank her for looking after his son and then some to pay for Divine's school fees.

During their discussion, she had mentioned to him how her husband had died of lung cancer in a mine hospital, in South Africa. She spoke of how much the xenophobia there had stripped down most of her relatives who had gone there in search of the greener pastures. Her son Divine, now twelve was good at maths. She had told Nyasha that she hoped he'd pass his grade seven and continue schooling. Nkosilathi was happy to see a doll and a box of chocolates in his father's car. He left Divine just a few and then got in the car as they headed back home.

Erica had succeeded in persuading her brother to leave. She claimed that it was for his own good that he go away from the boredom surrounding his home. He had refused to get in the bus without bidding his daughter farewell but Erica had told him that she would call her and tell her since she was still studying at school in preparation for the examinations. Max watched the whole drama quietly until his father finally agreed and got on the bus.

"So when will he come back?" Max said as they got into the house.

"I don't know yet. I'll figure out something soon," Erica said as she poured herself some whisky and then sat on the couch.

Max looked at her with a narrowed gaze," What are you up to aunt?"

Erica turned her gaze and looked at her nephew, "What?"

"You heard me, I said what are you up to?"

Erica stood up from her seat and then she walked towards her nephew, "Nothing, I am up to saving my brother's life. Elvis doesn't deserve pain and sorrow," Erica looked away from Max and continued, "He deserves joy, happiness and peace of mind."

Max just stared and then after some time decided to leave.

It was almost midnight when Tashinga came over to Margaret's home. She was standing at the gate shaking when she decided to call Tinashe. He answered her lazily but when he learned that she was in dire need of his help he crept out of the house and rushed to the gate.

"Tashi, are you okay?" he asked as he hugged her little body which was now cold since the weather was chilly that night.

"I am sorry... I am sorry...but...b..." she was trembling uncontrollably.

Tinashe hushed her as he carried her into the house and straight to his room. He waited before shutting the door since he felt that someone had seen him carry Tashinga to his room but he saw no one.

The next day at dawn, Nomagugu woke up and began to work in the kitchen. Nyasha was woken up by the noise she was making downstairs. He had told her how he had had Nkosilathi with Nomaqhawe. She had danced and ululated, she had wished that Nomaqhawe would have lived and obviously that Charity had died.

Nyasha went and stood at the door as he rubbed his forehead with sleep still in his eyes.

"And now?" Nomagugu asked as soon as she saw her son standing at the door.

"You woke me up."

"What, are you trying to tell me that the aroma of my traditional porridge woke you up son? I have always told you that I am a great cook. Your father died knowing that he had married the best chef in this whole wide world. Many women in the village envied me. MaMoyo you know her right? She even tried to kill me because she was jealous of my great talent. The way I cooked son even made your father refuse to take in a second wife, he called me his one and *oniri*. Your fath…"

"No mum, please. You're making noise with those pots. That's why I had to wake up," Nyasha said as he walked towards the fridge. He took a bottle of cold water and gulped it down.

There was a little moment of silence until Nomagugu said in a low voice, "I am sorry son. You know I always wonder why you hate me this much…um if ther…"

Nyasha quickly looked at his mother and then he hugged her shoulders from the back, "I do not hate you mama. I know what you're trying to do. You want me to tell you that your food tastes better than any woman's."

Nomagugu looked at her son over the shoulder and smiled, "Yes. And I did not know that it was that difficult."

Nyasha let go of his mother and stood before her, "You're the best mum and grandma in the world ma. I love you so much and I thank God because he made you my mum."

Nomagugu's smile widened, "Wow, I did not ask for that one. So it's true that I am so good."

He was about to leave when he looked at his mother and asked, "Now, my kind-hearted mother, may you please do me a favour?"

"Anything for you my duckling," Nomagugu said squeezing Nyasha's cheeks with her hands covered with the white maize-meal powder.

Nyasha heaved a sigh, "I want Charity to come back home. You know Nkosilathi needs a mother's love."

Nomagugu turned her gaze away from Nyasha, "I did not send her away from you my son. She left you *pano* I did no…"

"I know mother, I didn't say that you sent her away. You were giving her a hard time," Nomagugu turned to look at her son who raised a finger as if in realisation, " I did not say you sent her away mother. Anyway I'm going to bring her back on the sixteenth," Nyasha said as he left the kitchen and then shouted as he climbed the stairs, "One more thing mum, the porridge is smelling good!"

Nomagugu heaved a sigh as she turned to look at her boiling pot which was on the gas stove.

Tinashe woke up late that night and saw that Tashinga had already left. He went to the bathroom and turned on the tap. He forgot to turn it off as water began to spill from the bath tub to the floor. Margaret rushed in and turned off the tap for him since he had also forgotten to lock the door.

"Tinashe are you okay? "Margaret asked as soon as she turned the tap off.

"No," Charity said with her hands folded, "He is not fine at all."

Margaret turned to look at Charity and then ignored her. She repeated her question and again Charity answered it.

"He had some girl in his room last night. I guess that explains everything to you mum."

Margaret turned to look at Tinashe with a narrowed gaze, "Is it true Tinashe?"

Tinashe looked away and heaved a sigh, "Yes… but it's not what you think aunt."

"Then what is it? Do you want to be like Cephas? You want to get some girl pregnant? Your father and everybody else won't blame you but me! Are you getting all this from my son? If you're copying his ways then I'll have to ca…"

"No! Don't! She was helpless aunt. She needed me… she has always needed my help aunt," Tinashe said as tears began to flow down his cheeks, "I'm her only true friend. She didn't choose them but she was forced by circumstance aunt. You know how much Tashinga is trying to cope."

Margaret heaved a sigh and then Charity came and stood beside him, "I'm so sorry I didn't know sh…"

"No it's ok. I understand," Tinashe said as he turned to look at Charity who looked away for some time and then back at him.

"I would like to meet her. Is it possible for me to… you know…"

"Yes, she will be so glad."

Charity nodded, "Ok, but I want you to be very careful. Girls in this hood are whores. You're a good young man Tinashe, I don't want you to get all messed up."

Tinashe smiled, "Ok thanks very much for your concern," Charity nodded once again and left. Margaret squeezed his elbow.

"Don't stress over it son, Tashinga is a very strong woman she will be fine."

Tinashe nodded as his aunt got out of the bathroom.

Later that morning when the doctor came to inject Fatso, she found that he had already died and so she called the landlord and informed him. Fortunately, he knew that Fatso

139

had no family but some friends and so he informed one of his gang mates, Gejo. Gejo later informed the entire gang about their colleague's death.

That afternoon Max received a call from their gang leader. He demanded that all the members of the gang meet at their meeting place at exactly one. Max slowly prepared to go. He arrived almost an hour later. Lucifer's anger was kindled.

"Your bitch of a sister killed one of my favourite men here and you come at the time that you want? I am your leader so you sh..."

"No," Max said as he walked away from Lucifer, "I am my own man now. You do not tell me what to do Lucifer. All my life I have been listening to you but now..." Max turned to look at his boss whose eyes were now bloodshot due to anger, "I own myself."

Lucifer kept staring at him as his colleagues just glared at him, "I am still mourning my sister but you do not consider that. I will make everyone pay if you dare force me to bury a man I hate so much!" Max said vehemently and as he was about to leave, Lucifer screamed out his name. Max stopped with his back facing Lucifer.

"You're free to leave but you are certainly going to pay for your disloyalty, you will pay me with something special," Max turned to look at his boss, "Your father is the price I am charging you. You are a Samurai and Samurais are brave... *hadzizi mbwende*. You should stop acting cowardly...this is your home but if you have decided to leave then it's okay. But be ready to pay the price," Lucifer hissed as he signalled to one of his men for a cigarette. The young man put it in his mouth for him and then lit it up. Max watched as smoke coming from the cigarette almost choked him.

Max was tongue-tied as his boss continued to speak, "He is on his way to Lusaka right now. Max after all I have done for you, you just can't abandon me, abandon us," Lucifer said with his hands out stretched in the direction of all the men surrounding him.

Lucifer then took out a remote control, "There is a bomb under his bus and your answer to my question will determine whether he lives or dies," Max swallowed hard, "Do you still wish to leave the brotherhood?" Lucifer asked with a strong Ndebele accent in his voice. Max shook his head as he let out a "No" Lucifer smiled and then walked towards Max.

"That's the spirit my son," he said in a hoarse voice, "Now come and help us bury a brother."

Erica was sitting on an armchair just outside Elvis' house when her cell phone rang. She slowly took it from her pocket and answered it.

"What?" she said in a low but firm tone.

"We have traced the bus. So what do we do now?"

"Follow it until he has reached Lusaka. And from there I will tell you what to do with him."

"Yes Ma'am," the unknown person's voice said and then Erica hung up. She pursed her lips and began to talk to herself as she stared blankly at the gate which was adjacent to where she was sitting outside on the brownish but well-trimmed lawn.

"Your end is approaching my darling brother, wait till you see that Erica is not just a name but a personality," she raised her glass as if in a toast, filled with cheap, local beer, "For his end." Erica let out an evil laugh as she spilled some of it on the ground.

The sixteenth of January, a day everyone was waiting for had come. Margaret woke up early and then after taking a bath she realised that Cephas had not brought her car back home. She cursed under her breath, and then decided that she would board a *kombi*. She was dressed in her favourite dress and as for the new suit that Charity had bought her she kept it safe in her little bag. She arrived at the chapel at exactly half past five. The preparations were almost complete.

"Are the fridges in the room upstairs working?" Margaret asked one of the cooks who shook her head.

"I do not know aunty. We're using the ones downstairs."

Margaret looked at the plastic bags filled with large boxes of ice-cream, "The cream will melt and the dessert might be ruined. You should have checked. Anyway, continue with the marinating of those chicken pieces, I'll go and check," Margaret said and left the kitchen downstairs.

She felt that someone was following her up the stairs and she let out a cry when she turned and saw the trespasser who was none other than Cephas.

"You…you scared me. What are you doing here anyway, and where is my car?" Margaret asked even though the sparkle in her son's eyes made her feel uncomfortable.

"Shhh," Cephas hushed her and then said in a whisper, "Just give me the money."

"What money?" Margaret asked in an almost audible voice.

"I said quiet! They paid you *hanty*. I hear the Machinguras are very rich people," Cephas took a knife from the back pocket of his pair of shorts he was wearing, "Now you choose mother, life or death."

Margaret was now trembling, "Put the knife down Cephas. Please we can sett…"

"I said give me the money!" Cephas said in a loud whisper looking around and then he beckoned to someone who came from behind the old cupboards upstairs but he had a mask on his face.

Margaret began to look for the money in her little bag but before she had handed him the money they heard a whistle. Someone was coming towards the room. Margaret let out a loud scream, Cephas was angry that he pushed his mother who fell down the stairs. She suddenly collapsed. Cephas was startled, he then used his shirt to rub his finger prints from the rails of the stair case and left together with his unknown friend in a hurry with the money in their hands.

The owner of the whistle was Tinashe, he ran to the room and saw his aunt lying on the floor for he had heard the scream. He had come to the chapel to meet Tashinga. She had told him she was in the kitchen and he thought that she was in the kitchen which was upstairs. He went over to where his aunt was lying. He began to shake her so that she would wake up. Tashinga came up the stairs and saw Margaret lying on the floor.

She gasped, "What...what happened Tinashe? How did she...?"

"I don't know I just saw her lying here. Sh..."

One of the cooks also came up the stairs and saw what had happened she let out such a loud scream that everyone else rushed towards the room including the bride who had come to see if the preparations were going smoothly. Tinashe was asked what had happened but he kept telling everyone that he had seen his aunt lying on the floor and nothing else. Blood now oozed from her mouth. The police were called and Tinashe was their prime suspect!

11

The next day Tinashe woke up in the police station. He was called in for some questioning. All he kept saying were the words 'I didn't do it,' with tears flowing down his cheeks. Many people had protested against his arrest but the policemen and detectives claimed that his finger prints alone were found on Margaret's body. Margaret had died and so this made it difficult for Tinashe to prove his innocence. The police officers were so brutal towards Tinashe since they believed that he was in actual fact hiding the truth from them. He had sores and swellings all over his face. His father kept visiting him and he would always leave the police station with tears in his eyes. Misheck wasn't that rich, therefore he could not afford to hire a lawyer to defend his son from the policemen and court's allegations.

Cephas came back when he heard that his mother was dead. He cried and everyone just glared at him during the funeral and refused to comfort him. He began to drink and go to a lot of parties especially when he got the news that Kindra had died. He missed her so much and this time she wasn't there to give him the comfort that he needed. He would drink with friends, drive his mother's car and bring naked women into the house even in broad day light. He became every location's topic of discussion during gossip. He enjoyed it a lot...he was becoming famous. Only Margaret knew that her son had sounded a death knell for her that very day when she conceived him.

Life seemed to have gone back to normal for Charity, especially with a child in their house. Nyasha looked happier than ever, until one day when Nomagugu came with a stranger in their house. Nyasha was having breakfast with both his wife and son.

"Hello everyone," Nomagugu said as soon as she had entered the dining room with the strange young woman. Nyasha and Charity just looked at her and continued eating.

"Hezvo? I said hello or is it because you're not happy to see me at all?"

Charity forced a smile as she stood up and took hold of Nomagugu's bags, "You're welcome mama," she said curtsying.

Nomagugu pushed her away, Charity staggered and fell on the floor, "Away *muroyi!* Are you out of your mind? *He-e.* How dare you lay your filthy fingers on my bag?"

Nyasha stood up with his mouth agape. He could not believe his eyes. Charity stood up and dusted herself. Nyasha went over to his wife and held her shoulders to comfort her.

"Mother what is the meaning of this? You just pushed my wife away from you and you almost hurt her."

Nomagugu burst out laughing, *"Heede!* You call that a wife, she is not a wife, that woman is a man my son. Look at her womb, it's stuck inside *kuita kunge kamwana keku* Somalia *karohwa nenzara.* Do you know the pain and humiliation that I am going through Nyasha because of this faggot you call a wife?! She is a witch, look at how her family ruined my last-born son's wedding. They murder each other during festivals and celebrations. They do not have any shame in them. *Woti vanhu ivavo?* Please my son you should let this woman go!"

Charity burst into tears as she ran upstairs and then locked herself inside her bedroom. Nyasha watched his wife go and when she was out of sight he began to quarrel with his mother.

"We settled this misunderstanding long ago. I told you I love my wife but you keep tormenting her. Why do you hate her so much mother?"

Nomagugu looked at her son, "I warned you before you got married to that *twiza!* A great prophet whom I have consulted told me that your wife is a cursed woman. He said that during her youth she had six abortions and that is the reason why she can't conceive," Nomagugu said in a loud whisper.

Nyasha was quiet for some time, "But I don't believe in all that. These prophets are mere gold diggers and all that they are after is money and division of families."

"*Haiwa kani.* I am telling you the truth son. He went on to say that if you continue staying with her she might drag you into the mud and so I as your mother I do not want any harm to come your way son. I love you my son."

Nyasha heaved a sigh as he turned away from his mother, "I do not know why I always ask you for advice and solutions. So, what do I do now?"

"I have brought you Tapiwa from our village. She is a virgin, I want you to marry her and give us more grandchildren."

Nyasha turned to look at the girl and then his mother, at the girl again and then back at his mother. The girl looked down at the floor for she was so shy, "How old are you?" Nyasha asked the girl with his eyes glued on his mother's face.

The girl was quiet for some time until Nomagugu pinched her, "Sixteen my husband."

"Hell no mama! She is just a kid!"

"A kid is a goat's young one my son. She is a woman, a full woman. So are you saying that all the elders from our village are stupid huh? It took us three days to come to a conclusion."

Nomagugu then pulled the girl to stand in front of her, "Look at her Nyasha she has round and full breasts, a nice, round bottom, the waist is just so marvel…"

"*Amai* please! What are you doing? I have said no to it. My no is a no, don't you get it?" Nyasha bellowed, "Have you lost your wits?" he said pointing his head, he took his coat from the hook behind the door and left.

Tashinga decided to go and see Tinashe at the police station. She hadn't stopped crying from the day the incident had happened.

"I can't believe it Nashe. You ca…"

"It's okay all I know is that my God will fight this battle for me."

Tashinga looked away as fresh tears gushed out from her eyes, "You believe me, don't you? You know I didn't do it right?"

Tashinga nodded her head as she extended her arm to touch Tinashe's but the police officer in charge shouted, "No touching!" Tashinga quickly removed her hand.

She swallowed hard as she promised him that she was going to make sure he won the case, "I will work hard in school, do a law degree and then…"

Tinashe forced a smile, "That's a long period. Tashi look I'll…"

"No, I am the one who should set you free. It's my turn now. I know I no longer have a job but our God will definitely make a way for us. Continue praying Nashe and I'll do just the same thing, okay? God is never going to let us down," they both nodded with tears in their eyes and the police officer shouted, "Time up!"

Tinashe and Tashinga stood up, "I did not have money this afternoon but I'm definitely going to bring you something to eat in the evening, " Tinashe nodded his head as he stood up and was pushed by the police officer all the way back to the cell.

Erica was crying when Max came back from his gang meeting place. She had a bottle of whisky in her left hand.

"What's up aunt, are you okay?" he asked as he crouched down opposite her.

"No. How can I be fine when everyone in this family, I mean…when my entire family is perishing?"

Max straightened up as if in realisation, "What? What do you mean aunt?"

"Elvis. Your father is gone, Max."

Max stood up in a jerk as a sign of disbelief filled his eyes, "What? But how?"

"He had gone to the beach with Silas and so some men I hear…um had heard he was from Zimbabwe. They followed him and killed him. His body was found today in the bushes which are near the beach. Silas told me all this."

Erica's tears continued to flow as she kept stamping her feet against the floor. Max let out a loud cry. He then just got out of the house. Erica began to scream after him, "Max! Please Max! My son please do not do anything stupid! Max!" Max ignored her as he got out of the gate and went where he did not know. Erica smiled to herself. She dropped the bottle of whisky on the armchair humming an unknown hymn. She went into the house and headed straight for Elvis' portrait which was hanging on the wall.

"Hello brother. You have always considered your mind as full of wisdom, many have called you clever and brilliant when

148

it came to scheming ugly machinations to destroy the innocent. But no. Maybe I was born for a purpose, I was born to prove you wrong my beloved brother. You thought wrong, your thoughts have always been wrong and you will always be wrong…even in your grave, " Erica began walking round the living room with a couch cushion in her hands, "You thought that I wasn't going to come back for you but look here I am. I will not surrender until my hands are covered with your blood, because you ruined my life Elvis," she hissed as she turned back to look at the portrait once again with a fierce look on her face.

When Nyasha came back from work he saw his wife sitting in front of a long mirror in their bedroom. She was putting on a black Indian sari. She had bought this to express the sorrow she had in losing her mother. She was staring at her reflection with tears flowing down her cheeks. Nyasha turned his gaze away from her when he had entered the room. She hadn't seen him come in until he spoke.

"Are you okay, honey?"

She turned to look at him as she sniffed, "Oh you're back. How was work?"

"It was good. And you? How was your day?"

There was a little moment of silence. Charity stood up and began pacing around the room, "You know what baby? I have realised something."

Nyasha looked at his wife with a quizzical expression on his face, "And that is?"

"*Muchato wedu.* Our wedding was a huge mistake that the two of us have ever made. It was maybe a sin before God because I do not understand the reason why I'm tortured almost every single second in my own house," Charity's voice was now hoarse due to crying. She began to shake her head,

"I…I am tired. I love you so much but I'm so tired. Maybe we were not meant to be together but we…"

Nyasha walked towards his wife and held her frail body in his arms. He kissed her forehead and they both sat on the bed, "You shouldn't get weary. What have I done wrong Charity?" Nyasha asked in a gentle voice.

Charity raised her gaze and then she looked at her husband, "It's not you…and it has never been you honey. It has always been your mother! She taunts me day and night. Don't you see it? And all you do is calm her down," Charity stood up and walked from her husband, "There is something you should make her understand. We're married. And you should also tell her that *haisi mhosva yangu* that we do not have kids! It's not my fault that I'm barren!"

Nyasha looked at his wife. He heaved a sigh, stood up and walked out of the room. Charity wiped the tears off her face with the back of her hand, she walked towards her chair and then sat back down in front of the long mirror in their room.

Susan and Christopher were having coffee whilst in bed. They seemed to be enjoying their conversation when Susan let out a cry in a shrill voice.

Christopher then jumped from the bed, he ran to their bathroom and came back holding a hockey stick in his hand.

"Where is it?" he asked his wife with his eyes wide open. Susan wanted to laugh but she failed.

She screamed once again, "I said where is the damn thing Sue?"

"It…It's coming, aaaahhh! No! It's coming Kirisi *kani!*"

Christopher looked around confused, "The baby! I'm having *macontractions*. I do not know… but I'm supposed to be due this *w…wi …wiki!*"

150

Christopher threw the hockey stick away in realisation, "I thought you had seen a scorpion!" he exclaimed as he helped her on the bed, "Sit I'll call the do…"

"No. I do not want to *siti dhauni.*"

Christopher looked at his wife with a quizzical expression on his face, "So what should we do?"

"Take me outside. *Kune suwimingi puru,* I'm feeling hot… like all over," Susan said fanning herself with her weak palm. She groaned as Christopher kept staring at her.

"What are you looking at? Take me outside *mhani! Hindava so?* I'm in pain *kaini,*" Susan was getting angry now. Christopher hesitated but he later helped her outside. They went over to the pool and then he took out his mobile phone and called the ambulance. Susan began to climb down the stairs.

"Hey! Susan, *unopenga here?* Do you want to die? Look it's okay if you want to but please spare my baby!" Christopher said with the cell phone stuck on his ear but Susan ignored him and continued to get inside the pool until she began to wade inside and then went and stood in the middle. She let out another frantic cry, it was so loud that Christopher almost jumped.

"Baby please not so loud. The ambulance people said they're on their way. You're beginning to scare me now, "Christopher said looking around.

Susan began to groan, cry and scream at the same time. She almost fell in the pool as her husband looked on. Christopher then removed his shoes and then dived in the chilly waters. He let out a cry for the water was beyond coolness. He waded towards his wife, she was now trembling, the weather was chilly cold that night. Susan held Christopher's strong arms for support and continued with her groaning. Christopher was so scared, she looked up at him shivering, "T...the baby is coming," she said whispering. He smiled as her grip on his hand tightened. The ambulance arrived. Christopher shouted and so they ran at the backyard only to see husband and wife delivering their child in the pool. Susan then let out a much louder cry that alarmed almost everyone present at that moment, and with her hand she reached for the baby who had just popped out of her abdomen and like a trophy she held it up high for everyone to see. Christopher's tears came out of his eyes as he and his wife's gazes locked. One of the ambulance people reached for the baby and wrapped it in warm cloths and Christopher helped his wife out of the water.

That night Nyasha had gone to his mother's room and saw that she and Tapiwa had gone out. He had sat in the lounge waiting for them. He decided then he would talk to them tomorrow but as he was about to stand up and go to bed the door was opened and Nomagugu walked in singing a Ndebele church hymn. She stopped humming as soon as she saw her son sitting on the couch.

"*Ei mfana*, why are you not in bed? It's almost twelve midnight."

Nyasha stood up and walked towards his mother, "Please mother do not get me wrong, I appreciate your being here but your taunting has gone too far."

Nomagugu frowned a little as she moved away from her son, "Did that faggot tell you to inform me that I am so unbearable? This is just the beginning. Where is she?" Nomagugu said heading for the stairs. "*Wena mthakati*! Charity, *iwe mwana wemuroyi buda mumba umo!*"

Nyasha hurried towards his mother, he gently pulled her by the arm, "No! You will not say another word to my wife! I

152

have heard enough, this is going too far mother. Remember that this is my house and that it is I who decides what goes on here."

Nomagugu looked away from her son, "And what if I disagree with you?"

Nyasha looked straight into his mother's eyes, "You leave my house," he hissed and got out of the room leaving Nomagugu amazed, her mouth agape.

The next morning Charity received a call from Christopher telling her that Susan had a baby girl. She was so overjoyed that she told her husband and they both agreed on buying Susan a gift for her new born baby. Nomagugu walked into the lounge and heard their discussion.

She pursed her lips and then sat down, "I can't believe this, you buy gifts for other people because they have babies. What are they ever going to buy for you? For what exactly? Will they be gifts for *amabirthdays, amaweddings? Haiwa* you're already wedded" Nomagugu turned to look at her son, "You want to send me out of your house but as long as you're with this *Kizito* you will always be mocked, gossiped about and seen as a worthless bull in its kraal."

Nyasha looked down on the floor together with his wife and then Nomagugu stood up and went to her room.

Max was pacing around the lounge when Erica walked in with a vase in her hands. The people were already gathered outside waiting for the funeral to begin. Erica had said she was going to collect his father's body from the airport. Max turned to look at his aunt as soon as she entered the lounge.

"The body, did you get it?"

"Yes," Erica nodded her head, "Come on let's do this," Erica said as they walked out of the lounge to where the people were seated. Max suddenly stopped as he saw that there was no coffin or any sign that Elvis' body had come.

"Where is it?"

Erica walked past him and then stood in the middle of the people, "I greet you all! Um… I would like to thank you all for coming here to mourn with us. You all know that we lost a child and now we have lost a brother…It's just so painful but you people have shown us love and care and I thank you, " Erica cleared her throat as she looked directly at the crowd, "I know that you have been waiting for my brother's body. I have it right here with me," she said as she opened the vase and held it high for the people to see.

Some gasped and some just looked on and seemed not to care about it. Max walked and stood beside his aunt, "And this?"

"They are your father's ashes," Erica said in a gentle voice as she turned to look at her nephew.

"But… but dad always told us that he never wanted to be cremated no matt…"

Erica looked away dismissively, "Are you saying I do not know what I'm doing?"

Max looked baffled. "Nope," he said and then he swallowed hard and put both his hands in his pockets.

"Then you should step back. I'm not some crazy woman Max. I did what I thought was right and cheap."

Max looked away with his jaw clenched and nodded his head in agreement. Erica decided to continue with her speech, "I will be going to Lake Chivero next week to get rid of his ashes. I… mean they have to be set free. Elvis has always been the man. He loved freedom and independence. And so, in order to fulfil my brother's wishes I will do what I have said."

The people nodded their heads and with a crocodile tear flowing from her right eye she left. Max looked after her thoughtfully and then back at the crowd. The people were dispersing for food was now being served.

Charity decided to take Nkosilathi for shopping. Nkosi was so excited and it rubbed off on Charity who had never taken any child with her for any special occasion. Charity bought him a lot of chocolates and a few gifts for Susan's baby. She also bought her husband a Giorgio Armani shirt and an Antonio Banderas Dior. The shopkeeper was helping her with the packages when she realised that Nkosi was missing. She looked around for him but she didn't see him. She then ran out of the parking lot to look for her son and then she saw him trying to cross the road. She dropped all the packages that she was holding and called out his name. Nkosi stopped but as he was about to run back to his mother a car knocked him down. Charity felt her legs become numb. She fell down and began to crawl towards her son and the car which had just hit him. She began to cry and scream. In no time a lot of people had surrounded her. An ambulance was called and her son was taken to the hospital.

When Chipo, Susan and Christopher received the sad message they decided to go and see her and the child at the hospital. When they arrived, they saw Nomagugu shouting and dragging Charity about. Charity was just crying, the nurses tried to calm Nomagugu down but to no avail. Nyasha came in a hurry. He asked what had happened and then the nurses informed him. Nyasha wasn't allowed to enter the ward. Everyone was silent for some time until the doctor walked out of the ward. Everyone stood up. Charity's eyes were now swollen from crying.

"How is my son doctor?" Nyasha said as he took hold of the doctor's arm.

The doctor was quiet for some time, "He is in a very critical condition but we will try our very best to save his life."

"What do you mean by critical condition doctor?"

"He was hit on the head, and so that is actually the reason why he is still unconscious. He is also finding it very hard to breathe, but like I said we'll d..."

The doctor was cut in the middle when Nyasha turned to look at his wife, "You see? Do you see this Charity? I'm going to lose this one and only son because of your carelessness! You miserable witch! How did I even get to know you, why did I fall in love with you?"

Fresh tears gushed from Charity's eyes as she sat down with Susan holding her by the shoulders. Nyasha walked towards her, "My mother has always been right. You come from a cursed people!"

Christopher wanted to answer him but Susan held him back with her hand and shook her head, "No," she said in a whisper. Christopher heaved a sigh, swallowed hard and then stood back leaning against the wall but with his fingers tapping against it.

Charity held her head with both hands, "I'm sorry...I am so sorry. I did not... see Nkosi leave me. I..." Charity broke into crying again, "I admit it now. I'm cursed...yes. I shouldn't have gotten married to you at all. I thought th..."

"To hell with your thoughts! You have always destroyed my joy. You have always blinded me with your pretentious love. Today you have made me realise how stupid I was to have stayed with you for ten years!"

Charity looked up at her husband astonished, "Nyasha I said I'm sorry. I said th..."

"No!" Nyasha bellowed he hit the walls with his fists, looked at everyone and then he left. Nomagugu looked at Charity with an evil expression on her face which told Charity that she was guilty of murder.

"Mama I…"

Nomagugu raised her arm to silence Charity, "Hey! Your mother is dead *ini handisi amai vako*. If you look at me carefully is there anywhere *pakanyorwa kuti* Margaret?"

Charity swallowed hard as she looked at her feet. She could not see them clearly for her vision was blurred by the tears. Nomagugu cursed and left. All her siblings surrounded her and began to comfort her including Susan who let her lie on her bosom.

Max decided to follow his aunt to where she used to stay. She entered a food outlet and then she bought food which was enough for two or more people. Max became so curious that he decided to continue following her. She then entered a bar and called a friend. A certain man arrived and they began to eat but they ate from the same dish. Max kept staring until his aunt stood up as if going to the toilet but in no time she was out of sight. Max kept waiting until he took a glance from his watch and realised that about fifteen minutes had passed since she left where she was sitting. He decided to return back to his house but something caught his attention. Erica came out a little later with a brown wig which was a substitute for her black hair. She changed her jacket, boots, skirt and handbag. Max who had been hiding in the market place did not even recognise her.

When she got home, Erica woke up her friend. The friend was always quiet. She never said anything much. When Erica gave her the food she mumbled a thank you. "What did you say your name was by the way?" The woman looked up at her, "Nowinnie." Erica smiled as she sat down beside the woman, "My friend you should always feel free when talking to me. We both share the same predicament. You said that you and your friend were gang raped and that she died on that spot?" Nowinnie nodded her head, "That's right."

Erica smiled but the smile suddenly vanished from her lips, "I am not saying rape is good but I find your situation a little understandable compared to mine. I was raped by my own brother. I'm not talking about a cousin or half-brother…I mean a blood brother."

Nowinnie kept staring at Erica, "I have just begun my mission of exacting my revenge upon him. He ruined my life and I think that you should do the same too. A bad past should be burned to ashes my dear. It is not meant to live… but to die."

Nowinnie looked away from Erica, "You're right *shamwari*. I'm hurt because I lost a friend who was more of a sister to me than just a friend."

There was a moment of silence until Nowinnie spoke up, "Eish, so how do I do this? Won't the guy who did it try to kill me?"

"Who was the guy? I think I know everyone in our hood."

"It was Max," Erica felt as if she was hit by a huge blow. She sat up straight and found it hard to swallow her food, "One of the popular Samurais."

Nowinnie began to laugh, "I know he is your nephew…but are you just going to help him take off with blood in his hands. Your nephew is a murderer *sisi*. He killed my friend and I'm having a hard time trying to forgive him and all those men. Promise me that you'll never betray me."

"Nowinnie, Max isn't just a nephew…he is a son. Max is my biological son," Erica swallowed and then continued, "I was fourteen years old when my brother Elvis raped me. I fell pregnant and so I told him that I wanted to abort but he stopped me from doing that…he threatened me," Erica took a deep breath before continuing.

"He told me that if I was going to do it he was going to kill me…I was so scared…he said that he would give me up to his friends so that they have sex with me endlessly…I was perturbed…and so I kept the pregnancy. And as soon as I was delivered I went and gave him his child but he refused it and said that I must keep him until he was weaned…I had no choice. My brother destroyed my life…like every other teenage girl I had dreams and goals but he destroyed everything for me Nowinnie."

Nowinnie heaved a sigh, "I'm so sorry Erica…it's painful to have a brother treat you like that!"

There was silence for some time, "I'll try and help you Winnie even though it pains me for Max is my son."

Nowinnie smiled as they continued to have their supper.

Tashinga now concentrated on her studies but still she continued to visit Tinashe at the police station. She'd bring him food and some old novels. Tinashe loved this. On his birthday, she brought him an old bible which he had given to her when they were still kids. She kept encouraging him until the date of his trial had arrived. The judge was so mean and she did not tolerate any explanations. Tinashe was sentenced twenty years' imprisonment. He changed into jail clothes and was then put into a bus for prisoners and then he was taken to the maximum prison…he was taken to hell…the bus sent Tinashe to Hwahwa Maximum prison. And with tears in his eyes he murmured with his eyes looking at the sky, "May your will be done, *Baba.*"

Charity decided to stay in the hospital for the whole night. The doctor then called her from the waiting room and suggested that she come and sit beside her unconscious stepson's bed in the ward. The collar of her dress was drenched in tears, it was very cold at night but she didn't feel the chilly weather. She slowly sat down beside Nkosilathi. Fresh tears began to flow down her cheeks as she watched the bandages tied around his head, she held his hand and then leaned against the bed with her head.

"Baby, I… I am so sorry I wasn't careful. I do not care if my marriage falls apart. The most important thing is that you live. You mean the world to my husband and myself baby. It was not my intention to hurt you. Please forgive me…do not die," Charity said shaking due to both the cold and the tears. After some time she fell asleep and then she began to dream.

She was walking in a lonely and abandoned city with Nkosilathi when a certain woman in animal skin clothes approached. She had decayed teeth and a severely pierced ear. Charity wanted to run but the woman held her by the arm. It was so painful.

"*Ukuda kutiza zvivi zvako?* No…I will not let you. You have a lot of blood on your hands and so I myself have decided that every child who comes near you or any woman is to die." The woman tried to grab Nkosilathi but Charity held on tight on him screaming, "No! No! Noooooooo!" and then she woke up. She saw that she was sweating. It was already morning. She yawned as she looked at Nkosi's still body and began pacing around the room praying. She was asking God to protect the boy but she stopped suddenly as she tried to remember the last

160

time she ever tried to talk to God. It was long ago when she was still in the primary school when all the children were lined up to repeat the Lord's Prayer. She heaved a sigh as she remembered how Margaret had warned her against the abortions. Charity sat back down in her chair with a plumb. She turned to look at Nkosilathi who did not show any sign of life in his body. The doctor walked in and asked how he had slept. She forced a smile and answered, "There is no change doctor."

The doctor began to check on Nkosilathi when Charity approached him, "Do you think my son is going to live?"

The doctor turned to look at her with gentleness in his eyes, "Yes, but I advise you to pray very hard so that Jesus Christ can save him. With God nothing is impossible."

With these words the doctor finished his task and walked out of the ward. Charity got out of the ward with a smile and went to look for a church nearby.

Susan was folding the baby's clothes when Christopher walked in holding two ties, a red one and a blue one.

"Which one is suitable for the occasion?"

Susan looked up and whispered, "The one on your right."

Christopher looked at the blue tie which was in his right hand and nodded, "Where is the angel?"

Susan smiled at him, "Asleep in her room. You want her to say bye?"

Christopher smiled too, "No. The mother can say that for her."

Susan stood up and walked in Christopher's arms, he kissed her on her cheek and they bid each other farewell. But before he had gone out Susan stopped him.

"I hope you're praying for *tete*, she's having a *tofu* time."

Christopher heaved a sigh and again he nodded his head, "Yes. I am."

Susan smiled and they kissed again before Chris left for work.

Cephas had parked his mother's car beside a park where some children were playing when he received a call from his brother Christopher.

"Sup big bro?"

"How are you Cephas?"

"Good. Any problem?"

Christopher was quiet for some time, "I have called to inform you that Charity is having a tough time here and so that is the reason why we are delaying that program of sharing…um distributing mother's belongings amongst us and other relatives."

"No that is not a problem it's ok. I am actually looking after all these for you. You know you can always trust me brother."

Again Christopher was silent and then he said, "If anything goes wrong I'll make sure your ass gets locked up in jail," Christopher said and hung up. Cephas cursed as he returned his mobile phone in one of the side pockets of his pair of expensive denim jeans. He leaned against the car with his back and took out a cigarette from the other one and began smoking. He was suddenly attacked by some men he could not identify because they were putting on some masks. They hit him before putting him in the car.

They then arrived at a place he did not know. It looked like a dumping place but it was clear that no one would ever come to the place for it was a bushy area. He was put in an old torn leather seat by the men. They made him sit before a short and stout man who was wearing sun glasses and a cap on his head. He had a scruffy moustache and shrivelled hair. His cap was not worn properly. Cephas groaned in his seat as the man began to walk around him. He made about ten rounds. The man then asked one of his men to hand him a cigarette. He put the burning cigarette in his mouth and then he was also handed a seat. He sat down slowly with his eyes on Cephas as if to carefully scrutinise the teenage boy. The man took his time in everything. He rested his chin on the back of his palm which was leaning against the armchair on which he was seated. The man cleared his throat.

"Do you remember me boy?"

Cephas was shivering, "No…no sir I don't."

The man burst out laughing and then he suddenly stopped and the friendly expression which had formed on his face disappeared, "I am Lucifer. The one that was cast out of the great heavens."

Cephas stared the man as he removed his sun glasses and let Cephas see one of his blotted eyes, "*Ukuona ziso rangu iri*, I call it a merit of a job well done. I actually sent my men to get you so that you could work for me. I want you to come and join us here and stop working for S. S is a son of a b…"

Cephas stopped the man, "You can't insult my leader in my presence."

Again, Lucifer roared with laughter, "Loyal dog! S is dead now. We raided his camp last night. There's no more Bra S," the man hissed as he took a newspaper from under his seat and threw it to Cephas for him to see. The headline was written in deep scarlet, a colour which looked like blood:

Cephas could not believe his eyes and ears. He flinched as the man walked towards him with a knife in his hand.

"I spared you so that you could work for me. I even spared a pal for you," the man let out a whistle and a boy who was almost Cephas' height was escorted by two men. He was made to stand before Cephas who recognised him, "Rusv…" Cephas was tongue-tied when he saw his friend's swollen face. Rusvingo had cuts on his body. Lucifer took hold of Ruvingo's arm and put it before Cephas to show him the cuts. Rusvingo winced in pain, "This is what we call the initiation."

Cephas swallowed as he felt a knot tie in his throat, "So are you in? If you do not want tell us…be quick my boy. We will then take you to the guillotine," the man said in a strong Ndebele accent. One of Lucifer's men pointed in the direction where there was an old and useless tyre covered in dust, "We call it *chuma,* the necklace."

Cephas looked at Rusvingo who was also shivering and then back at Lucifer, "So what do you think?"

Cephas wanted to say something rude but Rusvingo shook his head and so Cephas nodded his head, "I'll join you."

Lucifer walked towards Cephas with a scary look on his face, "Are you serious my boy, because no one plays around with the king of the dungeon"

Cephas nodded his head again and then Lucifer lowered his face and then his and Cephas' gazes locked, "Do you mean it? I want the truth and commitment because a Samurai is identified by those qualities."

Cephas looked at Rusvingo who nodded again and then he agreed. Lucifer bit his lower lip and then clicked his fingers, "Clean him up boys!" he said and his men carried Cephas from the clearance to the bush where they beat him to a pulp. Lucifer said it was necessary for the sharpening of the brain.

When Charity had gone to church she met the pastor who gave her a bible to read after she had told him her story. He prayed with her. Charity repented of her sins and after a brief moment of counselling she went back to the hospital. She bought herself some fries, a burger and two bottles of juice. She brought the bible with her. Her gaze met with Nyasha's as she entered the ward. She greeted him but he ignored her, same applied to Nomagugu who seemed not to be in the mood of taunting Charity. Charity went out of the ward and then returned later on when Nyasha and his mother had left.

She started to cry and then she knelt down and began to pray, "My God, my Master and Saviour Lord Jesus Christ of Nazareth I come before you my God. I know you know that I made a mistake and that it wasn't my intention to hurt Nkosilathi. My family has turned away from me at this critical moment. God please forgive me all my sins and please Heavenly Father grant me this wish…I need you to heal my son for me. I have killed many children in my past but you still showed me your Mercy and Grace by giving Nkosilathi to me. *Siyabonga Nkosi yami. Ndinotenda Jehovah nekundirangarira kwamaita.* Now I beg you to heal him my God. In the name of the Father, the Son and the Holy Ghost. Amen and Amen," Charity said as she rose up on her feet, she felt relieved after saying out the prayer and so she began to eat her food.

After about two days Cephas asked Ruvingo about their leader and colleagues.

"They came without warning *shaa*, I'm so scared because I do not even know what I am going tell BaTsitsi my uncle. You know he is so harsh… this Lucifer guy is just so wicked. He burned up everything including the garage. The stuff was burned to ashes man. Bra S was shot. I do not know if he is still alive and the other boys…they're all dead," Rusvingo said as tears stung his eyes.

"And *isu?* What exactly does he want?"

"To work for him, that's what he told me…one of his men Zenze told him about us…Yes now you tell me did you by any chance tell Zenze about our camping?" Rusvingo asked with realisation in his eyes. Cephas was quiet for some time. He slowly dropped his gaze from his best friend and nodded his head.

"Oh shit! Shit man! You screwed!" Rusvingo cried out as he stood up from where he was sitting beside Cephas.

"I did not know that he was going to tell. I told him to keep it a secret!" Cephas said trying to defend himself.

"Did you go on a mission with any of his guys or Zenze himself?"

Cephas looked away from his friend as the scary thought got into his mind. He could see his mother's face, how she fell down the stairs and shut her eyes forever. Cephas took so long time to answer that Rusvingo began to shake him.

"Hey! I asked you a question, you better tell me the truth because I want to help you man," again Cephas dropped his gaze from Rusvingo.

"You're beginning to scare me *mhani,*" Cephas said with stinging tears in his eyes.

"Answer the question did you by any means agree to go on a mission with them?"

Cephas nodded his head, "I knew it!" Rusvingo clapped his hands as he paced around the room, "You made the worst mistake of your life. Which mission did you go on?"

Cephas stood up and refused to say a word, "No, I can't tell you. Just tell me the reason why you're asking me all these questions"

Rusvingo heaved a sigh and then he looked away from Cephas, "You killed your mother right?"

Cephas felt as if he has been hit by a huge fist just above the temples of his head. Rusvingo turned to look at him, "That's how they are going to manipulate you. I know everything that happened on that day. Poor aunt, she had a beautiful heart. Sorry that she is gone now."

Cephas fell on the ground with his bottom. He was panting and choked on his words, "How…how…how did you know?"

"My name is Rusvingo Cephas. Rusvingo means a wall. Everyone in this hood is inside the wall. Just like the walls of Jericho I am surrounding this hood and whatever which happens I'm bound to find out even before the criminals have committed the crime. You killed that woman, I assure you my friend that your end will b…"

"Shut up! Just shut up! You son of a bitch!" Cephas said with his eyes wide open, he moved closer to Rusvingo and put his forehead against his, "I killed my mother yes but if you play *dilly dally* with me Rusvingo I'll make sure you follow…you go the same path. Trust me," Cephas said poking Rusvingo's chest with his forefinger, "I'm no longer afraid of taking away any dog's life."

Rusvingo was now panting, "I am not afraid of you Cephas."

"I mean it! I will kill you, don't push me because I have always looked upon you as my soul brother," Cephas said as their gazes remained locked, "I don't want to be guilty of murder…again."

167

That evening Charity went back home. She was so tired and felt that she needed some rest. She had sung Nkosilathi all the lullabies she thought she knew and had read some bible verses for him. She even made up some stories and told him. She clapped her hands and told herself, "Bravo mama *vaNkosi* your son is extremely proud of you!"

As she opened the door, everyone turned to look at her. Charity noticed that Tanaka and Kundai had been invited for dinner. Nyasha had invited some guests without letting his wife know about it? She smiled at the visitors and waved at them but they remained stiff in their seats. Only Kundai smiled and waved back and also whispered a "hello". Charity climbed the stairs and then went to their room. She fell on the bed. She realised she could not resist the comfort that her bed was offering. The door was opened as soon as she shut her eyes. She opened them quickly as Nyasha walked inside. She just looked at him and shut them again. Nyasha heaved a sigh, he sounded irritated... with what? Charity tried to guess but she realised that she did not know.

"I cannot tolerate this anymore Charity, so I suggest that you start packing and leave my house!" Nyasha demanded with his hands on his hips.

Charity slowly opened her eyes, "Sorry, are you talking to me?"

Nyasha chuckled in a way that made Charity feel so stupid, "Who else is in this room besides you and I? It seems like your wickedness has taken control of everything!"

Charity looked calm, "Aaron this too is my house. So I am not going to leave."

Nyasha heaved a sigh as he watched his wife shut her eyes again, "Do not make me drag you out of this house Charity!" there was an element of anger in his voice.

Charity slightly opened them as she watched him pace about the room scratching his chin, "Do not make me drag you out! You have just murdered my son and all you're doing right now is spitting shit! Get out of my house!"

Charity realised that Nyasha was in his element she looked startled as she jumped off the bed, "I did not think it was this serious Nyasha. It's not my fault that your son is in hospital!"

"Just pack your bags and go! Right now!" Nyasha shouted as he pointed in the direction of their closet.

Charity was shaking her head, "No. I am not going anywhere. Where am I supposed to go? My mother is gone. I am not sounding helpless but as a married woman I belong here!" Charity said trying to affirm her voice though it was still shaky.

Nyasha stopped shouting and then he looked at her, he began to walk towards her slowly. Charity moved backwards until she reached the wall. She felt trapped as her back touched the wall. Nyasha lowered his face and then he brought it closer to his wife's, "I said pack your bags and leave my house!" Nyasha screamed almost to his lungs.

Again Charity shook her head and whispered, "No."

There was a moment of silence until Charity felt a sharp pain surge in her nose. She lost her balance and fell on the floor. She screamed out loud especially when she saw blood coming from her nose. Nyasha began to pull her clothes from the hangers in the closet and throw them on the floor. He pulled the suitcase from behind the closet door and threw it to Charity who took it and threw it away. She was crying now. He stopped and then he looked at her with his bloodshot eyes. He walked towards her and began to pull her out of the house, the guests rushed upstairs to see what was happening. Tanaka tried to hold his brother but Nyasha pushed him away and he continued to drag his wife down stairs. Nomagugu smiled and then she pursed her lips in triumph. Charity begged Nomagugu to stop Nyasha but Nomagugu ignored her as she ululated and even helped Nyasha with his wife's bags. Kundai held Nomagugu's arm, "Mama please you should stop him, he might hurt her please."

Nomagugu looked at Kundai in a way that made her feel so stupid. Kundai stopped begging and then went to the bathroom upstairs. Tanaka followed her.

"Are you okay baby?"

Kundai who was looking at her face in the mirror turned to look at her fiancé, "No. What Nyasha is doing is just not right don't you see it? He shouldn't be treating *amaiguru* like that. She made a mistake yes…but is this the way in which he should treat her?"

Tanaka heaved a sigh, "Nyasha is not himself babes, he'll calm down soon."

"Really? Are you telling me that no one in this house can stop him? Mama could have done something!"

Tanaka shook his head and then heaved a sigh, Kundai's tears began to flow down her cheeks, "And now? Why are you crying?"

Tanaka drew closer and held his wife's shoulders, "I am so scared. What if this happens to me too…like I get to find out later that I'm barren. This whole family will turn against me and starts to treat me like I'm some piece of trash. You'll pull me round the house like some piece of shi…" Tanaka quickly put his finger on her lips and hushed her in a gentle manner. They were looking into each other's eyes.

"No…I promise you that it's never going to happen to you. *Mina nawe* will have a lot of children around us and we will live happily ever after so you should not worry my baby."

Kundai looked away from Tanaka as he wiped her tears away, he smiled at her, "I do not want to see you cry my lovey. I married you and so whatever you go through or I go through we will get through it together," Kundai smiled.

Tanaka took her hand, "Let us go back."

Kundai forced a smile, "*Ndukutevera,* just give me a sec baby."

Tanaka then wiped a tear from her left eye and smiled, "Don't stress okay?"

Tanaka smiled and left. Charity's cries had subsided. Kundai took out her cell phone and dialled Christopher's number. She told him what had happened to Charity. He asked her how she had got his number but she told him that for now that wasn't important because Charity's life was at stake.

Charity was stranded, Nyasha had forced her to leave everything including the car. She stood beside the road trembling. It was so cold. She looked at her watch it was already past nine. The moon was hidden in the clouds. She decided to cross the road and went to sit on a stone just outside the road. She took out her phone, the battery was low. She heaved a sigh when she saw a car coming her direction. She was frightened, she had read newspapers, magazines and even novels which had stories of women who were mugged and by strangers in fancy cars. The car seemed to pass her by but it stopped. Charity stood up, she was ready for take-off when the owner of the car shouted, "Charity!"

She stopped, turned round and saw that it was her brother and so she ran to him and they hugged. He told her to get into the car as he put her bags in the car for her.

12

Susan opened the door for them when they had arrived at Christopher's house. She hugged Charity and then led her to the guest room. Christopher followed them with the heavy bags in his hands. Susan gave Charity some warm blankets. Christopher was in the lounge waiting for his sister to come and tell him all that had happened. Susan applied some betadine on Charity's wound which was on her nose. She carefully dressed it as Charity winced in pain.

"I'll make you a cup of coffee," Susan said with a smile on her face. Charity looked up at her and thanked her. Charity then went to the lounge where Christopher was waiting for her. She was wearing a robe over the night gown. She went and sat on the couch which was opposite him.

"I thought you were tired," Christopher said to Charity as he watched his wife serve them coffee.

Charity heaved a sigh as she looked up at Susan, "Thank you."

Susan was about to answer her when the baby began to cry, 'You're welcome. I am sorry I can't stay the baby is…"

Charity nodded her head and Susan excused them. There was a long moment of silence. Charity picked up the mug and noticed that her hands were shaky.

"He sent me out. He said it's probably over between us. I don't know but…I have a feeling Nyasha hates me so much now."

Christopher picked up his mug, "Why do you say so sis? Nyasha is angry that's all."

Charity looked away from her brother, "He was so angry…so fierce…so devastated you should have seen his face.

172

I…" hot tears spilt from her eyes as she spoke, "I…I was so scared."

Christopher quickly put his coffee mug back on the table without taking another sip from it, "Did he hit you?"

Charity remained silent as she bit her lower lip, "I said did he hit you? Tell me damn it!"

Susan came running from her bedroom where she was about to sleep, "Charity I asked you a question," Christopher had now stood up from his seat, "Did that bastard lay his filthy hands on you? I said tell me!" Christopher demanded.

Charity was now so frightened that she just nodded her head and then Christopher reached for his car keys which were on the coffee table. Charity held him by the arm, "No Chris you're not going ba…" Christopher pushed her away.

Susan hurried and stood before her husband, "No, no Kirisi. You're not going anywhere. Can't you *weiti* for tomorrow and then you can settle this *dhisiputi?* No I'm going to stand here in front of the door *kusvika* Amen," Susan said as she barred his way with both her legs and arms.

Christopher looked down at her and heaved a sigh. He turned to look at his sister who had stopped crying but her eyes were swollen from crying.

"Please don't go," Charity begged him with her hands joined together as if in prayer. He looked back at his wife.

"You'll deal with this tomorrow. There is always tomorrow my *dharingi.*"

Christopher heaved a sigh and then went to bed because Charity had told them that she wanted to be alone. Susan came back to check up on her as soon as Christopher had started snoring.

"I never knew you had a big heart Sue. Please forgive me… I was always mean to you."

Susan smiled back, "It's okay. Come you should go to bed now. I'm here *furu taimi*. You can tell me everything that happened. I think *kuti* I can be of some help."

Charity smiled and they both stood up and hugged each other but as Charity was about to go to her room Susan stopped her.

"No committing suicide *atete*. You will go to hell and hell is not very *gudhu*, it's always hot. There's no fan, no *suwimingi puru neeya kundishina*. There's fire *oniri* so do not make a mistake of *kiringi* yourself."

Charity laughed as she nodded her head and they both went to bed.

After two days Charity decided to go and see Nkosilathi. She had called the doctor and he had told her that Nkosilathi was still in a coma. She went and sat beside his bed. She began to speak to the boy. Suddenly the door was opened as Nyasha and his mother walked in and chased Charity away. The doctor later told them to leave saying that the patient needed some rest. Charity then went to Nomaqhawe's grave. She brought some fresh flowers with her and put them on top. Charity sat down and began to speak to the grave. She lit up a candle and put it on top of the grave.

"When I saw you I knew you had good intentions. I was angry at first when I heard about your past with my husband Aaron. I later realised that everything had happened for a purpose. Please I'm begging you to save your son. I know you have always wished that good things happen to him. I wasn't looking forward to losing him…to losing him this way. Nkosi means the world to me…and you should forgive me for my negligence," Charity's tears spilled from her eyes as she toyed with the soil on Nomaqhawe's grave, "I need your help Qhawe. I do not believe in talking to the dead…but I just have

174

a feeling that you can hear me. I want Nkosilathi to live!" the candle was suddenly blown out. Charity looked around her, there was no sign of the wind. She had a feeling that she was answered. The bible also fell open on the ground, it was open on the scriptures John chapter 14:1 which reads 'Let not your heart be troubled you believe in God and also believe in Me. ' Charity looked up high in the sky with a smile. She knelt down with her hands raised up high, "Thank you Jesus my Lord, Master and Saviour. It is done!"

Rusvingo and Cephas were commanded to begin their mission that day. They had to go to the border of South Africa and Zimbabwe where they were supposed to rob at least three cars for a start. They had Max, Zenze and Wizzy to guide them. They had guns on them and knives. They were all dressed up. Cephas was so excited except for Rusvingo who did not utter a single word that day.

When Charity arrived at the hospital she saw that there was no one. She crept into her son's ward with the bible in her hands and began to praise God. She then sat down on a chair and began to read him some scriptures. After that she said a little prayer and then began to sing him some lullabies. Nkosilathi began to move his fingers, Charity did not see it until he pressed her palm. She was so overjoyed that she ran to the doctor's office and called him to witness the miracle. When the doctor got in the ward Nkosi had opened his eyes. Charity almost jumped from her shoes with joy for she was very happy. She hugged her son and then she knelt down to thank God.

"I thank you my God for your mercy and grace. I'll always worship you," she said as she smiled at her son.

After another two days Cephas and his friends arrived at the border. They took out their weapons and hid them under some fake uniforms which they were putting on. They pretended to be some workmen who issued permits for the new vehicles. Everything was working out as planned however, until one of them pressed a certain button mistakenly as the cars were taken in the opposite direction of their destination. The police force was alarmed. The police began to chase after the robbers with ammunition in their trucks. The police began to shoot. Cephas and his colleagues jumped in their vehicle and began to drive away in the direction of Zimbabwe. Rusvingo tried to shoot back but he was shot by the neck. He almost fell from the car but Max pulled him back. He then took off his shirt and pressed it against Rusvingo's neck to stop the blood from flowing. The car was driven at a higher speed by Zenze who kept looking back for any sign of the police coming nearer. They managed to escape and arrived in Zimbabwe safely. The vehicle which they had used during their expedition was burnt to ashes. They carried Rusvingo back home and he was finding it hard to breathe. Max put him down and they all surrounded him with their eyes filled with anxiety. Cephas then knelt beside his friend with his hand below his head to support him, "I'm sorry…I did not mean those words brother…I did no…"

Rusvingo looked at Cephas, he forced a smile and blood continued to flow from his mouth, "I'll be…I…I…love you…Ceph…I did not take th…at…serio…usly. I knew…you'd ne…ve. . r kill a…soul bro…broth…er," Rusvingo was finding it difficult to speak. Cephas looked around him.

"Can't anybody do something to save him? Please save my friend…save my brother!" Cephas began to cry out loud with

Rusvingo's head in his hands. He screamed out loud as his friend began to pant like a weary dog and breathed his last. Cephas cried so hard. He had never felt anything like this before. He had lost a real friend...a true friend. Rusvingo's body was carried by the other men they put it in a scrap car and burned it to ashes. Cephas screamed out loud as he watched the hungry flames turn his friend into a black mound of ash.

Nowinnie had just finished washing the clothes and was putting them on the washing line to dry up when Erica approached her.

"I'm feeling dizzy today but I do not know why."

Nowinnie looked at her a little surprised, "Ha! *Sisi hanty* you came back home drunk yesterday."

Erica smiled as she scratched her neck, "Life is so hard my dear...some things that happen to us are so unbearable."

Nowinnie nodded her head and then looked away from her friend, "Max and those goons destroyed my life. They stole everything from me...my pride, happiness, peace of mind, my best friend and my kind heart. I'll never forget what they did to me, and like a tiger I'm going to hunt them down," Nowinnie turned her gaze back to Erica who was smiling, "One by one."

Her tone was so frightening but Erica clapped her hands and then walked towards her, "Now that's the spirit honey! You should kill your prey before it's too late!"

They clapped their hands and hugged each other.

Tashinga felt lonely...fate had always made fun of her. Fate had always taken from her the people, memories and events she treasured the most. She realised she missed Tinashe so much. She reached for the bible beside her bed which Margaret had given to her as a gift. She smiled before opening it. Tashinga then read a scripture by candle light and then she knelt down to pray. She wanted to pray for him…she knew that if she continued praying for him he would always be fine. Her exams were starting tomorrow. She had to pass, that was the only way to make him proud of her.

Charity was sitting beside her son's bed feeding him when Nyasha and Nomagugu walked in. They were so surprised when they saw him awake. Nkosilathi forced a smile as he reached out his hand to touch his father's arm. Nyasha hurried towards his son and hugged him. Charity quickly stood up and went out of the room, she went and waited outside. She would go in after they had left, she told herself quietly. It was warm outside, she looked at the sky and loved the way it blended with the shining sun. She smiled to herself as she folded her arms in admiration of the fluttering butterflies. After about twelve minutes Nyasha came outside. He kept staring at his wife who had not yet noticed him for she was standing with her back facing the exit.

"Thank you," Nyasha said after clearing his throat. Charity gasped she had not expected it.

She looked at him and forced a smile, "Oh… no don't mention. It's God not me."

"But you've always been there for him."

"Yeah, since I'm the one who made the mistake and was negligent, I was bound to take responsibility," Charity said before biting her lower lip. There was a moment of silence until Nyasha decided to break it.

"I'm so sorry…I'm sorry about the way in which I tr…"

Charity quickly cut him, she did not want to hear him say it, "It's not a problem. You were angry that's all. You were upset."

Nyasha looked at his wife "But I really shouldn't have vented my anger on you, you're my wife!"

Charity looked away from his eyes as tears began to sting her eyes, "Like I said it wasn't your fault."

Charity took a glance from her watch, "I have to go."

Nyasha quickly took hold of her arm, "I need you to forgive me and come back home."

Charity pulled her arm from his grip as Nomagugu came out and stood where they were, "I'll think about it," Charity said and then she left.

Nyasha sighed as he looked at Charity leaving, "*Hona*, she is always running away from her crimes. I just wonder what you see in that woman," Nomagugu said as she stood closer to her son but when she tried to hold his arm he stopped her.

"Don't even think about it mama," Nyasha said in a firm voice and left his mother alone. She was watching the direction in which Charity had gone with a narrowed gaze.

"Why does she always win? She's so evil but she always triumphs… no her end is drawing nearer and nearer I'll see to it that I sound her death knell!" Nomagugu said in a low but firm voice and went back inside the hospital.

It was late in the evening when Tashinga was coming from a friend's house. She had just finished writing her O'level exams. A certain young man greeted her, she recognised the voice but did not see the face of the speaker. There was no one on the street, Tashinga felt that the man was up to no good. She increased her pace but the man also increased his as he turned round and began to follow her. Tashinga was almost

179

running when the man held her arm and pulled her from the road. Tashinga tried to scream but the young man slapped her across the face that she lost her balance and fell on the ground. He was removing his pants already when Tashinga looked up at him. Tashinga began to struggle with the man. She bit his arm. She felt her teeth dig deeper into his skin after she had kicked him in between his legs. He let out a loud cry and the man let go off her and Tashinga began to run. She ran as fast as she could. When she reached her home she quickly locked the door and pulled her old closet and laid it against the door. She then noticed that she had blood on her lips, she had no idea how deep her teeth had dug into his skin. She sat on the bed, her heart was beating fast, she closed her eyes and murmured some words of thanks to God for saving her life. She then pulled her blanket to cover herself and fell asleep.

Later that same evening Nyasha called his wife and asked her to come and meet him so that they could have dinner. Charity tried to turn him down but he persisted until she agreed. She put on a simple dinner dress which was turquoise in colour. She wore a pearl necklace which she had bought during their honeymoon in Belgium and then some Corsican fashioned heels. She got there right on time. When she had arrived Nyasha pulled out a chair for her to sit on. She thanked him with a smile and sat down. The waiter came and poured them some wine. It was red sparkling wine. Charity took a sip from her glass as she waited for Nyasha to speak.

"You look great," he said with a smile on his face.

Charity smiled back, "Thank you."

There was a long moment of silence until Nyasha decided to break it again, "Um… I have actually called you for dinner because I want to apologise to you. I was wrong I shouldn't have sent you away. I'm sorry."

Charity was silent she just looked at him and then away.

"I know you're angry with me but I really need you to forgive me. I was wrong and the slap I. . ."

Charity's tears began to flow down her cheeks. She wiped them away with a silky piece of cloth, "There is a secret that I have kept away from you for years. I...I wanted to tell you but I was afraid you'd refuse me...like dump me. I was afraid of being dumped."

The gentleness in Nyasha's eyes increased, "What secret?"

Charity looked up at him but the words could not come out. She imagined how her husband was going to take it. She then decided to look for words to say, "That I...in my family most women are barren *handina kumbobvira ndazvifunga kuti ndingangoitawo* that same problem, I am sorry," she said looking away from him. She lied.

"It's not your fault that you're barren. It's natural and I have come to terms with our predicament so why worry?"

Charity forced a smile as she watched her husband take a sip from his glass, "So *wandiregerera here?*"

Charity nodded her head, "Yes, you're forgiven."

They both stood up and hugged each other, "I love you," Charity whispered in Nyasha's ear.

"I love you more," Nyasha said as he tightened his hug around her.

That night Cephas went over to Max's place. He was holding his wrist. Max opened the door. He was already preparing his dinner.

"And now?"

"Let me in please... I am in pain. I am bleeding!"

Max opened the door a little wider for Cephas to enter, Cephas got in and went to sit in the living room and Max followed him.

"What happened?"

Cephas looked up at him, "I was trying to have a good time with some bitch and she bit my arm. Eish I'm in great pain."

Max roared with laughter that he even fell off the couch laughing.

"That's not funny. The lady kicked my balls!" Cephas said as he wiped the blood off his arm with his t-shirt.

"Well I find it amusing. Why didn't you ask her nicely? Like hey babes want some sugar?"

Max said and then they both roared with laughter, "Who is the girl?"

Cephas rolled his eyes, "I do not know I jus…"

Again Max burst out laughing, "*Haaa ende kuzungaira kwacho kwakanyanya.* I have never met anyone this stupid. You're my first."

There was a moment of silence until Cephas looked up at the roof which now had a lot of spider webs hanging from it, "You're lonely bro right?"

Max looked at Cephas with his blood shot eyes as he lit a twisted paper filled with weed, "Why do you think that?"

"I can feel and see your loneliness. Kindra was a great ki…"

"Don't you dare talk about my sister like a saint!" Max shouted as he removed the blunt from his lips and smoke poured out of his mouth as if it emitted from some chimney, "You came here and fucked her in my absence now you come and tell me shit?"

Cephas swallowed hard, "I'm sorry I did not me…"

"Shut up boy," Max hit against the table which was between them." She was a stupid doll, so innocent and naïve. She never listened to me. I warned her against stray dogs like you and Fatso but what did she do? She turned a deaf ear to sound advice."

Cephas was still looking at Max until Max asked him to leave, "Did you have sex with Kindra?"

Cephas felt an icy cold feeling flow down his spine, "Don't lie to me *tsaga*, because I can beat you up…I'll kill you for just one lie," Max had stood up and was now standing towering over Cephas.

"I…I…I…we…she…"Cephas stammered.

"Get out!" Max said vehemently and Cephas hurried out. He was glad to have gone out without being tortured by Max's huge round fists.

It's been six days since Charity came back to her house. The happiness in the family had increased from the time Nkosilathi had regained consciousness. Susan decided to visit Charity at her house. She came with her baby. Everyone was so glad to see the baby except for Nomagugu.

"Have you come here to make fun of my son's house because there is only one heir? Have you come here to show us that you're always awake in your homes at night and that you're not lazy like my daughter in-law here? Huh? You have come here to showcase your fruits!" Nomagugu began to pace about in the lounge shouting, *"Mwana wangu ingochani! Kubva aroora umwe murume here? Hezvo havana vana!* No wonder people say my son is a homo! Look he doesn't have a child with this woman! My son got married to a man!"

Charity and Susan just looked at each other as they shook their heads.

"How do you stay with her? Because she is more of a sounding *gon'o.*"

Charity smiled, "You're asking me that? I think I have gotten used to all her mockery, scorn and taunts. I just look at her and ignore her. She'll get tired."

"Ah *ndiyo taipi inoneta here iyo.* She's never going to give up."

"Well that's her business not mine. Anyway we are not here to discuss craziness," Charity snapped and they laughed, "So tell me what should I offer you?"

"Water. Very cold water," Susan said as Charity stood up and went to the kitchen.

There was knock at the door when Charity came back to the lounge and gave Susan her glass of water.

"Thank you," Susan said clapping her cupped hands. Charity went and opened the door and saw that it was Kundai. They hugged each other.

"Come on in, what a pleasant surprise," Charity said with a smile as Kundai entered the house. They both went to the lounge where Susan was sitting cradling her baby. Susan and Kundai hugged as they greeted each other.

"Wow I wasn't expecting this…thank you so much," Charity said as Kundai turned to look at Susan.

"Actually this wasn't my plan, it was Sue's. She said you needed some company and to tell the truth I certainly agreed with her…so now here we are," they all roared with laughter.

"Thank you so much ladies, so what do I offer you now? Susan I guess you were waiting for Kundi and maybe that's the reason why you refused lunch?"

Susan laughed, "Yes, *gudhu gesi.*"

Charity smiled and then she went to the kitchen to prepare them some food. The women followed her to the kitchen with Susan tying her baby on her back.

"How is mother?" Kundai asked as she chopped some carrots.

"She is fine, I think you should go and say hi," Charity said opening her pot of relish which was steaming on the stove.

Kundai shook her head and whispered, "She is so scary…she might be in her element. I really don't want to upset her."

Charity smiled, "She likes you so much, just go and say hi because if she sees you down here and gets to know the reason why you did not greet her *inoita nyaya*."

Kundai put down her knife and then removed her apron but as she was getting out of the kitchen she bumped into Nomagugu who frowned her face.

"*Makadii mama?*" Kundai greeted her mother in-law curtesying.

"*Tiripo*. How is my son?"

"He is fine he said I should say hi."

"Oh…so what are you doing here?"

"Excuse me?"

"*Ndati ukudei pano?* So you have come all the way from your house to gossip about me with that spider?" Nomagugu said as she turned to look at Charity who pretended to have not heard it.

"No mama actually the thing is that I had actually visited you. I…I had a dream about you last night…um you were…I thought that maybe if I tell you the dream you might be able to interpret it for me."

Nomagugu burst out laughing, she held the sides of the huge mahogany table in Charity's kitchen for support. Kundai was smiling when Nomagugu suddenly stopped laughing, "Hey *musikana* do I look like an interpreter of dreams here?"

Kundai smiled, "I didn't say that…did I?"

Nomagugu was getting bored by the conversation until Kundai came up with a new idea, "Um mama you were in a jet. Your own jet. And um…it had the name…**Noma's space ship!** You were very popular and I d…"

"Hey… are you here to play games with me *netumanyepo twako?* Can't you see you're wasting my time?" Nomagugu said as she pushed Kundai out of the way. Kundai looked after her mother in-law.

"The woman is so full of herself. Tanaka should have told me he had a beast for a mom," Kundai said and then they all roared with laughter as she imitated Nomagugu.

Chipo was enjoying himself at his new workplace. Florence who was a receptionist for the company was his former school mate in high school. When she heard that he was struggling she suggested that he look for the job at her workplace. She was then asked by the CEO of Ruregerero Holdings to call Chipo and tell him that he goes to the CEO's office with immediate effect. Chipo hurried to his boss' office. He knocked the door and was told to enter. He saw her turning around in her chair with a pen in her mouth. She was so beautiful especially with her spectacles on. Chipo walked towards her and stood behind her desk.

"I heard that you called for me Ma'am," Chipo said with his head bowed down a little.

"Yes, you're Chipo Khumalo right?" the lady said toying with the pen in her hand now.

"Yes that's right."

"You can take a seat," Chipo sat down after saying thank you.

"Well, the company is impressed by your hard work and commitment…a lot of potential is seen in you. My father

Albert Ruregerero was quite impressed. He is actually the owner of this company. He is after excellency and excellency seems to be your priority too as an individual Mr Khumalo. Congratulations!" the woman said as she gave him a handshake, "I would like you to attend the board meeting. It's starting in the next few minutes, that's where you are going to be informed about the rest," the woman said with a smile on her lips.

Chipo swallowed and then answered, "Thank you very much Ma'am. I'll be there on time."

"Good," the woman said in a firmer voice as she watched Chipo leave her office.

After some time Chipo was called to the board room where he got the best news ever. He went out of the board room after the meeting walking like a gentleman but as soon as his bosses were out of sight he began to dance and sway around.

On his way to the office he met Florence, "What did she want?"

Chipo smiled, "I got a promotion. I'm going to Australia to be CEO there! I can't wait Fulo. I have been working for this and guess what baby? I nailed it!"

Florence was silent, "And now? Why are you quiet?"

Florence looked up at him, "So are you going to leave me here? Like leave me behind?"

Chipo looked at her and burst out laughing, "What do you mean?"

"I knew it! That you're some selfish, arrogant and impulsive nerd. You know what? I did not think what I said was that funny," Florence said and left. Chipo looked after her as she banged his door. He heaved a sigh and sat back down in his chair.

That day Tashinga went to the prison to see Tinashe. She told him about the incident where she was almost raped by someone she thought she knew. Tinashe advised her to change where she lived.

"But where exactly do you want me to go? I don't have another place to stay."

Tinashe's tears flowed down his cheeks, "I hate to see you go through all this. You can ask some friends to help you… the ones you go with to the studies."

There was a moment of silence until she thought of someone else, "I have a friend, may be she can help me."

Tinashe nodded his head as he opened the food Tashinga had prepared and began to eat it. Tashinga watched him as he breathlessly attacked the food and finished it all. He belched after drinking the cold water she had also brought him.

"Thanks, I had missed homemade food."

"Anything for you Nashe," she said with a smile on her lips.

That evening Chipo visited Florence at her house, she had refused to open the door for him but after he had insisted that she open for him she then went and opened it. They went and sat in the lounge where there was no one. Florence lived with her sister, Faith who had three children. Faith had been divorced her husband since he had come from China with a new wife. The new wife was a Chinese woman with two children but she had also left them with her husband Mao back in China.

The children were getting ready for bed when Chipo and Florence began to discuss their issue in the lounge.

"You're upset with me…did I do anything wrong?"

Florence who was sitting opposite Chipo stood up and began to pace about the room, "I thought we were together…I thought we were a team."

"So? What went wrong?" Chipo asked sounding a little confused.

Florence laughed with scorn in her voice, "Look who's asking! That promotion is supposed to benefit the two of us my boy. Remember I forged those papers to make it easy for you to get a job. Ruregerero Holdings *haisi* company *yaana museamwa kaiyi*. When I did that for you my reputation, job and life were on the line."

Chipo stood up and walked towards her, "I know… and I haven't forgotten all your sacrifices. What do you want me to do for you in return?"

Florence looked up at him smiling, "I want a better rank in that company and I don't care what branch."

Chipo chuckled, "I know exactly what you deserve. I haven't forgotten how much I owe you," Chipo took a glance from his watch, "Meet me tomorrow at Maguta Delicacies at lunch time, I have to go right now."

Florence's smile widened, "Okay, will be there," Chipo turned to look at her smiling and left.

Florence jumped and shouted a "Yes!" after closing the door. Faith who was with the children came to where her sister was dancing and smiling.

"Uh huh? What's all the *chibilika* mood about?"

"I helped someone out with a project and so he asked me what I want in return and I told him a promotion. So he said we meet at an inn to complete the deal."

Faith burst out laughing, "And you believed him? *Hai mhani* Florence I thought you were intelligent."

Florence was disappointed by what Faith had said but she smiled again, "Yes I am intelligent *sisi* wait until I prove it to you tomorrow," Florence said clicking her fingers and went to bed.

Late in the afternoon the next day Charity was sleeping on the couch in her lounge. She was making some movements which showed that she was having nightmares. There in the dream she saw a woman sitting with her back facing her and that woman was putting on a black gown. Charity approached the woman and patted her shoulder. She saw that the woman was her mother, Margaret.

"Mama? Oh mom I'm so glad you're alive! Ev…"

Margaret cut her daughter's statement as she stood up holding her arms, "I do not have much time with you child. You should tell Nyasha the secret or your marriage will be destroyed."

Charity could not believe her mother's words, "What? Mama you want me to tell Nyasha that I used to sleep around with boys at school an…"

"Just don't say that I didn't warn you…I have to go now," Margaret began to walk away and Charity followed her. Margaret stopped and turned suddenly to look at her daughter, "Do not follow me. You can't come along."

"But mother I want to come al…"

"No, impossible… they don't want you there. I…"

"Mother please my life is unbearable here I want to com…"

Margaret began to run away from Charity who decided to follow her screaming, "Wait! *Amai kani mirai!* Wait for me please mamaa!" Charity then saw that Margaret was out of sight and so she woke up screaming, "Nooo! Don't go…Wait!"

Nomagugu was leaning against the couch looking at Charity as if she was some crazy woman.

Charity woke up, she looked startled and was panting with the left hand on her chest. Nomagugu roared with laughter as she watched.

"*Ehe mthakathi, chii?* Tell me what has the witch seen in her vision that has made her look so baffled?"

Charity looked at Nomagugu and ignored what she said. She decided to go to her room. Nomagugu sat down, took the remote control and switched on the television. She let out a loud and provoking laugh that made Charity turn to look at her and shake her head.

That afternoon Florence and Chipo met at the inn. They sat quietly and did not order any food. Florence looked at him and then away until a smartly dressed chauffeur approached their table. He looked at Florence and asked with a smile, "Are you Miss Florence Ncube?"

Florence nodded her head, "Yes but wh…" she was short of words.

"Follow me please," the chauffeur said extending his hand to her. Florence stood up and turned to look at Chipo who smiled, put his hands in both pockets and followed the two outside.

They went to the parking lot and saw a car which was packed on its own, "A limousine?" Florence asked with one hand covering her mouth.

"Yes, you want a ride?" the chauffeur said as he opened the car door for her.

Florence looked at Chipo who shrugged and looked away, "Yes but with Mr Khumalo."

The chauffeur nodded his head and they both got into the car. No one spoke to another. Chipo then suggested that they drink some wine. Florence told him she wasn't in the mood of drinking anything. No one spoke to another until they reached their destination. The chauffeur opened the car door for them. They stepped out and saw that they had come to Meikles hotel.

Florence gasped as the chauffeur led them in, "No wait. Are you taking us inside? This is one of the best hotels in town and it is very expensive…by the way who are you?"

The chauffeur smiled, "I'm just a servant doing his job Ma'am and as for the one responsible for all this you'll soon find out."

Florence looked and Chipo with a quizzical expression on her face but he shrugged, "Let's go in and find out," they then hurried inside.

A waiter welcomed them and showed them a table to sit on. It had a candle on it and was at the far end of the dining hall. It was a little dimmer that side and had rose petals sprinkled all over. Florence suddenly turned to leave, "I'm sorry but you must have mistaken me for some one els…"

Chipo took hold of her hand and gently led her to the table. They both sat down looking at each other.

"What are you doing? Maybe the chauffeur made a mistake, do you want us to be on the front page of some newspaper?" Florence whispered over the table, "*Handei varidzi vetable vasati vauya*…I don't want to be humiliated, remember important people have their dinners here…*maministers, mapresidents, masenators nema…*"

Chipo held her hand in his, "Calm down I'm sure the person who has done this is on his way…um I have to go to the loo just give me a sec please and don't go anyway, "Chipo said as he stood up and left the table.

Florence who was still holding her purse continued to look around. Chipo took a lot of time whilst in the loo, Florence was getting impatient and then the chauffeur approached her.

"He's here," he said with his hands on his back.

"Oh, that's good, "Florence said nodding her head, "But um…call Mr Khumalo for me please he went to the loo."

The chauffeur smiled and nodded, but before he could leave Chipo called out to Florence, "I'm the one you're looking for," Florence turned and looked at him amazed.

He had changed his clothes, he was wearing a blue tuxedo on top of a white shirt and a pair of black Giorgio Armani trousers. He walked towards Florence with a bouquet of flowers, "For you," he said handing them over to her. Florence took them in disbelief and put them on the table, Chipo helped her to sit down. She sat down slowly with her eyes still on Chipo.

"I have come to give you what you asked for yesterday, you said you wanted a promotion *handiti?*" Chipo asked and Florence slowly nodded her head in disbelief.

"You're going with me to Australia, a place for you has been decided in the company. You'll be the director…it's a new company and so they want real expertise."

Florence covered her mouth with both hands amazed, she stood up and hugged Chipo, "Thank you but how did you…how did you….?"

Chipo decided to continue, "There is more to it," Chipo said putting his hand in his pocket and took out a little red box. He went over to where she had sat and knelt down on one knee, "Will you marry me, Florence Ncube?"

Florence was tongue-tied, tears of joy spilled from her eyes as she stretched her arm and showed her fingers to Chipo, "Yes," she said sobbing and Chipo put the ring on her finger and then there was loud clapping from the other people in the restaurant who had witnessed the good deed.

They both stood up and kissed and then hugged each other, "You're coming with me right?"

Florence looked up at him, "Why not?"

They laughed and embraced once again.

Nyasha had come back from work and Charity was preparing dinner when her phone rang, it was Christopher.

"Chipo is going to Australia, did he tell you?"

"Yes he called. He was so excited that advising him against it would have been futile."

"Ya, you can say that again," there was a brief moment of silence before he continued, "I have called you so that we can make arrangements. Mother's belongings are not yet distributed. We have to do it soon before he leaves."

"Okay, he's getting married too. He told you that right?"

"Yes…he is growing up isn't he?"

"Yes, I'm just so proud of him…at least he is doing the right thing."

"I agree with you sister."

"And the little girl…is she growing up?"

"Yes she is fine, I hope her aunt is doing good together with Nkosi."

"He's fine…the wound on his forehead is also healing."

"Wow that's great news," Christopher and Charity talked until they told each other to pass on greetings to their family members and then they hung up. Nyasha then entered the kitchen and asked his wife who she was talking to on the phone.

"It was Chris…he was telling me about the distribution of mama's clothes and the other stuff. He says it's going to take place next week."

"Oh, that's great," Nyasha came and hugged his wife from behind her shoulders and let his chin lean against it, "I just want you to know that I love you and I trust you."

Charity moved her eyes from side to side she wanted to tell him the secret but the words could not come out. She heaved a sigh as her husband lingered around her.

"Um…baby you know I have to prepare dinner before Nkosi starts complaining."

"So are you saying that I shouldn't have some sweet moments with my wife?"

Charity turned around to look at him and put her arms round his neck, "No…I didn't say that. It's just that I am a mother now and so my attention is divided. You need attention same applies to Nkosi he needs me…more."

Nyasha lowered his head and kissed her forehead, "You're so caring and loving. You know every time I thank God for you," Charity smiled as she kissed his lips.

"Same applies to me."

"Ok then I have to go…you said you want to cook right?"
"Yes…"

"Make sure then it's something yummy," Nyasha said as he tickled his wife who chased him around the kitchen with a cooking stick and frying pan in her hands.

The date which had been set for the distribution of Margaret's belongings arrived. Cephas was not home and so everyone decided to wait for him. It was two hours later when he drove Margaret's car inside the compound with music playing at a very high volume. He came out of the car holding a bottle of very expensive liquor with two women dancing in the car. They were wearing bum shorts and some blouses which left their backs uncovered.

"Ayo wassup my bros and sis?" he said as he got out of the car.

Christopher's face had already turned red with anger, he began to walk slowly towards the boy and gave him a hard slap across the face. The slap landed on Cephas so hard that he lost his balance and fell down holding his cheek. The people were shocked by the slap. There was silence amongst everyone, the girls who were with Cephas stopped dancing but the loud and irritating noise from the playing music kept on playing.

"Can someone stop that trash!" Christopher demanded and one of the women who were with Cepahas bent and then stopped it.

The women were now shaking with fear when they saw Christopher walking towards them, "And you *makamirirei ipapo?* Is the car yours *kuzoitsamira kani?* I want you to leave this place right now. Get out! I am giving you two seconds...out!" the two women removed their high heeled shoes and ran out of the gate. "Dogs!" Christopher cursed under his breath and spat on the ground. He came and stood beside Cephas who was still lying on the ground.

"Aren't you ashamed of yourself, you knew we were coming but you did not do anything at least to cover up your madness."

Cephas groaned as he rose and sat up straight, "Come on Chris everybody knows who Cephas is so why cover up...I am not a hypocrite like everyone here...I show people my true colours."

Christopher heaved a sigh and then he crouched beside his brother and shouted in a loud voice, "We're going to distribute everything our mother owned among ourselves but Cephas is not going to get a single dime!"

Cephas looked up at him astonished, "Yes, you are not going to inherit anything."

"Why if I may ask?" Cephas said with a frown on his face.

Christopher lowered his voice as if to whisper in Cephas' ears, "Because you have been nothing but a burden, a problem and a disgrace to our mother!"

Cephas was dumbfounded, he struggled up for he was drunk, "That is not going to happen Christopher…I'll not let you!"

Charity looked at Cephas in disgust, "Who the hell do you think you are?

"Shut up you crazy bitch!" Cephas said taking another gulp from his bottle, he began to walk towards Charity, "You haven't told him have you? I…I mean the little secret you've been keeping away from him all this while."

Charity looked baffled, "What secret are you talking about, Cephas?"

Cephas roared with laughter, "I said it didn't I? That everyone standing on this ground is a hypocrite, look at how she is pretending not to know what I have just said."

Charity swallowed hard as she looked up at Nyasha who had a confused expression on his face. Cephas walked past Charity to Nyasha and patted Nyasha on the shoulder, "Brother in-law is it? My sister here is a real criminal…she…she…"

"Don't you dare sa…" Charity said pulling away Cephas from her husband but Nyasha stopped her.

"Let him say whatever he wants to say," Nyasha said in a firm voice. Charity left him and folded her arms as she looked aside.

"Do you know the reason why she cannot conceive?"

Nyasha did not respond he just kept staring at Cephas as if he had smeared his entire body with smelly dung.

"She had six abortions during her 'hay days', Charity would sleep around with any boy she chose, wanted and desired. Every guy claimed her to be his. She would go to gigs, bunk her lessons and lectures …and um…she used to love them old…I mean the big guys with round tummies…she almost got AIDS, but it seems miracles happen every time my in-law, " Cephas took a gulp from his bottle, "She decided to get married and settle down. She was rich in a sec," Cephas said clicking his fingers.

Nyasha burst out laughing, "Thanks for telling me Cephas," Nyasha turned to Christopher, "Let's start the event. We're running out of time."

Charity was so relieved at Nyasha's reaction though she had not expected it.

Everyone was relieved by his remark because he had chosen to ignore Ceohas. The distributions were made and everyone got what they deserved but Cephas did not get anything except for his clothes which were thrown outside.

When they reached home Charity was so relieved. She eased herself on the couch in their bed room after she had poured herself a glass of red wine. Nyasha seemed to be out of his element even as he was driving them home. Charity noticed it and got from the couch and walked up to him. She put her hands around his neck, "What is the problem baby? You were not happy since we came back home… is something the matter?"

Nyasha looked down at her, "I just want the truth…we have been married for ten years and still you hid such important information from me?"

Charity removed her hands from his neck and looked away from him, "You believed him? Honey I can't believe this...Cephas is a maniac and you know that!"

"A drunken man tells no lies Charity," Nyasha was getting angry, he threw his jacket which he had just removed on the bed, "I want an answer is it true? Did you have sex with other men before getting married to me?"

Charity began to walk away, "No! I did not!" Charity shouted trying to defend herself, "Cephas is a devil! He is a lunatic, he just wants to create friction between us that's all."

"No, you are lying to me! So is it true then that you lied about you being raped when you were still a teenage girl because when I married you, you were not a virgin!"

Charity turned to look at her husband, "Nyasha!"

"Do not fret Charity! Just answer the damn question!"

Charity leaned against a wall as hot tears spilled from her eyes, "If I tell you the truth, promise me one thing...you won't do anything stupid."

Nyasha turned to look at her, "I'm listening."

"Whatever Cephas has told you...is... is true. I had the abortions and that's the reason why we can't have children. The accident that Nkosi had was a result of the sins that I committed in my past...a woman came into my dreams and told me that I was cursed," Charity began to cry aloud, "I'm sorry Nyasha...I have always wanted to tell you but."

"But what Charity? But what?" Nyasha turned his gaze away from her to the walls and he hit against them with his fist.

Charity who had sat on the floor walked up to her husband and touched his shoulder, "Don't you dare lay your filthy hands on me woman!" tears came out of his eyes, "For all these years that we have been together I have showed you nothing but love and all you pay me back with is betrayal?"

Charity tried to touch him again but he pushed her away, she lost her balance and fell on the bed, "I hate to say this but my mother has always been right about you. How could you? You hid such important things from me? You know what *uri dhimoni chairo...uri dhimoni parimire zvaro*...because how can a normal person who is actually a woman kill six babies?"

Charity got off the bed, "Nyasha I said I am sorry, I was ignorant... *ndangandisitombori* a true believer in Christ... I was still a lost soul by then."

There was a moment of silence until Nyasha shouted, "Get out of my house!"

"And go where? I am your wife I made a mistake I know but *ngiyacela murume wangu* please forgive me. I am not a god I am a human being...and that makes me liable to making mistakes!"

Nyasha was now shivering with tears and mucus pouring from both his eyes and nose respectively, "Count the number of your mistakes Charity, they are a thousand and I'm just so fed up!"

"Nyasha please if I..."

Nyasha took hold of her neck and attempted to strangle her to death, Charity reached for her wine glass and hit it against his head. He let go of her neck and fell on the floor. Charity decided to run away. She quickly got into her car and left.

13

Nomagugu who was picking some grapes heard the noise and ran inside the house. She saw her son lying on the floor blood oozing from his head. She tried to help him up but he was just too heavy for her. She decided to call an ambulance but before she could even dial the number she heard the car tyres screech outside as it took off.

Charity went over to Christopher's house and banged the door with her hand. Christopher went over and opened it and she barged inside, she told him to lock it as soon as she was inside the house.

"*Hezvo sisi,* what's the problem, is something chasing you?"

"No…um…yes…uh," Charity stammered with her hands round her neck and eyes hovering at the door.

Christopher looked at the door and then back at her, "What happened?"

Charity looked distraught, she began to pace around the room turning all the time to look back at the door. Susan just stood and watched. Christopher walked up to his sister and held her arm. He helped her sit down and they both sat down, "What's going on?"

Charity looked up at him, "He wants to kill me…he's so devastated to an extent that he's never going to spare me."

"Who?"

"Nyasha, I told him the whole truth about my past…everything is upside down Chris. I am finished…I'm in real trouble."

Christopher looked away and heaved a sigh, "Everything had begun to flow…now look at me it has fallen apart…" she said as she looked up at her brother helplessly, "I just wish I was never born."

Christopher shook his head, "No it's going to be fine. Both of you need time to calm down. All you need is rest right now," Christopher then beckoned to his wife, "Take her to bed please Susan."

Susan nodded and then she helped Charity up and escorted her to the guest room. Christopher shook his head as he stared after his wife and sister.

Max went over to the graveyard where Kindra was buried. He put some flowers on her grave and began to speak to it.

"I made a lot of mistakes in the past and I want to correct them sis. I am sorry because I wasn't a real brother with love and care for you… I was selfish, stupid and reckless in everything. I just cannot believe that I wasn't there to protect you. You died with me ignorant of your whereabouts… I'm so sorry Kin, I let you down. Dad is gone and I'm so lonely…" Max felt tears sting his eyes and a hot pressure flow from within his nose, "Losing the two of you has made me realise how important family is in one's life. I now realise the pain of being left all alone in the world. I wasn't a good son to Pa nor… was I a good brother to you," he wiped the tears off his face with the back of his hand.

"I really want to change the way I am living my life and I'll be doing this for you and father. Please forgive me my sister…I don't know how I'm going to do it and when but I believe the time will come…" Max put the flowers on the grave, cupped the dust on his sister's grave with his hand and poured it back as he began to cry out loud, shaking uncontrollably.

"Farewell my sister but I'll be back here to tell you how far I've gone…even though it's already too late, " Max said and left.

Nyasha was discharged from the hospital after about two days. He went back home with his mother. The doctor had told Nomagugu that her son was depressed and so he needed attention and that she should make sure that no one said anything to upset him for this would worsen his condition. When he was fast asleep she decided to go downstairs and prepare some food for him. She decided to cook maize meal porridge with some peanut butter. It has always been his favourite since he was a small child. She began to hum a certain church hymn as she did her work. She was so absorbed in her singing that she did not see her son creep from his room and leave the house. A taxi was passing by and so Nyasha stopped it and told the driver to take him to the old chapel. Nyasha still had a bandage on his head. He had taken along with him a jug of petrol from his garage.

The driver dropped him off when they had reached the chapel and took off. Nyasha took out his mobile phone and called Charity to come to the chapel. Christopher had also barred Charity from leaving the house. At first Charity refused but Nyasha insisted that she come and he even made it difficult for her to resist, "You owe me remember?"

Charity just nodded her head and told him that she'd be there in a minute. Charity went over to the lounge where Susan was playing with her little baby and crept out of the house and went to the old chapel. When she got to the chapel she took in a deep breath and walked inside it. Nyasha was standing at the forefront with his back facing the entrance. When Charity arrived he did no turn to look back at her but just started speaking.

"I loved you with my all heart Charity…I never knew you'd lie to me and be a disgrace to my family. My father, Aaron Machingura had two sons only and I am the eldest. He left his legacy to me because he said I am the one who has the brains and am older. I needed a bride who had the same interests as far as maintaining and preserving a legacy is concerned. I thought that you were the right woman but little did I know that I had made the biggest and greatest mistake of my life by marrying you."

Charity looked around the chapel, "This was our wedding venue, so what are we doing here?"

Nyasha grinned as he turned to look at his wife, "I haven't finished telling you my story…the reason why we are here is part of the story…" Nyasha said walking towards Charity.

Charity felt that something was not right and so she turned to leave, "I can't do this… I think I should leave."

Nyasha held her arm with his right hand, "Not so fast my angelic wife…stay with me please. Why are you running away from your man?"

Charity looked at Nyasha deep in his eyes, "I never meant to hurt you, I love you so much…you're my everything and getting divorced would just devastate me."

Nyasha looked at her and then he hit one of the benches with spider webs with his fists, "Then why didn't you tell me about your real past? I wanted children…till now I need babies with Machingura blood to inherit my all. Nkosilathi is not enough!"

Charity looked away she did not know what to tell him, "Forgive me please, " Charity begged as her voice turned into almost a whisper.

"We have failed. This necklace I'm wearing is a sign of fertility and loyalty to my lineage. My father gave it to me but I have realised that it's of no use in my case," Nyasha said after removing the necklace and putting it on a bench next to him, "But there's only one thing that we can do," Nyasha suggested as his eyes signifying a scary sparkle in them, "I failed my fathers and ancestors...*tiri vanhu vakatukwa!*"

"No, don't say that we always have second chances, don't we? You can marry a second wife who's going to give us kids. Children with your blood my husband."

"It's too late for that *nekuti* my mind is already made," Nyasha began to shake his head, "Oh, why did I get involved with this deceitful woman?"

Charity wanted to run away but Nyasha always pulled her back to him and her head would always hit his chest. Nyasha gently took hold of her shoulders as he turned her round to look around the chapel, "We wedded here, but what do the people say about this chapel?"

"They say it's haunted..." Charity answered shivering, "But we do not believe in ghosts Nyasha. We're not other people!"

"But take a look at our marriage, *muchato wedu unengozi* Charity. My problem is I have always listened to you but you have never listened to me."

Charity moved to free herself from his grip but he tightened it, "No...you cannot leave me. I want you to see me sanctify myself!"

Back at home Nomagugu was looking for her son, she first thought that he had gone into the bathroom but after about ten minutes she realised he was nowhere to be found. She began to walk around looking for him. She then asked the gardener who said he saw him go out through the gate holding something in his hands.

Susan's baby began to cry she called Charity because she wanted to leave her with the baby and make the baby some porridge. She looked everywhere and saw that Charity was nowhere to be found. She even went to her room and saw that she was not there. Susan then opened the cupboard in Charity's room in search for some hospital documents which stated that Charity was pregnant and apologised for the mistake of having been mistaken for a certain patient. Susan then realised that Charity had gone to meet with Nyasha, she then called her husband who was at work.

"Kirisi it is me *yesi*…I can't see *tete* anywhere. I think she is *misingi.*"

"Have you tried calling her?"

"Yes but she is not *pikingi opu* my calls."

"Okay, um don't stress baby, she's an adult anyway she can look after herself," Christopher said and they both hung up but Susan felt that Charity was up to something dangerous.

Charity nodded her head and Nyasha left her, she fell on the wooden floor and then she watched her husband go to the podium. He took a lighter from his pocket.

"I have poured petrol in this chapel and outside, I want to die with you," Nyasha said holding the lighter in his hand, "Let's burn together my love."

Charity stood up slowly from where she was sitting, she kept staring at Nyasha, "No! Don't do it! The doctors said there is still hope for me to get pregnant again."

"You find pleasure in lying to me right?"

207

"No…I'm telling you the truth," she opened her purse and took out a piece of paper, "Here is the proof. I wanted it to be a great surprise for you."

Nyasha walked slowly towards his wife and then he took the paper from Charity's outstretched hand. He began to read through it. It was true, he began to smile but the smile suddenly disappeared from his lips, "Some bribed doctor is capable of forging so…"

"No that report is a genuine report Nyasha," she took out the second paper and gave him. This time he looked at his wife in disbelief. Charity was two months pregnant. He hugged her. He was so happy that he decided to name his child, "She is going to be a girl and so we will call her Hauziveremangwana," and again with the lighter still in his hands he embraced his wife and mistakenly lit the pregnant test papers. The burned papers' ambers fell to the floor and sparked a fire which spread out in the entire hall. The whole chapel was lit in no time. They panicked and so they dashed for the exit but Nyasha suddenly remembered, that he had forgotten his lucky charm which was a necklace his father had left him when he was still a child and as he turned back to fetch it a beam holding the church's roof fell down and so it closed the way out for him. He struggled to get out. Charity screamed out loud, she wanted to save her husband. As Nyasha tried to cross the barrier another beam with fire fell and hit him on the head. He let out a loud cry for he was burning. Charity decided to go back and save him but her foot got stuck in the old wooden floor on which a crack had formed due to the pressure of the beams. Nyasha tried to save his wife but the two actually died trying to save each other. Then the fire brigade arrived a little later, the whole church had burned down including the beautiful couple and their unborn child, Hauziveremangwana which means that one does not know about tomorrow. They only managed to find their charred remains - teeth, eyes and bones but everything else had been burned to ASHES.

The funeral took place at their beautiful mansion in Borrowdale Brook. Their remains were the ones which were buried at the city's cemetery, Charity's were buried beside a river since she died a pregnant woman. Some said they died a peaceful death for they were husband and wife already and some say it was an unfair death since Charity was pregnant at last. People said a lot about their death...

Tanaka and Kundai adopted Nkosilathi and they agreed on treating him like their own son.

The South African and Zimbabwean police joined forces in order to track down the robbers who had tried to steal the cars on the border the previous month. Lucifer and his men were taken by surprise, they had not expected it at all. Cephas was not around because he had been sent on an "errand" by his boss. Another mission that he had gone to complete was the collection of fake passports for Lucifer felt that something really bad was going to happen to him and his men. It was twelve midnight when the South African helicopter landed in Zimbabwe just near Lucifer's camp. These police officers were armed. The helicopter had landed a little further away from the spot. The Zimbabwean police officers had already invaded the territory. Lucifer was sitting in his "dungeon" when he felt something cold touch his neck. He stood up in a jerk but a strong hand took hold of his shoulder and forced him back in his seat. He looked around him and saw that he was surrounded by armed policemen. A certain man with numerous barges on his uniform reluctantly walked towards Lucifer, he took out his police ID and showed it to him.

"I'm…"

"Mufandayedza," Lucifer injected before the man had said out anything, "I know you very well."

The gentleman heaved a sigh as he looked at Lucifer from the corner of his eye, "I wasn't going to introduce myself anyway," the man returned his ID card to his pocket. He looked at the other gentleman with the same merits on his uniform but the uniforms were different.

"Wow Mr. Intelligence I bet you know him too," Mufandayedza said pointing to his fellow police officer wearing a different uniform from his own.

Lucifer turned his gaze away from the D. P. O as he shrugged his shoulders, "Why do you think that?"

"Anyway we aren't here to waste any of our time, he is Mr Senzo Moroka a South African D. P. O, " one of the police men pointing a gun to Lucifer began to put chain on his wrists, "You're under arrest for car theft and …"

"Whoa wait a min…" Lucifer tried to cut the D. P. O but he continued speaking.

"… for whatever you say right now can and will be used against you in the court of law."

Lucifer and all his men were arrested except for Max and Cephas who were not around. Max was already approaching their camp when he saw it surrounded by some police men. He decided to run back home. Cephas had already accomplished his mission when he saw the news on TV in a bank as he was withdrawing some money Lucifer had sent him to get. He had been sent to withdraw 10 million US dollars. The news reporter was congratulating both the police forces for the job well done for they had caught the culprits unaware. It was also reported on the news that two of the culprits were missing and then their photos were displayed on the screen for everyone to see.

Fortunately, Cephas had withdrawn the money when the news was reported, he quietly left the bank with no one noticing that he was one of the culprits. However he bumped into an old lady as he was heading for the exit and this attracted people's attention. One of the people in the bank recognised him but he left in such a rush that no one managed to catch him.

Chipo had already paid lobola to Florence's people and everyone was so excited about them leaving for Australia the next day. The day arrived and they left. Florence was so happy that she felt she could not thank Chipo enough. After a week Muza followed his friend to Australia and decided to go and stay in a hotel for some time. Muza was so friendly and so Florence was fond of him.

One day when Chipo had left for work he called back home and told Florence to look for a certain file. He told her that it was urgent and so she had to find it. Florence looked for it everywhere but she did not find it. She then took a stool and searched the shelves which were too high for her in the closet. A certain envelope then fell on the floor. It had the word **CONFIDENTIAL**. The envelope was so long and seemed to be carrying a lot of papers in it. She tried to put it back on its place but she later decided to open it and see what was inside.

Dear Mr C. Khumalo

We have sent you this letter to kindly inform you about your personality results subsequent to the personality test you had with us the previous year. Un/fortunately you have homosexual personality disorder. It is not that complicated for it can be easily addressed. We have also noted that your fiancé Muza has the same personality disorder. However since you too are already married we suggest th…"

Florence was taken by surprise. She quickly looked back at the piece of paper and decided to read it again,

The solution we can give you for the time being is that you should try getting married to a female…

She threw the letter on the bed and then took another paper from the envelope. In that paper was a photo with both Chipo and Muza naked in bed with each other. At the back of the photo were the words **honeymoon…best day of our lives… M & C**

Florence felt her legs becoming numb, she sat on the bed with a plumb. What had she gotten herself into? She was going to regret this all her life. She unfolded the paper which had the photo, it was a script with the information of a South African reverend who had wedded Chipo and Muza. The envelope had two rings in it. Both had golden and silver rims but one of them had a diamond on its back. Florence's tears began to flow down her cheeks. She then heard the living room door open. She quickly stood up from the bed, returned the envelope to its place and then opened the lower drawer of the closet and took out the file. Chipo then walked in. She smiled as she handed him the file.

"You took a very long time to…"

Florence quickly nodded her head and appeared to be uneasy.

"Are you okay?" Chipo asked as he put his hand against her forehead as if to check her temperature.

Florence looked at him quickly and shrugged, "I'm fine. Why? What is it?"

"You're behaving like you've just seen a ghost."

"Um…really? No…I'm good anyway," Florence said getting her purse from their dressing table, "I am running late for work. I'll see you there. Goodbye," Florence said and left in a rush. Chipo stared after her but as he was about to leave their bedroom he saw a white paper on the floor where

Florence was standing. He picked it up and saw that it was his engagement certificate with Muza. He heaved a sigh and decided to follow Florence to work.

When he reached their workplace Florence was nowhere to be seen. He decided to ask a security guard at the gate and he too said he had seen Florence enter only. Chipo decided to ask the cook and they said that they saw her run towards the pool. Chipo almost panicked, he then went to the pool but when he reached there he saw Florence standing a little further away from it staring blankly in the space. Chipo cleared his throat but Florence did not move an inch, she didn't even turn her head to look at him.

"You went through my things," Chipo said waving the file in the air. Florence slowly turned to look at him.

"Why didn't you tell me that you were gay?"

"What?" Chipo pretended not to have heard what she had said.

"*Wazvinzwa*, I can't believe I'm some guinea pig in our marriage…you married me only to see if you'd cope with a woman in your life instead of a man. This is pure betrayal. I can't believe it…I did not know you were this wicked Chipo," Florence said almost in tears.

"It's nothing…I mean my relationship with Muza is just a fling. We're eve…"

"Stop! Do not patronise me! Are you saying that I am too dull to understand all that I have seen and read?"

"You just did not have the right to go over my personal things! Look at you… you are losing control of your emoti…"

Florence burst out laughing but this laugh was of scorn, "Losing control? A right to go over your things? Chipo we're married for goodness sake; no secret is to be found hidden by any one of us from each other…we made a vow on our wedding day that no secret was to be hidden by either of us from another!" Florence almost said in a scream, "I made a mistake…by trusting you, helping you and above all…loving you."

Chipo looked at her in disbelief, "What are you saying Fulo?"

"It's over between us and by the way don't call me that. It sucks!" Florence said and left.

She went back to their new home. She met Muza at the door and passed him.

"Hey Flora, how are you? Have you seen Ch…"

"You mean to say your fiancé? He's at work, excuse me," Florence said as she pushed him out of the way.

She got inside their bedroom and began to pack her clothes. She stuffed them in the bag without folding them. Chipo came running with Muza lagging behind. Chipo was panting.

"What are you doing babes?"

"What does it look like I'm doing? I am leaving you of course."

"No, you cannot do this to me…" Chipo said holding his head with both hands.

"Why? *Kuti ndiwe wakaita sei?* So you think that what you did to me was right huh?"

"No I did not sa…"

"Now you listen to me. You've caused me great pain and I know exactly how to pay you back…I want to make you famous…best gay couple trick innocent girl into marriage. Now how is that?"

Muza was getting annoyed by what Florence was saying, "Will you shut up you slut! You were the one following my man… you even got upset when you discovered that he had got a promotion and was transferred to Australia. You're the one who is not supposed to be here, now out. *Hamba!*" Muza said walking towards Florence who was taken by surprise by his attitude.

Florence burst out laughing, "You really are not ashamed," Florence said shaking her head with pity.

"*Haikona* you're the shameless Jezebel because, you're just so desperate to the extent that you follow a gay and married man for riches and reputation. You are nothing but a smelly and torn rug left for the dogs to lick," Muza said as he spat on the floor.

"Hey ladies!" Chipo shouted.

Florence who was enraged picked up the stool on which she once stood and hit Muza with it on the head. He fell on the floor. Her anger had gone beyond limits for she continued to hit him with it until he could no longer breathe. Chipo looked on with his mouth agape. Blood now covered Muza's head and face as some even stained the green shirt that he was putting on. Florence was panting. She quickly let go of the stool and began shaking Muza's body. This time Chipo had already left for the police station which was a stone's throw from their new home. When he arrived with the police Florence was nowhere to be found and the house was already burning down.

"She turned the gas on!" one of the police officers said as he reached for his phone to call the fire brigade. The other police officers left as they began to try and follow her after finding out that she wasn't in the house.

Two days later Florence was caught at a railway station in New Zealand heading to a place she herself did not know. She was desperate…she had killed a man for the first time but she did not want to go to jail, she wanted to go home. They arrested her and she was sentenced twenty-five years imprisonment. She was never going back home, she thought as tiny beads of tears rolled down her cheeks.

Chipo was fired and was told to go back to Zimbabwe the following day for everything had been arranged for him by Ruregerero Holdings...passport, flying ticket and other necessities needed when travelling. He did not board a flight back to Zimbabwe but rather he took a short cut for everything about his life was over. He had lost everything...the good job, wife, friend, ambition... he was left homeless when his house was burned down...he now stayed in a hotel room and how was he going to pay for the expenses? He had no idea.

He committed suicide. He tied himself to a shower head...the gardener saw him kill himself through the open bathroom window. He tried to open the door to save Chipo but the door was locked from the inside. He then hurried to the reception in search of help. They were late for they found him hanging on his shower...lifeless.

A year passed and Max and Cephas had still not been caught. It seemed like the police had forgotten all about them. Lucifer escaped from prison and was on the run. Cephas was now in England. He worked for a dry cleaning company in London. The owner who had gone to Paris for a vacation left the dry cleaning company in the hands of Cephas for he thought he could trust him.

Max decided to get married to his girlfriend Martha. The wedding had made people believe that he had changed for the better. Unfortunately fate had surprises in store for him since he had decided to forget his past. His past however continued to follow him. This all happened during the time whereby everyone was so attentive. Tashinga had decided to attend

Max's wedding for one sole reason, she wanted to get her revenge, she wanted to ruin him just in the same way he had ruined her. She had a gun in her purse and this she had stolen from her friend's brother who was a warden at Hwahwa maximum prison. She was about to stand up as Max was kissing his bride when a certain lady stood up before her. She called out Max's name…he was caught by surprise. She too had a gun in her hands…she was trembling maybe due to both fear and anger, "You thought you'd get away with this Max? You…bloody voyeur! They raped us…you raped my friend…those bulldogs did it and they killed her! Max you murdered my best friend and you think I am ju…" the lady was shaking with rage as she said this, she wanted to say a lot but anger, hatred and the desire to revenge could not let her and so she choked on some of the words.

When the people saw this they all poured out from the chapel and ran away including the reverend.

"Don't shoot please," Max said almost getting on his knees.

"Shut up! You do not tell me what to do, it's my turn now… "

Erica then stood up, "I directed her to you because what you did to her my son was very very wrong," Erica said this in a gentle voice.

"But why aunt I am like a son to you…I mean I have always been."

"Yes. You have always been my son… I am your biological mother. Years back your father who is also my brother raped me and I became pregnant for him with you. He tortured me and like a demon he continued to torment me Max. He did all kind of bad things to me and I adhered to every ruthless demand he made without question," Erica swallowed hard as she walked towards her son.

"Marilyn is and has never been your biological mother. She died but yes you can trust me on this one…I never had a hand in her death. That is because naturally she was a reckless woman. I knew she'd bring end upon herself."

Max heaved a sigh as he looked at Nowinnie who was still pointing a gun at him, "And dad? I know you're not that stupid to have tried to kill him," Max said shaking with fear.

Erica laughed an evil laugh, "They do not call me Erica for nothing. My name means eternal ruler and I'll forever be in command of everything that belongs to me. I killed him. He got kidnapped on his way to Zambia. He was put in an old stolen car," Erica stopped and turned her gaze back to her son, "And in it he was burnt alive…I meant to say he was burnt to ashes."

Max gasped…that was so inhumane he thought to himself. He fell down on the floor with both hands on his knees and without notice Nowinnie let go of the trigger and shot him. Erica screamed as she watched her son fall to the ground. She hurled insults at Nowinnie who remained calm.

"That wasn't part of the agreement…you shouldn't have killed my boy!" Erica screamed out loud as she rushed at her son who was lying on the floor fighting for his life.

"I rest my case!" Nowinnie said as she shot herself in the head and fell down, lifeless. Tashinga who witnessed this tragic event crept out of the chapel and as soon as she left the police arrived and Erica was arrested. She was sentenced to twenty years' imprisonment. She did not blame herself for anything rather she congratulated herself for a job well done!

14

Six years passed. Tashinga was now planning to go back to her mother country Zimbabwe. She had been granted a scholarship to England to complete her studies in the degree of social work. She missed Tinashe. She had promised him that she'd come back and set him free. She turned to look at the calendars on her desk in her office. Years have passed, she thought as she took a sip of coffee from her mug. A lot had also happened during the course of the years. She picked up a photo in a picture frame. It was Dean, the man she was in love with. He was a gentle man, no man on this planet could ever replace him in her heart. She put the photo a little bit closer to her lips as if to kiss it when her door suddenly opened. The photo fell down and as she bent down to pick it up the person who had got into her office gasped. Two ladies walked in to her office with packages in their hands. These were her friends from the university, Jessica Jude and Rudy Mope. Jessica had blonde hair and Rudy's was chestnut red.

"Tashi, don't tell me that you are on about the pic again, it's just a piece of paper for goodness sake," Jessica said picking up Dean's photo.

Jessica was a detective already and a Rudy lawyer. Jessica and Rudy were so fond of Tashinga and chose her to be their roommate while they were still in college. They had the same interests…in fact they found out that they shared a lot in common.

"I know but to me the photo is different from the other photos," Tashinga said dreamily as she sat on a chair behind her desk.

"Mmmm, I hope he feels the same for you, " Jessica said sitting down on one of the chairs opposite Tashinga's, "Anyway I have come to tell you that we're leaving on Tuesday next week so you should be ready."

Tashinga smiled, "Wow, I can't wait. I miss home, I miss my friend…I miss everything."

Jessica then unpacked a little bag in her hands, it had chocolate muffins and some orange cupcakes. She stood up and switched on the water heater, "Ugggh it's cold outside. I hate the snow," Jessica said rubbing her hands together.

Tashinga laughed, "You'll be leaving Britain in four days time so why the grumpy attitude?"

"I hope Africa is not this cold," Rudy said as she sat on the other chair which was adjacent to Jessica's chair.

"Have you ever read anything about the savannah? It's good out there, the warmth, the sunrise and sunset are the most beautiful and dazzling moments of my life. That's what's making my heart ache for home!" Tashinga said almost shouting.

Jessica and Rudy looked at her admiringly and Dean walked in. He had a bouquet of beautiful roses in his hands.

"Hello ladies, I hope I'm not interrupting anything?"

"No. We were leaving… we needed some air," Jessica said standing up.

"No guys, you stay, you were complaining about the cold and you wanted to have your cupcakes and choco muffins. Your tea is even ready," Tashinga said as she removed her coat from the hook which was behind the door, "Dean and I will go out."

Jessica smiled with an expression that told Tashinga that, 'I was hoping you would say that!!"

"Ok Tashi, thanks. And Dean imagine me as her brother…take very good care of my sister!" Rudy said in a deep voice and they all laughed as Dean made a little bow, nodding his head. Tashinga then left with Dean following behind her.

"You think he loves her?" Jessica said as soon as Tashinga and Dean had left.

"No…not that again. You've been on about this for a very long time Jess. If he doesn't so what, who cares?" Rudy said pouring some coffee in her mug.

"What? I don't think that is a character quality of a true friend," Jessica said shaking her head.

"Really? Look, it's her life why should I worry about her whilst I have my own problems to solve. I want to enjoy this hot cup of coffee, so may I have a moment of silence," Rudy said as she chewed her muffin and took a sip from her mug with her eyes completely shut. Jessica looked on. She later stood up and poured herself some.

They went on to the food outlet and ordered their favourites. Tashinga and Dean began to talk over their lunch.

"Do you think it right to have dinner with me again today?"

Tashinga laughed, "It's okay but do you really have to ask?"

"Yes, you're not just a girlfriend, you're a queen to me. Queen of my heart, " Dean said taking a sip from his wine glass with his eyes carefully watching her, Tashinga then extended her hand to hold his hand but he flinched as if in pain.

"Are you okay?"

"Yes…I… it's a little scratch…I was helping the plumber fix one of the staff toilets at the dry cleaners and…and… so the toilet seat mistakenly fell on me from where I had put it… but I'm fine, " Dean said quickly forcing a smile.

Tashinga also forced a smile but she wasn't convinced by what Dean had said.

"So tell me Tashi, do you want us to go and watch the Ballet Dance Competition?"

"Yes, that'll be awesome," Tashinga said brightening up. They ate their food and left the food outlet. They walked the streets arm in arm. They joked, laughed, embraced and kissed. They went over to a certain park and sat on one of the benches.

"There's something strange about you Dean"

Dean looked at Tashinga, a little startled, he removed his hand from her back and then held her hands in his as if to warm them, "What is it my love?"

"Your clothes…I mean you're always wearing long sleeved shirts…um it's unlike most men," Tashinga said looking deep down in his eyes. Dean burst out laughing as he tightened his grip on his girlfriend's hands but the grip was gentle.

"I am not most men. I thought it was every woman's dream to have a unique man in her life… actually I have allergies from the cold weather. So to avoid such the doctors said I should wear warm clothes," Dean swallowed hard as he turned his gaze away from Tashinga's which was earnest, demanding and defied all discretion.

"Wow, that's great then."

"You want some ice cream?" Dean said as the ice cream man passed by them. Tashinga nodded her head with a smile on her face. They had some ice cream and after that she went back home. On their way home, Dean suddenly stopped holding Tashinga's hand in his.

"On the day I declared my love to you, you requested that we do something."

Tashinga turned to look at him, he had spoken at last for all the way back home he was silent, "Yes…what?"

"You said we have to set boundaries…I liked that. You showed me your uniqueness."

Tashinga smiled as he kissed her on the lips, "I love you so much Tashinga. And I appreciate the fact that you feel the same for me."

"Yes…you mean more to me. You know, I never thought I'd meet a guy who would love me unconditionally like you Dean Hopkins…thank you, " Tashinga said smiling and then she left him standing on the road watching her. She smiled back at him as he waved watching her shut the door.

Tuesday arrived and then the three Jessica, Tashinga and Rudy boarded a flight to Zimbabwe. They had found a place to stay in Mount Pleasant Heights, a low density suburb. They had purchased it whilst in England. As they got there they suddenly fell in love with it for it was so beautiful. They decided to paint the walls a different colour for they disliked the pink paint. They painted all their walls white, brown and cream. Jessica preferred brown for she claimed that it matched their African environment.

"I don't know but brown is the only colour that makes me feel and see Africa as a beautiful continent."

Tashinga shrugged, "Wow that's good, I always thought that colours operated as stimuli to me only but now you've showed me something. And in England which one was the stimuli?"

"Every colour made me feel comfortable in England, maybe because it's my home," Jessica smiled as they finished painting the last wall in their lounge cream.

"I'll bake the muffins," Tashinga said straightening up from her crouching position

"When did Dean say he was coming?" Rudy asked as she chewed a gum.

"Next week but he suggested that soon after paying the lobola we'll return to London."

"Why? But this is your home Tashi," Jessica said as she followed Tashinga to the kitchen.

"I do not know but I think he's right because Zim is filled with bad memories."

"No… why do I have a feeling that this man is controlling you?"

Tashinga quickly turned to look at Jessica, "What?"

"Yes because whatever he says goes."

"No… I think you're becoming jealous Jess. You're my friend and that same part you occupy in my heart will always exist…no one can ever take it away from you, okay?"

Rudy nodded her head, "That's right. I'll be in my room," Rudy said and went to her room.

"I'm not being jealous…I…all I want…okay you got me! I feel Dean is pushing me away from you. Look every time we're together he arrives suddenly… he's becoming more of an intruder than a proper boyfriend…and I wonder why he is always in long sleeved shirts?" Jessica snapped.

Tashinga's smile disappeared from her lips, "He says that he has allergies and so the doctors suggested he wears 'warm clothes'", Tashinga said as she poured some flour in a bowl, "I found it hard to believe… when he said it I felt that he was actually hiding something from me, " Tashinga said as she shrugged.

Jessica who remained silent with a thoughtful expression on her face mumbled that there was something wrong with Dean.

"What?" Tashinga asked as she added some ingredients to the flour and began mixing it up.

"Nothing, I'll make us lemonade juice," Jessica said wearing her sandals, "I'm going to the nearby supermarket to buy the lemons."

Jessica said and left Tashinga mixing the flour humming a song.

Christopher decided to go to the graveyard and put flowers on his sister and brother in-law's graves. He felt tears stinging his eyes as he knelt beside Charity's grave.

"I didn't expect to lose you that way sister. You've always been there for me… and whenever I remember the times we used to be together when we were still kids, the pain I feel is just unbearable. You used to remind me of mama… and now that you're gone who is ever going to heal that pain of losing *amai?* No one *sisi* can ever replace you…" Christopher sniffed as he wiped away the beady tears rolling down his cheeks, "I am left alone in this world… I have lost all my family members… maybe I was destined to be lonely… you never know… Chipo killed himself… who knew that our brother *yangaitori ngochani zvayo*…" Christopher laughed and then continued, "I still remember your words on the phone you mentioned how proud you were of him… you did not know that he was deceiving us all this while. I miss you so much. I have brought you these flowers *sisi* may your soul rest in eternal peace… I love you… so much," Christopher said as he put the flowers on his sister's grave and remained crouching for some time and then he left.

Tashinga was already preparing to go out for dinner with Jessica and Rudy when her mobile phone rang. She answered it hurriedly for the taxi driver was sounding his hoot for her under Rudy's orders.

"Hi babes," Tashinga said with a smile on her face. She continued talking to Dean until she hung up. She pulled a face as she walked to the car.

"What was that for?" Tashinga asked as she got inside the cab.

"You always did that to us when we were still staying in England. It's so annoying. Right?" Jessica asked Tashinga teasingly.

"You know what? There's always tomorrow, I'm definitely going to teach some ladies a lesson," Tashinga said triumphantly and they all roared with laughter.

"Oh before I forget, Dean called and he told me to get ready becauusse," Tashinga said dragging the word, "He's coming back tomorrow!" Tashinga exclaimed and they all screamed out loud excited.

"Wow that's great, hope he lands safely," Jessica said as they got off the cab, "I do not want him messing up... I mean I don't want anything bad to happen to him because if anything happens you'll be heartbroken and that might spoil our moments in Zim... altogether."

Tashinga was quiet for some time until she spoke out as they sat down on an unoccupied table just outside the restaurant when Rudy had stood up to visit the toilet, "Do you think he's the right guy for me?"

Jessica was a little puzzled by the question, "Um...what do you mean...why are you asking this question now?"

Tashinga heaved a sigh, "I don't know...this may sound crazy but I am scared of Dean."

Jessica felt as if she was being hit by a loud and heavy blow. She swallowed hard and she felt a knot tie in her throat she wanted to say something but she failed, "Yes and I think you were right when you said that he was pushing me around... I feel it and I know it. I feel that there is something familiar about his man."

"What?" Jessica said after gasping for air.

"I think I share a past with him... I mean when I tried to touch his hand he flinched as if in pain... I do not know but... he seemed not to... me touching that part of his hand," Tasinga said thoughtfully.

The waiter approached them as they were getting deeper into the discussion, "Good evening ladies?"

"Hello, um just give us some wine for the mean time. Red wine... we're waiting for a friend... she has gone to the loo," Jessica said with her gaze still on Tashinga's face. The waiter nodded and left. He came back with the red wine on a platter and then poured it in the two ladies' glasses. Jessica nodded briefly at him after he had poured the wine and then he left.

"What exactly do you mean Tashi?"

Tashinga felt a cold shiver flow down her spine, "Do you still remember the guy I told you about who tried to rape me that time when I was just nineteen?"

"Yes," Jessica said nodding her head.

"I think the man is Dean!" Tashinga said not believing what she had said, "I know...it's him."

"B...but...but what makes you think that?"

"I bit the man on the wrist... the wound is supposed to be deep because I bit him on that with my entire strength. He bled heavily on that wrist... the scar has teeth marks on it. I saw it six days after I had met him, I think he knows that I'm the girl he tried to rape," Tashinga said almost getting hysterical and the two friends shuddered with fear.

"You're right, maybe that's why he is all dressed up in long sleeved shirts all the time!" Jessica said in an almost loud voice banging the table with her fist so hard that the cutlery made a noise, and the people in the restaurant turned to look at them. The two women looked away so as to avoid people's stares.

Tashinga was now shaking all over, "I think it's time I go and see my old friend tomorrow. I had said I'd go and see him next week but I guess I have to do it soon!"

"But how is he going to help you? Prisoners are always helpless whenever they go out of prison," Jessica said taking a sip from her wine glass.

"I have a job, I won't be helpless and I promised him that as soon as I finish studying and find some where suitable to stay I'll bail him out," Tashinga said in a firm voice. Jessica nodded.

After some time Jessica touched Tashinga's hand which was on the table, the weather was now a little bit cold, "You're shaking?"

Tashinga nodded her head in agreement, "Must be the cold."

"You're lying… you're scared of what Dean is going to do to you. Don't be scared. We're a team. We can team up and find out what his real motives are."

"But don't you think I'm becoming a little irrational… I mean by thinking that he is the man who tried to rape me."

"What more proof do you want? You saw the scar with marks of some human teeth on them…those teeth might be yours!"

"I'm scared and I think we should go home right now… I need to be somewhere quiet and peaceful," Tashinga said looking around frightened. Rudy came back a little later looking uneasy. Jessica and Tashinga stared at her as she struggled to sit down.

"What?" Jessica asked as soon as Rudy had sat down.

"My worst moments! I am having my period… I forgot to count the dates now I have messed this beautiful gown," she said wringing the hem of the long dress in her hands. So I want to go home right now!" she tried to whisper but some people sitting on a table beside theirs turned to look at her and her friends as soon as she finished her statement.

"Okay," Jessica said standing up but she suddenly took hold of Tashinga's hand, "She too wants to go back home… she's shaking. . . must be the cold."

Tashinga nodded her head and they paid for their wine and left. But as soon as they reached home Rudy hurried to her bedroom and then Jessica took hold of Tashinga's hand, "I want you to give me a chance to investigate what Hopkins' real motives are."

Tashinga looked at her friend in disbelief and silently nodded her head.

The next day Tashinga travelled all the way to the city of Gweru to see Tinashe. He had grown pale due to the poor conditions in maximum prisons she thought. She sat in a chair opposite him. He was so quiet and he seemed to be more reserved than ever before.

"I want to help you get out of prison like I promised you the last time I came here," Tashinga said with her gaze fixed on Tinashe's.

"No… there's no need, it's over."

"What? What do you mean it's over? You do not mean to give up so soon do you?"

Tinashe stood up from the chair and hit the table between him and Tashinga with his fists, "Look at you… what did I get myself into… you're successful and so what about me? Why? Why me?"

A police officer came to escort Tinashe back to his cell for he was becoming violent, "I have got the prison as my home because I was always nice to everyone!" Tinashe shouted as if to jump from his chair to Tashinga's.

"No! It's not what you thi. . ."

"*Iwe handei!*" the warden said pointing his sjambok at Tinashe. Tinashe looked at Tashinga with eyes full of blame, shame and rage and then he left.

Tashinga remained sitting on the chair until she took a glance at her watch and walked out of the prison. She decided not to leave Gweru until she had managed to convince Tinashe that he had done great things by sacrificing a lot for her. She had to get him out of prison no matter what!

She reached for her mobile phone as soon as she got inside her car.

"Jess?" Tashinga said as soon as Jessica's phone was answered.

"Yeah it's me I'm at work right now… is there any problem?"

"I think things have become a little complicated this side…Tinashe said he does not want to get out of prison."

"What? No. You have to convince him… I suggest you try a bit harder to make him understand why you're doing all this.

"He seems to be regretting ever helping me out…"

"He needs you right now… I think you should get him a psychologist. A qualified professional… and remember it's him who can lead us to the real culprit. I mean the one who murdered Margaret."

Tashinga felt hope building up inside her, "You're right. I guess I should go and look for the psychologist right now. Thanks, you're a true friend and I appreciate that." Jessica smiled, "You can always count on me," she said and they hung up.

Later that day in the afternoon, Dean arrived at the airport in Zimbabwe and then called Tashinga to tell her that he had come back home.

"Wow that's good babes but I'm not at home right now. You can go and meet Jess at her work place. I'm in Gweru doing some work."

"Well…what? Gweru…? What kind of work is it that you're doing there?"

"I… um I'm at Blue Hills the probation centre for kids you know it right?"

"Yeah?"

"The children need counselling and so that is what I'm doing."

"Wow great… I'll see you later then… are you coming back home today?"

"No…I don't think so maybe next week."

"Oh good," Dean said biting his lower lip, "I love you."

"I love you too," Tashinga said with a frown on her face and they both hung up.

Dean went over to Jessica's workplace and saw her talking to a certain guy who was telling her that he too was British and stayed in some other part of London. Dean waved at her, Jessica saw him and smiled. She walked up to him and hugged him.

"Welcome back home, you're looking good," she said pointing at his jersey.

"Thanks Tashi bought it for me…I called Tashi and she sa…"

"No… it's okay. She called me too. We'll take a taxi home and maybe I can leave you there."

"That's great!" Dean said as they walked out of the complex. They took a taxi home and Jessica showed him his room.

"You won't be using the same room with Tashi bec…"

"I know," Dean said in a brisk voice, he then walked towards Jessica, "I know everything that you're up to Jude. You want to separate Tashi and I but that ain't going to work!" Dean said in a whisper though it was scary. Jessica felt a cold shiver flow down her spine. She swallowed hard.

"What makes you think that Dean? Tashi is my friend and I swear I'd never do a thing to hurt her. She loves you and separating you two will just break her heart."

"Well we'll see about that," Dean said as he put his bag on the bed, "Now leave my room please."

Jessica shrugged and walked out of the room.

Tashinga was lying on her bed in one of the expensive hotels in the city of Gweru. She was holding a diary in her hands and she still looking for the best psychologist for Tinashe. She smiled as she screamed, "Gotcha!"

She dialled the number on her mobile and the phone was answered after the first ring.

"Hello Doctor Nduru speaking."

"Hi I'm Tashinga Makombe and I'm a social worker. I hear you're one of the best psychologists in Zim residing in Gweru. Do you mind if we meet tomorrow in Sugar'n Spice at one at noon. I'm in dire need of your help."

"I'll inform you tomorrow at eight in the morning after I have checked my schedule."

"Okay thank you," Tashinga said and she hung up. She heaved a sigh and then she called Jessica on her phone. Jessica who was peeping through the bathroom door watching Dean quickly ran back to her room and answered the phone. She thanked God that it was on silent and the noise the shower was making did the trick, Dean hadn't noticed her.

"What's up Jess?"

"I saw the damn scar on his arm, just near his wrist!" Jessica said in a whisper after locking her door, "I can't believe I'm going to spend another six days with a rapist under my roof!"

"I'm sorry it's all because of me that I…"

"Don't mention… I did not mean to complain… by the way that culprit who tried to rape you where exactly did you bite him?"

"On his hand, just near the wrist," Tashinga said trying to remember the scary moment.

"Which hand precisely?"

"I… um… I can't remember anymore."

"Oh come on try…"

"I… his hand… I'm sorry…" Tashinga stammered again.

"No it's okay," Jessica said as she heard the shower stop running, I have to go," Jessica said and hung up.

The next day Tashinga went and met the psychologist. They agreed on the amount she was going to pay her until Tinashe had recovered. They then paid him a visit at the prison. At first Tinashe refused to come and meet her but then he later agreed after his jail mates had convinced him to.

"Why are you doing this Nashe… you know how much I wish to pay you back for all the good deeds you did for me. I owe you," Tashinga said almost breaking up into tears, "I want the best for you and that's what I've been working for all these years!"

Tinashe was standing with his back at her, Tashinga decided to leave but he stopped her, "Stop! Do you really want to help me get out of this place?"

Now there was one of the prisoners passing by them who was eavesdropping on their conversation.

"Yes," Tashinga nodded desperately, Tinashe then sat down on the chair opposite Tashinga.

"I think I know the person who murdered aunt that day, it was Cephas."

Tashinga looked at him quizzically, "But he wasn't there at the wedding how com..."

"He attempted to kill her a lot of times for money and the car. He might have been the one who pushed her down the staircase... remember her purse was found empty when the police searched it for more evidence," the man eaves dropping on their conversation looked at Tinashe and Tashinga with the corner of his eye.

Tashinga leaned back against her chair as she and the psychologist looked at each other, "Now you're talking... I'm going to do some more research. You know I saw Cephas once. That day when I came looking for you. What exactly does he look like? Do you mind describing him?"

Tinashe began to describe Cephas and when he finished Tashinga almost fell on the floor.

"What... are you okay?" Tinashe asked as the psychologist held her back.

"That man is Dean Hop... my fiancé to be... he is also the man who tried to rape me! The guy I told you about the last time I visited you Nashe!"

"Fiancé to be...bu...but how?" Tinashe asked, sounding disappointed.

"Yes, I met him in England, I'll explain that later. Right now I have to do something real fast!" Tashinga stood up and then she left the psychologist and Tinashe staring after her a little confused by her actions. The prisoner who has been watching and listening to Tinashe reached for the phone and began to dial some digits. The phone was answered in no time.

"Yes, how can I help you?"

"*Wena* Satan! Judahs…so you're back? You know a Samurai is no deceiver!"

Dean looked confused, "Who are you?"

The man let out a little laugh, "You *forogeti* so soon huh? It's *de* one and only king Zenze."

Dean felt as if he had been hit in the head, "Wha…wha…whaaat? But…how did you know th…?"

"Your bitch was here…I can see you're enjoying yourself… we worked for that mammon remember… me, our boss and *de oda* masters… but I just cannot believe *dat* you… a son of a b…"

"Look I don't have time for you, okay?" Cephas was about to hang up when the man shouted that he dare not.

"No don't you dare! I got all *de* digits. You have committed a sin against everyone so in order for me to *forogivhu* you I have one request… if you want me to give you more information on *dis* just visit me *kuprison* and bail me out."

Dean was silent for some time and then he told the man he'd think about it and they hung up. He sat with a plumb in his chair as Jessica crept away from his bedroom door feeling suspicious.

There was a little moment of silence until Tinashe spoke out to the psychologist.

"Do you mind telling me what's going on?"

"I too need an explanation but as far as you and I are concerned I'm your psychologist and you my patient. I suggest we begin the session right now," the psychologist said opening up her file.

Tashinga called Jessica as soon as she reached her hotel and was in her hotel room. She threw her purse on the bed as she dialled Jessica's number. Jessica was at work when Tashinga called her phone.

"Yes? Found anything?" Jessica asked as she answered Tashinga.

"Yes. I went to see Tinashe and asked him to describe his cousin… the one he suspects to have killed his aunt and the description matched with Dean's appearance when he was still a lad!" Tashinga almost screamed out of her lungs.

"What? I can't believe this so do you think that Dean… you know?"

"Yes… yes yes yes!" Tashinga said almost whispering and looking around as if she knew someone was watching her, she was pacing round her room closing up the windows and curtains, "And you did you find out anything?"

"No… I mean yes, the scar… they are human teeth. I took a pic of his wounded wrist and made some investigations on the photo. I took it to a friend who specialises in that and he said they are female teeth… a teenage woman's teeth."

Tashinga lost her balance and fell on the bed, "O…kay. Does he know what we're doing… I mean anything about the investigation?"

"No. But I think he's beginning to suspect something. So don't take long because I heard him talking to someone on the phone but I did not hear what they were talking about exactly" Jessica turned round and saw Dean greeting her colleague Simones, "He's here I'll call you later. She hung up and turned to look at Dean who was already standing at her back. Before Jessica could say a word, Rudy approached them with a smile on her face. She had been sitting on Jessica's desk for she had brought her some lunch.

"Dean what a pleasant surprise! You want some tea, coffee?"

Dean shook his head with a smile on his face, "No...I came here to ask about Tashinga...what kind of job is she taking care of in Gweru, Jess?"

"Did you try calling her? She told me it's a social work project concerning child delinquency. I hope she told you the same?" Jessica said with a quizzical expression on her face.

"Oh yes, she mentioned that to me but I thought there was something more to it."

"No, why do you think that? If there was something she could have told me about it...it's just that project...she'll come home soon. She mentioned to me this morning that she had missed you I hope she... um... told you the same?"

"Yeah she did," Dean said nodding his head with a clenched jaw.

"So... I guess I should get back to work now," Jessica said toying with a file in her hands.

"Yes, that's right," Dean forced a smile and Jessica left. Rudy then took the opportunity to talk to him.

"Yes, the child delinquency thing," Rudy injected, "I wonder why she doesn't have time for you... I can take you out for lunch and maybe you might find something in me that Tashi doesn't have," Rudy said licking her lips. Dean looked at her and whispered in her ear. Rudy giggled mischievously.

"Later," Dean said and left.

Jessica adjusted her spectacles as she watched Dean leave and Rudy smile to herself and hold her fist just below her waist line in triumph and hissed a "yes!"

Rudy turned to look at her back to check if Jessica had heard or seen anything but Jessica began to hum a song and pretended to be busy with some files. Rudy pursed her lips and walked out of the Zimbabwean CID building.

That night Rudy put on her best denim jeans and a see-through blouse. She took a jacket and put it on. She put on Tashinga's perfume. She then went into the lounge where Jessica was having a cup of coffee and arranging her files.

Jessica raised her head as soon as Rudy walked in putting on her jacket.

"Wow, you never told me you had plans for tonight?"

"Yes, I had plans, actually I have just come up with the plans," Rudy took a sip from Jessica's mug, "So bye dearie."

"Wait. You're wearing Tashi's deodorant?"

"Yes, I like her choices. Heard it drives the guys crazy," Rudy said with a widened grin on her face and walked out of the house. Jessica raised her eyebrows, shrugged and then she resumed her work.

Dean was having a glass of whisky when he received a call from Zenze who had been imprisoned with Lucifer their gang leader.

"Promise me *dat* you'll help me get out if I give you some important info *bout* your girlfriend."

"Who are you? And what exactly do you want from me?"

"I can't believe it! You forget so soon… it is me, your brother from *anodah modah*… Zenze."

Dean held the phone closer to his ears, "Your girlfriend is planning your arrest…remember you're *de* one who killed Margaret *dat* day."

Dean stood with his mouh agape, "Tinashe will get out soon and you…you will come here and stay with us… so just think *bout* it. Remain free *oro* you'll come *kwatiri kunoku!*"

Dean heaved a sigh and there was a knock on his door, "Thank you brother I'll see what I can do for you. I'll call you later," Dean said and hung up. He heaved another sigh and went over to open his door. Rudy was standing outside shivering for the weather had become chilly.

"I came at the right time right?" Rudy said smiling wildly.

"Yes," Dean forced a smile as he shut the door after she had got inside.

"So what are you doing… I mean why are you still up? It's late at night"

Dean turned to look at her as he sat back in his couch, "Having whisky…you want some?"

Rudy remained standing looking at Dean with a narrowed gaze, "I'm leaving."

"Why? What? So soon?" Dean said as he leaned his head against the couch but his gaze still on Rudy.

"You do not seem to be in the mood…we talked about this early in the morning but you seem to have forgotten about everything so… bye bye" Rudy turned to leave but Dean leaped off the couch and took hold of her hand.

"Look, I'm sorry. I am having some problems right now… but I think I need you for the night."

Their gazes locked and Rudy then removed the jacket from her body and let it fall to the floor. Dean's gaze dropped to her chest and then she moved a few steps towards him and then took his hand in hers, "That's Tashi's …you've…" he said in a hoarse voice but Rudy put her finger across his lips as if to hush him.

"Just wanted to show you that I am a very bad girl," she rolled her tongue seductively and Dean quickly swept her up from her feet into his arms, they both laughed wildly as they went to Dean's bedroom.

It was already three in the morning when Rudy woke up and heard Dean talking on the phone. He was talking about how he had murdered Margaret and then how he was going to murder Tashinga. She felt an icy cold shiver flow along her spine. She got out of the covers naked but before she could do anything, Dean walked in with a knife in his hand.

"You must have heard my conversation on the phone," he said walking slowly towards her.

"No…" Rudy said moving backwards, "I'm telling you I didn't hear you say a thing!" tears spilled down from her eyes.

Dean had almost reached her when she shouted, "Look at your back!" Dean turned to look and she ran over the bed and then was almost getting inside his lounge when he got hold of of her. Rudy lost her balance and fell down on the floor. Dean pounced on her and mercilessly stabbed her in the chest several times. He let go of her lifeless but still warm body and went to the kitchen with the knife still in his hand. He washed his hands in the sink together with the knife. He then dragged her body and put it behind the couch. He wiped the blood off the floor and threw away the rug. He poured himself a glass of whisky and went back to bed.

It was ten in the morning when Jessica received a call from Mzeki Firm where Rudy was now working as an advocate. They were asking for her but she told them that she went out last night and had not seen her that morning. Jessica tried calling her on her mobile but it just rang and wasn't answered. Jessica called Tashinga and told her that their friend was missing but she told her not to panic because she was going to investigate the case. Tashinga then told Jessica that she was coming back home but would go and see Tinashe first. They told each other to be careful and then they hung up.

Tinashe was called to come and see her. He walked and sat on the chair which was opposite Tashinga's.

"I'm going back to Harare today. Something came up. The lawyer who was supposed to help you with your case has gone missing."

"What? And do you know the reason why?"

"I'm afraid no… so that's why I think it's best to go back to Harare but I'll be in touch."

Tinashe looked away from Tashinga with a frown on his face, "Are you okay?" Tashinga asked rubbing his hand but the police officer bellowed, "No touching!"

They both looked baffled and then Tinashe spoke in a voice that alarmed Tashinga.

"You betrayed me…I never thought I'd be let down by you."

"W…what do you mean Nashe? What did I do?"

Tinashe looked away from her, "You know what? Just go!"

"No! I am not going anywhere until you tell me what I have done to you!"

Tinashe buried his face in his hands as tears spilled out from his eyes, "You planned on getting married to some guy because I have been arrested for a crime you know I didn't commit. I didn't murder Margaret and you know it!"

"I believe you… I'm so sorry Tinashe. I didn't know *kuti* you had feelings for me. I wasn't aware of the fact that you loved me. You know what? I was happy when Dean… I mean Cephas proposed to me because I thought that no man would accept me after I had told him my history. You knew a lot about me. I was raped, I was a prostitute, a stripper. All that I di…"

Tinashe suddenly turned to look at her as tears flowed down her cheeks. He saw that they were tears of pain. He extended his hand and wiped them away. This time however the warden did not shout because he too felt pity for Tashinga.

Zenze who had requested to make a call felt sympathy for he was eavesdropping Tashinga and Tinashe's conversation. He then asked the warden escorting him.

"Is he going to be tried again?"

"Yes," the warden nodded, "His trial is tomorrow."

"I would like to testify," Zenze said as he turned back to go to his cell.

"You don't want to make the call again?" the warden asked and Zenze shook his completely shaven head.

Tinashe then understood that whatever Tashinga was doing for him was genuine. Before leaving, Tashinga told him that she was going to find another lawyer but one residing in the city and she was going to fly to Gweru the next day.

15

It was already three in the afternoon when Tashinga arrived the city of Harare. She boarded a taxi to their new home. Jessica had been impatiently waiting for her. Tashinga threw her little bag on the floor as Jessica hurried to shut the doors and windows, in case Dean was nearby to eavesdrop their conversation.

"So where do you think she went? Because she never mentioned anything about a relative when we were still in England," Tashinga said as she sat down.

"I don't know… I don't have any clue."

"Have you tried her mobile?"

"Yes! But she is not picking up!"

"The trial is tomorrow… so I don't know what to do. She is supposed to stand in as Tinashe's advocate!"

There was a moment of silence until Jessica approached her friend from her back and took hold of her shoulder, I suggest we look for someone else today and prepare for the trial. In case she does not turn up."

Jessica reached for the phone and called the Mzeki Firm. They agreed and then they assigned a new lawyer to the case. Tasinga and Jessica heaved sighs of relief but with looks of dismay still on their faces.

That evening, Dean bought a beautiful emerald ring for Tashinga. He kept it safe in its little box. So when she called him and told him that she had come back to Harare he decided to take it along with him. He sounded the alarm on their door, and Jessica was the one who opened the door for him.

"Oh, it's Dean!" Jessica called out to Tashinga who was dressing up. Jessica opened the door wider and let Dean inside

"How is she?" Dean asked as Tashinga called out from her room, "I'm almost through!"

"Well, the disappearance of Rudy is making our lives miserable. I wonder where she went that night?" Jessica said thoughtfully as her eyes ran over Dean's face.

"Oh me too. Um… didn't she have a friend in this part of Harare or some relative?"

Jessica quickly shook her head, "No… I don't know because besides going to see a friend where would she have gone an…" Jessica was cut when Tashinga walked out in a dazzling red dress.

"Wow, you look ravishing," Dean said as he stood up and took hold of Tashinga's hand.

"Thank you," Tashinga said as she let him kiss her hand.

"I have something for you. It's something special," Dean fished for something in his pocket and then got on one knee as he opened the little box, "Will you marry me?"

Tashinga and Jessica gasped at the sight of the emerald ring. Tashinga looked in Dean's eyes for they had a sparkle of triumph showing in them. Jessica's facial expression of surprise suddenly changed into a cynical one as she moved a little closer to have a very good look at the ring.

"Um… Dean where did you get the emerald from?" Jessica said still looking at the green stone.

"India. Any problem?" Dean asked quickly as he got back on his feet.

"No… it's just that it is so beautiful and unique," Jessica looked at Tashinga, "You're so lucky dear. Most women receive diamond rings but you have received an emerald," Jessica forced a smile though Tashinga did not get any sense from her statement.

There was a moment of silence as they both stared at Jessica who cleared her throat, "Wow… um… I think I should excuse you guys and go to my room," Jessica left as she wiped off crocodile tears from her face.

"Is she that lonely?" Dean asked as soon as Jessica had left the room.

"Maybe…because she feels that since Rudy ha…"

"Damn it! Why is everyone on about her? It's always Rudy! Rudy!" Dean shouted. He then sat in an armchair with his face buried in his hands. "I'm sorry… it's just that I too am confused with this… I can't believe she is missing."

Tashinga nodded her head but the way that Dean had reacted had alarmed her.

"Um it's okay but I think you should leave now," Tashinga said rubbing her arm with her other hand.

Dean looked up at her as she tried to explain to him why she had suggested that he leave, "I understand," Dean said standing up and then put his hands in his pocket, "Tell Jude she'll find a good man soon."

Tashinga forced a smile as she turned on her heel as soon as Dean had walked out of the room. She ran to Jessica's room.

"Do you think…" Tashinga was quickly hushed by Jessica who suggested they communicate in writing. Jessica handed her a pen and a book.

"Do you think he is the one who did it? Like kidnap Rudy?" Tashinga was trembling and so the writing was not so clear.

Jessica who was sitting on her bed glued to her laptop quickly looked up at Tashinga, took the pen and scribbled on the paper, "Yes…it's obvious. Look, the emerald which you're putting on is nothing but a wired device. Whatever we might say against him might take us to our graves," Jessica wrote and then looked deeper in to her friends eyes who almost let out a scream in fear.

"So I guess I should remove it," Tashinga wrote and tried to remove the ring but it was already stuck on her finger.

"That was actually the bad news I wanted to tell you," Jessica wrote down and shrugged her shoulders.

Tashinga was now shaking. She sat on the bed with a plump and then she reached for the paper and pen.

"Do you think he is now aware of the mission on which I went on…in Gweru?"

Jessica grabbed it as soon as Tashinga raised it up to give it to her. Jessica nodded her head and Tashinga's tears of fear began to sting her eyes. Jessica went and sat beside her friend and hugged her as she wrote with one hand, "We're doomed!"

Tashinga looked up to Jessica with fear in her eyes but Jessica nodded her head in agreement as she patted her frightened friend's shaky palm.

The next morning Dean woke up and realised that he had slept in a bar. He woke up and wiped his mouth. He had drunk a lot of whisky the previous night. He drove home and then switched on his computer which he thought had the information Tashinga had said. There was nothing besides the conversation they had had before he left. He looked away with a narrowed look on his face and barked "JUDE!"

It was the day of Tinashe's trial. He was told to get ready. He asked the warden to call Tashinga for him and remind her but her mobile was unreachable. He tried it many times until he decided to give up and got on the prisoner's truck to be driven to court.

That same time Dean decided to go to Tashinga's place and take her out to some hotel. There he bought her some lunch and told her that they were going to stay together soon for their house was completed. Tashinga's smile suddenly disappeared from her face.

"Don't you think we're rushing things, Dean?"

"No...*asi iwe* you think we're..."

"No... I mean yes... it's just that since you came we haven't given each other time... um and I think you should wait a little bit... I mean the lobola thing should wait," Tashinga said with her eyes glued to his face.

"Why?"

"I don't know but I have a feeling that things are happening so fast and I just can't stand the speed, that's all."

Dean nodded his head as his left hand ran to and fro in his neatly cut hair.

"Um... you want some ice cream?"

"Yes," Tashinga forced a smile and then Dean stood up and went to the ice cream shop which was across the road. She tried removing the ring but to no avail. Dean delayed. He spent about an hour buying the ice cream. She could feel that he was up to no good and so she stood up in a jerk and went away. She boarded a taxi and went to Jessica's workplace. When she got there Simones who claimed to be attracted to Jessica answered her.

"I haven't seen her since morning!" Simones shouted from his desk, "Did you find your other friend?"

"Um...no...we're still working on it!"

"Oh good gracious! She must have been kidnapped! Or maybe she hates Africa!" Simones shouted again but Tashinga decided not to answer him back for she felt that something was wrong somewhere.

Tashinga just smiled and then she walked out of the building. She tried calling Jessica on her mobile and decided to go back home herself.

The other lawyer who had been assigned arrived at the court room just in time since she had taken a flight to Gweru. She had everything in order and before the judge could say anything a warden walked in with a piece of paper which was handed over to the judge and was read out loud:

I'm so sorry to have kept quiet about this all along. Tinashe is not the one responsible for Margaret's death. It was I and Cephas who went to steal some money from her. I was hiding behind the cupboards upstairs when he pushed his mother down the staircase. She had refused to give him the money and so he tried to take it by force. Cephas and I met in a cell and from that day when he provided me with the cocaine. I and my men had beaten him up, then we became allies. Ruregerero hama dzangu… Ndakabatikana kuona umwe uyu achishungurudzika ari mujeri iye asina mhosva. Cephas is using the forged passports and stolen money to make a living… he has actually changed his name from Cephas Khumalo to Dean Hopkins. He is about to get married to some innocent woman so that he'll be able to travel to Russia for a "honeymoon" and there he'll be able to meet Lucifer our great leader who escaped from prison the very day he got arrested… Cephas is staying In Highlands on 537 Alexander Avenue and everyone who gets to know what he is doing will have to face the consequences. Once again I repeat Tinashe did not kill Margaret but Cephas did…

And like a brave Samurai I rest my case…

Thank you for reading this for in this letter is the truth…

The entire court room was filled with murmuring as soon as the judge finished reading the letter. He then asked for the one who had wrote the letter to come inside.

"Actually the prisoner was found dead in his cell. He committed suicide," one warden said as he entered the courtroom, "He was part of a cult and by saying this he said that he has betrayed a brother and so he does not deserve to live."

The judge turned his gaze to Tinashe who was completely surprised by what was happening, "What can you say? Do you have anything to say? Who is the lawyer? Who is standing in for you?"

The lawyer stood up and defended her client. Before she had even finished a young woman walked in. She had a six year old child walking beside her. It was Lindiwe. She testified against Cephas and told the entire courtroom that she was now married to another man with whom she had the child. The judge then passed his judgement that Tinashe was innocent and so he was set free. He was so overjoyed to the extent that he walked towards his lawyer and hugged her including his psychologist Doctor Nduru. Tinashe's flight to Harare was organised so that he'd go and save Tashinga since he had asked for help for he suspected that she was in some form of trouble.

When Tashinga arrived at her apartment there were a lot of cars parked out and most of them were the police cars. One huge truck was the CID's and it had Jessica's workmates in it. Tashinga walked in and met Jessica's boss Leonard Saungweme.

"What happened?" Tashinga asked as the man led her towards Jessica's body. It was lying in a pool of blood and lifeless on the floor in their lounge. She was lying with her eyes wide open.

"Her murderer is a serial killer. Do you know him?"

Tashinga turned her frightened gaze from her friend's corpse and then she covered her mouth as tears spilled from her eyes. One of the female detectives Naomi Chagwanda approached Tashinga and Leonard who seemed to be in deep conversation.

"Do you have any idea of the person who has done this to your friend?"

Tashinga turned to look at her as the lady handed her a little white script, "What's this?" she almost choked on her words.

"A receipt of an emerald ring. We found it on top of Jessica Jude's body and this is the only thing that can lead us to the murderer."

Tashinga grabbed it from Naomi's hands and her eyes ran through it. She began to tremble in both fright and anger. She then dashed for the door but the detectives held her.

"I know the killer! He has killed both my friends!" Tashinga shouted as she fought the detectives.

A woman in a police uniform then walked into the lounge, "You mean Dean Hopkins? He is a dangerous criminal. A lady's body has been found in his apartment. It is said that her name is Rudy Mope. Both parents are British and she too resides in Britain she only came here with friends for a vacation," these words echoed in Tashinga's ears.

Tashinga lost control to the extent that she pushed both detectives away and ran out. They all shouted that people stop her but she got into one of the policemen's cars and drove away. The police tried to follow her but they soon lost her. They tried tracking her down but failed.

"There is a unique wire in the ring… that's why it's difficult to track her down," Naomi said as she adjusted her spectacles.

"Damn it!" Leonard said as he threw away the paper in his hand and hit the walls with a fist and let out a cry. He then turned to look at some police men standing at his back,

"Follow her! Look for her now! Go!" the police officers hurried outside, got inside a car and went after Tashinga.

Tashinga went to the burned down chapel where Charity and Nyasha had died. The church had not been repaired and so she went and stood on the bare ground when she received a call. It was from Dean.

"Hi honey," Tashinga could feel anger rise from within her she wanted to say something but Dean stopped her, "No no no no babes. Not so fast…how is Jess and Rudy? Hope you found them?"

"You know what? You're a wizard, a dog and a big fool! You've killed both my friends and you dare call me?"

Cephas let out a laugh, "Yes…anyway to cut the long story short, I'm standing two meters from you," Cephas said and Tashinga quickly turned to look at him and she shuddered with fear when she saw him slowly walking towards her.

The police were still trying to track her down and still the tracker was not functioning for the words **TRANSMISSION BLOCKED** kept appearing on the screen.

"We're never going to find this girl!" one of the police officers shouted as she typed something on the machine and still the words repeated themselves.

Tinashe was still on the plane when he and the others received a message that Tashinga had gone missing and that no one could track her down because of the emerald ring she was wearing.

"What? No… he can't kill Tashinga. She's…"

"It's going to be fine just let them do their job," Dr. Nduru said as she patted him on the shoulder.

Tinashe turned to look at her and then he sunk into his seat. An airhostess approached them and told them that they would be landing in twenty minutes.

Tashinga was trembling when Cephas touched the back of her neck with a gun in his other hand. She swallowed hard as he bent his head to kiss her on her lips. Suddenly he began to unbutton the buttons of her blouse but with her trembling hand she held his hand and shook her head, "No."

Cephas looked at her as he toyed with a toothpick in his mouth. She shuddered with fear as he tightened his grip on her neck.

"Come on let's go," Cephas said as he pulled her by the neck to follow him. Tashinga tried to resist the strength of his grip but to no avail, she staggered after him. There was a car parked beside the road, Tashinga gasped as he opened the front door and pushed her inside. He came and sat beside her, locked the doors and started the car.

"You're not going to kill me are you?" Tashinga asked as soon as he started driving.

"Shut up!" Cephas said in a firm voice as his car rushed along the road. Cephas suddenly got off the road and got in a certain bush. Tashinga wanted to scream but soon the path cleared and soon some houses could be seen from a distance. They then parked outside one of these beautiful houses and then he dragged Tashinga into the gate. The house was surrounded by trees and these actually blocked the sun's blazing light. She tried to fight him but he took hold of her hair and so she squirmed as he mercilessly dragged her with it into his house.

He stopped suddenly just outside the door and then he harshly pulled her face by her chin and forced her to look around the mansion and something suddenly caught her sight. It was a beautiful fountain painted in her favourite colour white but it had a spear in the middle. Its blade shined menacingly and showed that it was regularly polished, "I built this with my money for you but what do I get? Betrayal!"

Tashinga tried to remove his hand but he tightened the grip and resumed dragging her. She kept staring at the spear until he opened the front door and pushed her inside. She lost her balance and fell down on the floor. Tashinga let out a scream and then he laughed, "No one is going to hear you babes, so calm down."

Tashinga watched him walk into the kitchen with strands of her long hair covering her face, she stood up from where she was lying down and tried to escape but the door was locked. Cephas came back from the kitchen with two wine glasses and then roared with laughter as he watched Tashinga take hold of a china ornament.

"Auto lock," Cephas said showing her a remote control.

"Open the door or I'll hit you in the head."

Cephas ignored her as he put the glasses on the table and sat down on a couch opposite where she was standing. He raised his gaze but waved her away as he began to drink. Tashinga saw an alarm button on the walls she walked slowly towards it and pressed against it with her fore finger. It did not ring. Again Cephas roared with laughter and Tashinga felt very stupid and helpless in his presence.

"I'm not that stupid Tashi… honey I…"

"Don't call me that you merciless beast!" Tashinga said in an attempt to hurl more insults at him but he stood up and walked towards her.

"A beast is never merciful," he raised the gun and pointed it against her head, "I'm not a beast because if I were one you wouldn't have been here till now… so don't call me that!" Cephas said as he let a strand of her hair lean against the gun.

"Ok...the...n if you ain't a beast you should let me go..." Tashinga stammered as he pressed his nose against her neck and breathed in her fragrance.

"No... we're engaged... you belong to me, " he slowly removed his head and looked deeper into her eyes, " I know you've tried so hard to remove the ring... it's a sign that you and I can never be put asunder, " Cephas gestured as he turned his back to Tashinga.

Tashinga was trembling as her eyes darted from corner to corner in the beautiful and luxurious lounge in which they were standing. The designs were of a sophisticated nature with a little bit of an Italian touch though the entire room was furnished in an African style. Cephas kept on standing with his back facing Tashinga until she reached for the Chinese ornament and hit him against the temple of his head. He fell down on the floor and Tashinga ran up the stairs. She got inside a certain room which had the best of great African furniture and hid inside a closet. She then tried to remove the emerald ring from her finger. Cephas woke up a little later and began to look for her. Cephas took another remote from his pocket and started pressing buttons as he looked for Tashinga. Whenever he pressed a button on the remote Tashinga's ring made a sound. Tashinga who was hiding in one of the bedrooms got out of the closet and crouched beside a bed, she took hold of one leg of the bed and hit the ring. She began to beat against the emerald. She could hear him approaching. She began to hit faster and faster and... until the emerald came out of the ring and rolled away from her. Tashinga then crawled to the other side of the bed where the closet was and soon Cephas' remote denied him any connection.

The police officers' machine suddenly reflected that the signal was available. They had parked beside the burned chapel.

They were discussing Charity and Nyasha's tragic death as they waited helplessly for the signal to appear. Suddenly, their machine showed them that the network was now available. It showed them the address where Tashinga was and they decided to follow her there. They quickly reported to their boss Leonard who passed the message to the officers in the plane. Tinashe decided to go where Tashinga was exactly as soon as they had landed. He was escorted by some police officers including the lawyer and the psychologist who felt that they should not miss out on this interesting expedition.

Cephas cursed as he hit the remote control against his palm but to no avail. He checked the batteries and saw that they were still new. He threw away the remote control took out a gun from his pocket and began to call out for Tashinga.

"I know you're here baby... just be a good girl and come out in the clear because if I find you... I'm definitely going to kill you in the same way I killed Rudy and Jude!" Cephas was now passing by the guest room when he saw the emerald and then the metal ring. He cursed under his breath. He then put the gun down as he began to look deep in to the stone. Tashinga came out holding a plank and then she hit him hard on the head. She kicked the gun away from him. Cephas fell down as he lay motionless on the wooden floor. Tashinga began to run around the house looking for the auto lock. It was on the table in the living room but before she took hold of it Cephas walked in the living room and slapped her across the face. Tashinga lost her balance and fell down, he walked towards her and began to kick her in the stomach and face but she took hold of his leg and pulled him down. Cephas fell on his bottom and Tashinga staggered to her feet but still he pulled her. Tashinga took hold of the couch to maintain her balance. Cephas did all he could to pull her down but as she was screaming, she tried to take hold of the remote so she could open the door. Cephas reached for it first and threw it on the floor. Tashinga watched it smash into pieces. Cephas wiped the blood oozing from his head with the back of his hand and then he took hold of Tashinga by the neck. He lifted her up with his hand, Tashinga began to wriggle her feet gasping for air. She tore off Cephas' sleeve amidst the struggle and saw the wound. Her eyes threatened to pop out of their sockets as they were already reflecting some pain, they also showed realisation in them and then Cephas threw her down on the floor. She screamed as her back ached from the pain that surged round her waistline.

"You see what you did to me… huh bitch!" Cephas was panting as he pointed at the scar on his wrist. Tashinga just looked at the already dried up wound and continued to groan in agony. Cephas took a knife from his pocket but before he could even touch her Tashinga quickly got up on her feet and kicked his hand. His hand let go of the knife and then she forcefully put her fingers in his eyes as he pounced on her and kicked him between his legs. Cephas let out a loud cry as she ran up the stairs. She tried opening the windows but she failed. Again Cephas followed her upstairs with his belt in his hands. She took a deep breath and then he hit her just above her eye with his belt. She felt dizzy as blood oozed from her forehead and she watched him walk towards her. She let out a loud scream as she leaped and kicked him in the stomach, Cephas lost his balance and fell out through the window. He fell upon his fountain which had the large metal spear as part of its unique decoration and design. The spear tore his stomach apart for he fell with his face and all his bowels fell out from it. Tashinga looked away as blood and water mingled and the water's colour was instantly turned into deep scarlet. The

Samurai had performed the ritual, Seppuku by letting his bowels come out from his tummy. His mission was accomplished! Cephas shut his eyes as blood oozed from his mouth, he let out a weak groan as he watched Tashinga look down at him in fright but with an element of victory shown in her eyes and then he died on the spot.

Tashinga could not believe what had just happened. She came down the stairs looking a little bit shaken by the entire incident. She hit the door handle with the plank she had once used to hit Cephas on the head which broke but the door opened up and the tiny steaks of light piercing the tree leaves almost blinded her. She then saw cars approaching. Sirens could be heard from a distance. Tears of joy streamed down her cheeks as she felt relief melt her once frightened heart. It was all over and she was safe again.

Detectives Leonard and Naomi asked her if she was fine and all she said was, "You can see for yourself," Naomi patted her shoulder and followed Leonard in the mansion.

Paramedics hurried towards her with a stretcher. Tashinga quietly sat on it and then a certain black car parked a little further from where she was. Tinashe came out of it…he was still in his jail clothes. She got off the stretcher bed and ran towards him, the two hugged and hot tears spilled from her eyes. Tinashe kept patting her back whispering, "It's okay" in her ears.

Tashinga and Tinashe then looked in each other's eyes, "I love you," Tinashe said as he touched her lips. Hot tears spilled from her eyes again as he knelt down on one knee and asked her to marry him. Tashinga was quiet for some time until she jumped up and shouted a yes. The way she jumped reminded Tinashe of the old days when they were still kids and she found out that she had passed her exams. They kissed and embraced

Tashinga looked forward to her new life with Tinashe though she knew that it'd be shadowed with very bad memories...

The End!

Printed in the United States
By Bookmasters